Ghosts of the Lost Forest
Nimue Brown

Copyright © Nimue Brown 2024

Cover Art by Keith Errington

Back Cover photo by David Bridger

All rights reserved. No part of this publication may be reproduced, distributed or transmitted in any form or by any means, without prior written permission.

Private, personal use, printing bits off because you want to, loaning to friends and whatnot is all fine. Just keep my name on it, please.
.

Book Layout @ 2024 Steam-powered Books

Ghosts of the Lost Forest

We are all haunted by the past, whether we know it or not. Ghosts of our former selves, or the lives we might have lived and the spectres of choices we did not make. Our ancestors haunt us, and sometimes we will glimpse their faces looking back at us from mirrors. Nothing ever goes away. Not entirely. We can never be wholly free from all that went before.

Sometimes, when you dare to greet those ghosts, to name them and face them, everything changes.

Somewhere in the UK Midlands, somewhen at the end of the twentieth century...

By the light of a lone candle, a girl scratches runes into her pale skin. She works in silence, brow furrowed in concentration as she presses the sharp steel into her delicate flesh. Crimson blood blossoms along her arm, a single drop falling onto the bare floor beneath her. She watches it ooze, as though unaware that this is her life force. After all, she has seen her own blood every month for some time now. This is no big deal. There is a peculiar sheen in her eyes. Pain intoxicates her. With her full lips pursed, she works another mark into her body, then catches up a few drops of blood on her fingertips and repeats the design on the exposed floorboards. In her deep concentration she looks strangely childish, despite the violence she does to herself. Even so she can be little more than fourteen.

Chapter One

Scanning the back room of the pub, Steven realised he had no idea who he was looking for. All the people he could see appeared to be pretty normal. He had expected the group he sought to be overtly different in some way, and had assumed they would stand out. Working out how to identify this collection of strangers hadn't been part of his nervous preparations. Looking around again, he tried to take his time, to think carefully. 'Back room of the pub' was all he had to go on. The back room was busy and the place heaved. They might all fit the bill, or maybe none of them did. He couldn't tell. Steven felt entirely out of place and worried people might be judging him as he stood there flustered, with no idea what to do

Clearly he had to ask at the bar. Hopefully the people working here knew about the moot and didn't mind and wouldn't take issue with him. Steven had a knack for seeing the potential disaster in every situation, and pushing through it wasn't easy, but he managed.

"What can I get you?" the balding man behind the bar asked him.

"I heard there was supposed to be a moot in here." He had to shout over the noise and it made him desperately self-conscious.

"That's them, over in the far left hand corner. Most of them aren't in yet." The barman smiled as he spoke. "New are you?"

Steven nodded, wishing it wasn't quite so obvious. He bought a drink. Looking to the back corner, Steven identified a large table. He could see a young guy with a shaved head, a goth girl with painted face and black lace gloves, and an older man nursing a pint. Taking a deep breath, he walked over. The goth girl spotted him at once, and her dark eyes followed his hesitant advance. She smiled showing small, pearly teeth.

"I'm looking for John and Elspeth," Steven began. "That's not you by any chance is it?"

"Nah," said the goth girl. "I'm Mindy. John and Elspeth are late. They're pretty much always late for everything," she added.

"Pagan time," the skinhead next to her said, as though this explained everything.

"Have a chair," Mindy said. "So who are you, how did you find out about us? What's your thing?"

Startled by the sudden barrage of questions, Steven sat, wordless and struggling to formulate any kind of response. Talking about himself hadn't crossed his mind as a likelihood either. He'd imagined lurking in a corner, listening and seeing what he could learn. Three pairs of eyes turned his way. Three strangers who suddenly wanted to know all about him. He coughed, nervously.

"I'm Steven Cooper," he said, trying to recall the questions. "I saw a poster in the library, phoned the number off it, talked to John. He said to come along and ask for him and Elspeth, so here I am."

"And what are you into?" the goth girl pressed.

"Umm," Steven managed.

"Give him a break, woman," the older guy cut in. "He's only just got here. You don't have to give him the ninth degree, surely?"

Mindy pouted at this, but didn't seem too upset. "Just trying to be friendly," she said.

"I'm John," the older man said, offering his hand.

Steven shook it, somewhat reluctantly. "Oh," he managed, feeling even more confused.

"You talked to the other John, Wiccan John. I'm Heathen John," he explained.

"Nice to meet you."

"Neil," the skinhead offered, also stretching his arm across the table to make contact.

Mindy's hand shot up in the air and her copious amounts of silvery jewellery caught the light as she waved her hand.

"Over here!"

Steven couldn't resist looking round. He saw a middle-aged couple waving back and heading over. They looked quite unremarkable to him.

"I saw Diana outside," the new woman said.

"Better clear a space then." Neil leaped to his feet and started rearranging furniture.

Steven felt glad of the ensuing chaos, as it allowed him to slip out of the limelight for a while at least. Looking round he saw a woman in a wheelchair approaching and guessed this must be Diana. She stopped in the space Neil had made for her.

"Hey, how's it going," she said with a smile.

Steven smiled back and nodded, glad to find she didn't seem to want to interrogate him.

"Is Helen coming tonight?" someone asked.

"I saw her yesterday and she's too busy," Diana said. "She sends her love."

There were assorted chuckles at this, and Steven knew he'd missed some kind of in-joke. He didn't mind particularly. Another round of introductions began, during which he grasped that the new couple were called Carol and Sean. Steven wished that they were all a little less enthusiastic about wanting to know who he was.

Half an hour later than the moot was supposed to start, John and Elspeth arrived, setting off a round of hugs, welcomes and yet more introductions. They all seemed very touchy-feely, and he wasn't sure what to make of that. Steven was not accustomed to touching, or being touched, but nobody attempted to put hands on him, much to his relief.

"So you found us all right then?" Elspeth said, sitting down next to him. She was a mature and full figured woman, with a long floaty skirt and a voluminous top. She smelled of flowers.

"Yeah," Steven acknowledged.

"He's not a talker," Mindy announced. "We already tried to grill him but he's not told us anything much."

"Mindy tried to grill him," Heathen John corrected.

"You've not been to anything like this before then?" Elspeth asked, her tone gentle.

"No."

"We probably all seem a bit crazy to you. So what were you looking for, why did you want to come along?"

Steven met her clear blue gaze for a few seconds. "I don't exactly know," he confessed. "I'm looking for something, something different. I'm looking for meaning, I suppose. Something to help me make sense f my life. It's hard to explain. I looked at some stuff about Paganism on the internet and it just felt right. About nature, and magic, and old gods. I don't know anything much really. I just wanted to see what it's all about."

There were nods and smiles from around the table.

"We've all been there," Elspeth said. "Feel free to lurk and listen then. Ask questions if you want to, but don't feel obliged to do or say anything."

"Thanks."

Relieved by this, Steven settled more comfortably in his chair. For a while, the others talked about what they had been doing since their last meeting, much of which sounded rather mundane.

"Neil was in the papers again, did you see?" Diana asked. She produced a neatly folded cutting from her bag and opened it out.

"So what was it this time?" Wiccan John asked.

"Protest against tree felling," Neil said, smiling self-consciously.

"Three oak trees, all over two hundred years old according to estimates," Diana announced.

"Bloody council," Mindy scowled, running her fingers through her dyed black hair.

"No," Neil said. "The council fought it. High court and everything. Homeowners reckoned the trees were doing for their foundations. They won. Fucking bastards."

"They do that," Elspeth nodded. "Especially oaks. You get as much oak under the ground as you do above the surface."

"Oaks were there before the houses," Neil said. "Bloody tosspot idiots."

"I wonder what will happen when the roots rot?" Diana suggested.

"Nothing they don't deserve," Neil replied darkly.

Steven quite liked trees, but this passionate defence of them was new to him. He'd never considered them as individuals before, and didn't think he could tell an oak from anything else.

"Can I have a look at the article?" he asked.

"Sure." Diana passed it over to him.

A picture dominated the page. He could see Neil holding a placard, but he wasn't the focal point of the shot. A woman of indeterminate age stared out from the paper, her gaze searing, her expression unreadable but very intense. Sleek, dark hair framed the strong bones of her face. The expression in her eyes seemed to challenge and demand. Something stirred deep within Steven – a feeling he could not name, but which held his attention to the piece of paper in his hands, and to the eyes captured in black and white ink. It wasn't desire, as far as he knew. None the less, he could not resist the call of those eyes, even though he had no idea what he might be summoned to do. Scanning the article, he could find no names.

"Who is she?" he asked.

"No idea," Neil said. "Seen her at other protests."

Steven nodded, and quietly returned the cutting to Diana. The woman's face stayed with him, and he knew he would remember it as well as the poor print quality allowed.

The conversation shifted rapidly, from some TV program he hadn't seen, to a book he hadn't read, via several forays into more personal chat. He listened, quiet and polite, but unsure that this was what he wanted. They all seemed nice, but he'd hankered after something more overtly magical and different. They all seemed depressingly normal, and rather too much like him in some ways – social misfits perhaps, but not a world apart.

"Do you do a lot of protesting?" he asked Neil.

"Practical action," Neil said. "Protesting, tree planting, raising awareness. Making people think. That's me."

"So how do you get involved?" Steven asked.

"You interested? Sure."

Steven waited to see if there was more to come, and finding there wasn't he nodded in what he hoped was an encouraging way.

"Anti globalisation demonstration. Next week. Up in Birmingham. Come along."

"Where?"

"Floozy in the Jacuzzi, midday."

Steven nodded. Despite being fairly new to the area, he already knew that piece of public art well enough.

"You anti globalisation?" Neil asked.

"Yes," Steven said, even though he'd never really considered it before. He'd never had much time to invest in good causes, but he wanted to care more about the wider world and this seemed like as good a place to start as any. An irrational hope of finding the woman from the picture also contributed to his decision. Neil had said she went to protests. The idea of seeing her in person caught Steven's imagination. He wanted something to sweep him off his feet, and hoped she might be the one to do it. The memory of her eyes flickered through his mind. He knew perfectly well that the idea was slightly silly but that didn't seem so very important. He needed things that would make him feel something positive.

Watching them go their separate ways at the end of the evening, Steven thought the moot people weren't such a bad lot, even if he didn't really know what to make of any of them. After the initial awkwardness of presenting himself, they hadn't probed too deeply, for which he remained grateful.

Other pubs were emptying out into the street, with noisy groups of young men and women making their way home through the orange-lit streets. Looking at these merry-makers made him feel old. Not that he'd ever been like that himself, even in his teens. He had never been carefree and irresponsible, and wondered if he had missed out. What did it feel like to be responsible only for yourself? Steven had no idea, but realised that for the first time in his life, that was actually the size of it. The sheer possibility intimidated. He could do anything. What on earth was he going to do?

What do I want? That's the question. The problem was, he had no idea how to answer it. He had no idea how to live for himself, what to want, or where to go.

Standing in a darkened alleyway near his flat, he peered up between the buildings. Above him, a few stars twinkled, and Steven looked at them, thinking he had never paid them enough attention before. The world seemed full of details that he'd not previously had the time to notice. That would change. Everything would change.

Chapter Two

Centenary Square thronged with people. Steven had meant to lurk on the margins and be there while not quite part of the demonstration. Somehow he'd ended up in the middle of things, no longer able to see the edge of the crowd, or the many pairs of policeman watching the proceedings.

It occurred to him that the situation could get rough, dangerous even. He'd heard enough about rioting protesters from news programs. Anti globalisation was a term he associated with threat and otherness – a world to which he did not belong. Now he stood right in the middle of it, and so far nothing of any note had happened to him. He had no idea what normally went on at this kind of gathering aside from the much publicised violence and vandalism. With visions of anarchy and arrest in his head, he found the crush of people around him horribly oppressive, but try as he might, he couldn't get out of it. Not without pushing and shouting, and he didn't much fancy that either. For a while, he entertained visions of trying to force his way out, and unwittingly unleashing the chaos. Better to stay still.

Loud music blared from some nearby speaker, the pounding beats throbbing in his chest. Sunlight blazed down from above, burning the back of his neck where his hair didn't quite meet his collar. The sweat, heat and movement of tightly packed bodies disorientated him. Someone shouted through a loudspeaker, but he couldn't hear the words.

Steven wondered what he was doing. He didn't really understand the purpose of the event, and hadn't seen Neil anywhere. In this crowd the chances of spotting a familiar face seemed pretty low. He'd come on a whim, intoxicated by too much freedom. A bout of queasiness took him. Too hot. Too enclosed. He wanted to scream and flail about until he got free of this mess of people, but didn't act on the impulse. Remaining still took all the self control Steven could muster. Everything around him blurred. He staggered, bumping into a dreadlocked young woman. She pushed him away, shouting an indecipherable stream of words that sounded like an insult. The sounds flowing from her painted lips didn't quite make it into his head. Colours wheeled past him and he fell.

A face appeared over him. Dark eyes gazed down. A small, soft mouth formed unintelligible noises. Green hair. Impossibly green hair that must have come out of a bottle, swung over his face, tickling him. Serene eyes gazed down at him. The panic receded. He strained his ears, trying to make out what she said. Struggling with the sense of it, he tried to piece together the fragments. What did she want of him? A question? An offer of help? As he blinked the confusion out of his eyes, she slipped beyond his field of vision. Steven tried to pull himself up, but his head throbbed dangerously. She had gone, and in place of her face, he could see the dancing leaves of trees above him.

"You all right mate?" A gruff voice asked. Not unfriendly, he thought.

"Too hot," Steven croaked. "Better in a minute."

He lay on shaded flagstones, with no idea quite how he'd got there. The face belonging to the rough voice swam into view. He took in the uniform and realised he was seeing a policeman. He'd not expected them to be pleasant, given the circumstances. Nervousness squirmed in his stomach, tangoing with the effects of heatstroke until he felt sure he would vomit. He couldn't decide whether to feel reassured or threatened by the proximity of this policeman. It seemed easier just to lie still and stop thinking.

"Try and sit up. That's it. Put your head between your knees."

Steven followed the instructions, having no better ideas. Gradually the pounding in his head subsided.

"I'd go home if I were you," the policeman said. "Too hot for this sort of thing."

"Yeah," Steven replied, quite certain he wouldn't be moving for a while yet. He just wanted the man to leave him alone so that he could try and pin down the flitting ribbons of his heat-stricken memory. Dark eyes. Whispered words. Had that been real or just hallucination brought on by the noise and heat? Green wisps of hair blew across her face, and her voice had been low and rich in his ears, suggesting mystery but not actually making any sense. Steven shook his head, trying to shake out the mayhem, but it didn't help much.

Pulling himself to his feet, he stood in the shade of the nearby tree, glad of its cool protection from the blistering sun. The bright green shades of its leaves danced before his eyes, and he thought of her hair again, and laughed at himself for mistaking a tree for a person.

"All right?"

Looking round, he saw that a petite woman swathed in brightly coloured clothes had joined him in the small patch of shade. He nodded, having no idea what to say to her.

"Too hot for this," she said. "The forecast wasn't this hot, I'm sure it wasn't. Now I've lost my friends as well."

Steven nodded again, unable to think of anything to say. His eyes wandered towards the nearby throng, looking for a face that preyed on his mind.

"I haven't done one of these before, but I went to this green awareness thing last week, and there was this woman, and she told me about it so I thought I'd come along. I've always been really into trees anyway. I mean, I know it's not a tree protest or anything, but its all part of the bigger picture, isn't it?"

"It is?" Steven asked, wondering about the woman who had inspired this one along. He had no way of asking – not knowing the name that went with the remarkable face.

"Oh yeah. Like, I think everything happens for a reason, don't you? We're guided. Like maybe we were meant to run into each other here, today, under this tree."

"Why?"

She laughed at this. "How should I know? Maybe we won't realise for years why it was important. Tell you what, I'll give you one of these fliers and maybe it'll change your life. How does that sound?"

Steven smiled and accepted the flier. He pocketed it without looking at it. The brightly coloured creature remained rather too close to him for a while, then vanished off into the crowd again with a cheery farewell. He hoped she'd found her friends. She seemed weird, he thought. Nice as well though. As he thought about it, Steven realised his notion of 'normal' did not particularly include 'nice'. Normal people did not talk to strangers, or give you fliers, or offer to change your life. Steven smiled to himself, glad to have escaped from that way of looking at the world.

Later, while sat on the train he pulled the crumpled flier from his pocket and examined it. An advert for a new café stared back at him. *The Lemon Tree.* Located on his side of the city, he noticed as he scanned the tiny map, and vegan. Not his usual sort of thing. He thought about the unfamiliar young woman under the tree, and her talk about fate. Did he believe in fate? Steven decided he didn't much like the idea of everything following a plan. Even though his life to date hadn't been especially of his choosing, he hoped it would be possible to make his own decisions in the future. The notion of it all being mapped out by unknown forces seemed grim, but then, the world had not been especially kind to him so far. He supposed if you believed everything would to treat you kindly, destiny might not seem quite so nasty a prospect.

Staring through the scratched window-glass at a rapidly changing urban landscape beyond, it occurred to Steven that any choice he made could change his life. The decision to visit one place in preference to another. Whether to strike up idle conversation, or move on. He had been out today because of a picture in a newspaper and a chance conversation with a near-stranger in a pub. Now those seemingly random things had brought him to an unfamiliar young woman, and an advert for a café. *What if it is meant to be?* He could choose to follow these apparently meaningless threads, or he could do nothing. Steven hankered after change. He put the flier back in his pocket.

Rather than ride the train all the way back to his new hometown, he got off early, and followed the small map in search of *The Lemon Tree*. It took him down what looked weirdly like the high street of a small town. He supposed Birmingham had swallowed up other places as it grew. It wouldn't all have been houses once. There would have been gaps, he guessed. Fields. Streams. Hedges. A whole different world from this vast, urban expanse.

The café had a large, gaudy tree painted on its exterior, and pleasant cooking smells wafted from it, competing with the car fumes. Steven lingered outside, wondering if he should go in. Just the idea of eating around other people made him feel uncomfortable. The thought of consuming food in a public place felt embarrassing, threatening. He had no idea what would happen if he risked it. Still, he had come this far, he could at least buy a cup of tea. Drinking carried none of the same taboos in his mind.

"You don't need another drink," said a sharp voice, echoing from distant memory.

"But I'm thirsty. I'm dehydrated," his teenage self replied.

"You're too fat to be dehydrated. Fat people can't dehydrate."

He wanted to tell her that was camels, not people, but knew better than to press the point. Steven pushed the recollection to one side, not wanting to be caught up in the past.

Muted, formless music greeted him as he stepped inside. The small chime attached to the door brought a lanky youth to the counter. Steven mentally marked the lad down as a student. For a moment he wavered, trying to work out if he should sit down and then order, or do it the other way round.

"What can I get you?" the lad asked, resolving the problem.

"Just a tea, please."

"What sort of tea?"

"What sort of tea have you got?" Steven enquired, bemused.

"Organic fair traded, with caffeine or decaff. Green Tea. Red Bush. Any of these fruits and herbals on the back here. Cinnamon tea. I think that's the lot."

"Just ordinary tea please."

"Milk?"

"Please."

Steven paid, and took a tray to the nearest table. The allegedly normal tea tasted rather peculiar as he sipped at it. Then it dawned on him that whatever milk had gone into it had not originated in the udders of a cow. *What the hell kind of milk would a vegan café put in its tea?* He didn't quite have the nerve to ask. *Coconut milk maybe, or something else squeezed out of a plant?* From the flavour, he hadn't a clue. For want of anything else to do, Steven scanned the menu. The front read 'cruelty free eating - fairly traded organic food without animal products of any kind.' They seemed to have a lot of cakes on the list and he wondered how they managed that without eggs. Obviously there were ways. Thinking about food, without the stress of trying to eat it, was something he had secretly enjoyed for a long time. He could imagine all the tastes and textures, without the messy guilt of actually consuming anything. Sometimes he read the menus from fast food companies who delivered in his area.

Now what? He sat and drank and waited. If nothing came to him, then he knew this was just another of his mad ideas and he'd give it up. Steven had no sense of what he might be looking for – a chance word, another flier – there would be some clue to lead him on, or there would be nothing. Sipping at his tea, he reflected how nice it was to live from moment to moment, with no constraints, patterns or requirements. He rather liked it. The feeling of pleasure this gave him evoked a pang of guilt. This newly found freedom hadn't come without a price after all, and an uncomfortable price at that.

After half an hour, he slipped back into the street, resigned to discarding this latest whim as foolish. A gust of wind blew a piece of paper against his chest, and he grabbed it eagerly.

"Clearance Sale. Everything Must Go. Today only. Ends 5pm."

There was a map at the bottom, and as far as Steven could tell, he would only have to walk along a few streets to get there. With new found enthusiasm, he set off. It might be a game, but it was a serious game and he felt sure it would take him somewhere significant eventually. In a city this size the odds of finding one strange woman seemed slim, but if it was meant to be then perhaps he would find her. The more unlikely his journey became, the more certain he felt about it.

By the time he arrived, the sale had almost ended, but there were still a few people milling about, and the warehouse wasn't entirely empty. Steven wandered around aimlessly, not really wanting to buy anything. He watched the other people, and wondered what this meant for him and how he might proceed from here. A middle aged woman nearby pulled a toy witch from a pile of otherwise unremarkable looking soft toys. That seemed relevant. Steven followed her to the checkout, and then out into the carpark. He knew if she got in a vehicle, his luck would have run out. Instead, she set off on foot and he pursued at a safe distance, not wanting her to think he was following. He had no desire to alarm her, and it wasn't as though he meant her any harm, she was just another clue in his puzzle. He hadn't played this sort of game since his schooldays.

She walked down streets of tightly packed houses, all of which looked the same. Her pace remained even, unfaltering, and she never once looked back. More than a hundred yards behind her, Steven had no trouble keeping her in sight. He wondered if she was going home, and who she had bought the little fabric witch for. A child perhaps. Maybe she was old enough to have grandchildren. He couldn't tell and supposed it didn't really matter. She stopped briefly, gazing into the window of a shop. When Steven arrived at the same point a minute or so later, he gazed a she had done. A small sculpture stared back at him, its eyes full of challenge. He gazed back, trying to figure out what it was. It looked a bit like a pig, but it wasn't quite that. Compelled by the sculpted eyes, he entered the shop.

"You're just in time, we were closing," said a pleasant woman in a dark red suit. "How can I help you?"

"In the window. I'm not sure what it is, but it looks like a pig."

"A wild boar, hand carved in wood by a local artist, with a somewhat Pictish influence."

"A what?"

"Don't worry," she said, looking him up and down rather critically.

"No, I'm serious," he said, feeling suddenly defiant. "What's Pictish mean?"

"A group of people roughly contemporary with the ancient Celts who left us stylised depictions of certain animals."

"And wild boar, where did they come from?"

"They lived round here I expect," she said, and he had the nasty feeling she was teasing him.

"I'll buy it."

"It's sixty pounds."

Steven shrugged and pulled a handful of notes from his pocket, picking out three twenties.

"Deal."

She looked surprised, but said nothing. He carried the well-wrapped wooden boar carefully in his arms as he walked down the road, finding his wanderings had brought him back to the right train line. Chance indeed. He'd chased fate enough for one day, he thought. Time to take the wild boar home with him and do some intensive thinking.

Chapter Three

"Do you want to watch the midsummer sunrise with us?" Wiccan John asked.

Steven shifted the receiver into a more comfortable position before answering, "When?"

"Midsummer – early hours of the twenty-fourth. That's a Sunday this year. Makes it a bit easier on us wage slaves."

"Will I have to do anything?" Steven asked.

"Just turn up and bring some breakfast. We can pick you up if you need a lift."

"That would be good. Thanks."

"Give me your address, and we'll collect you at midnight. Oh, and bring a blanket, it gets very cold that time of night. You'll want a good coat, something waterproof if you have it, a drink, that sort of thing."

"Ok. Thanks"

"You don't drive then?" Elspeth said. "Or is it an ethical stance?"

"I don't drive anymore. I had a couple of prangs a few years ago, put my insurance through the roof. Couldn't afford to keep on." He had lost his nerve as well, but Steven saw no reason to include that detail.

"Neil is absolutely opposed to cars and won't even accept lifts," Elspeth added. "He's going to cycle tonight. I hate to think when he had to set off."

Little showed in the darkened countryside beyond as Steven gazed out of the car window. He had no idea what to expect from the night ahead.

"Aren't there hills nearer to town?" he asked.

"Oh yes," John replied. "But the sky stays orange from all the streetlights, and believe me, the sun coming up over Birmingham is not an inspiring sight. That's why we come out here instead."

They pulled into a darkened car-park. Carol, Sean, Mindy and Neil were all visible, huddled into a small car. Neil's bike leaned against a nearby fence. Apparently taking shelter in a car was ok, even if travelling that way wasn't acceptable to Neil. Steven trailed behind John and Elspeth as they went over.

"I had a call from Heathen John about ten minutes ago, he's running a bit late and said not to wait for him," Carol said.

"We might as well get going then," Elspeth suggested.

Steven placed himself at the back of the party as they set off. The path seemed firm and well maintained, although he couldn't really see it. He didn't own a torch, and couldn't see all that well in the dark. Ahead of him, a few small lights bobbed, and Neil complained sporadically about Mindy blinding him with her torch. As the path grew steeper, Steven puffed, struggling to keep pace. Although he walked as a mode of transport, that usually meant on the flat and with pavements under his feet. The way forwards changed into high steps, and his legs started to ache.

"Are you all right back there?" Wiccan John called down from somewhere ahead.

"I'm fine. Just not as fit as I could be," Steven said.

"You can't get lost so long as you keep going up," John said.

Listening to the pained thud of his heart, Steven kept going. His legs hurt and he felt unsteady – on this steep hillside in the dark, it seemed as though he could fall all too easily. Still, he felt acutely aware of himself and the sensation wasn't entirely unpleasant. Most of the time, his head had been be the only place where he lived, while his body remained something between an inconvenience, and a way of getting around. Panting for breath, he felt more solid and substantial than usual. The hill seemed to go on forever, he couldn't imagine how high they were, or how he would get down in the morning. He could hear distant sounds of talking ahead of him, and followed as best he could, stopping frequently to catch his breath. Then the sound of conversation came from behind him as well.

"I must be bloody loopy to let you talk me into this," a male voice said gruffly.

"Yep," replied a younger sounding female speaker.

He stopped to let them go by. They kept their torches low, and he caught a glimpse of a silver haired man and a younger woman. His first thought was that they must be father and daughter, but he noticed they were holding hands, and thought again.

Just as he made it to the top, a vaguely familiar voice said, "All right mate?"

"Yes, thank you," he said, awkwardly, not sure who had spoken to him.

The other man came up behind him and flashed his torchlight about fleetingly, illuminating a small cluster of people sitting in a dip on the hilltop.

"Put the pissing torch away," Neil objected. "Bloody blinding everyone."

"And a very good evening to you too, Neil," Heathen John said, making his way down into the dip.

In the near total darkness, Steven could see very little. The grass felt very cold beneath him as he sat.

"Are you expecting anyone else?" a soft and unfamiliar voice asked.

"I think this is the lot," Elspeth replied. She rattled off a list of names, and the others all offered greetings as she identified them.

"Vicky and Dan are from Worcester," Elspeth explained. "They emailed me a couple of days ago."

"Cool," said Mindy. "The more the merrier."

"Well, at least its better weather than last year," Wiccan John said.

"Bloody pissed it down," Neil added.

"The year before was good though, when we had that full moon set before the sun came up," Mindy said. "What phase of the moon are we at?"

"Waxing. The dark moon was about a week ago," Carol replied. "I think you can still see it if you go up on the edge and have a look, although it can't be far off setting."

Steven sat quietly for as long as he could, but the cold ground didn't lend itself to resting easily. He regretted not having brought a blanket. After a while, he rose, stretching his chilled and cramped limbs. Turning away from the little cluster of Pagans, he looked out across the darkened countryside. Here and there, small lights gleamed back at him, suggesting the presence of houses and villages. Away in the distance he could see the orange glow that might perhaps be Birmingham. Wind buffeted against him, the sound of it ringing slightly in his ears. Having lived all his life in urban places, he didn't think he had ever been anywhere so isolated and exposed before. A distant grumble and moving light spoke of a lone car in the lanes below. They were evidently a long way up. Moving cautiously, he walked round the small summit of the hilltop. It seemed improbably even in shape, and not very big. Almost like something a child might have drawn.

When he came back to the circle, they were talking about ghosts.

"I don't see things so much as feel them," Mindy announced. "Or I know, but not in a visual way."

"I've seen," the girl with the soft voice said. Steven had forgotten her name.

"So have I," the older man with her added. "We both saw the same person in fact."

"Dan didn't know her when she as alive, and he described her to me perfectly."

"How strange," Carol said. "I've never seen anything either, but I'm like Mindy, I feel things sometimes."

"Apparently my grandmother used to see ghosts," Heathen John put in. "I never did, but I do believe some people come back."

"Do you think they're aware; that they're spirits who stay, or just some kind of echo?" Wiccan John asked.

"I don't know," Mindy said, yawning loudly.

The night seemed to pass more slowly than any other he could remember. Steven had endured some long and slow nights in his life, but usually sleep caught up with him in the end. He felt far too cold to even think of trying, and sitting for long made him worse, so he walked the small circumference of the hilltop every so often, looking up at the vast sky above. Having no sense of direction, he couldn't work out where he should be looking for the sunrise. The conversation between them had all but died, and in its stead lay a companionable silence – none of them had anything more to say. Darkness, the hill and the cold night air had taken each of them away to some other place. Steven could feel it himself – the weight of the hill beneath him, and the enormity of the sky above demanded quiet reverence. Of all the things he had done of late, this felt the most significant. Being this cold and tired felt utterly real.

Eventually, the faintest hint of blue crept across the horizon. Steven noticed its presence as he took yet another turn about the hilltop. It was easier to see his immediate surroundings – the humps and bumps in the grass became more apparent, and the cluster of human forms, draped in blankets and sitting in ones and twos were visible as dark outlines.

"It's getting lighter," he called out softly.

Heads raised. In moments they were all on their feet. Mindy made it to his side first.

"I've done this loads of times, but I still end up wondering if the sun's going to come up at all. It's really magical, isn't it?" she said.

"Yes. How long before the actual sunrise?" Steven enquired.

"Oh, ages yet." She sat down on the ridge running round the summit. "Are you cold?"

"A bit."

"Want some blanket?"

"It's ok."

"Seriously," she persisted. "It's quite a big blanket and I'd feel totally guilty if you froze to death or something."

Steven didn't manage to protest quickly enough. Mindy peeled her blanket off one shoulder and wrapped it round his. The gesture seemed very intimate to him, but he felt warmer at once, then realised with a flush of embarrassment that it was due to her body heat locked in the cloth. He held the end of the blanket across his chest. One by one, the others came up to sit at the very top as well.

By imperceptibly small degrees, the sun climbed, and before it, the sky lightened, turning the horizon blue, and painting the few wisps of cloud with crimsons, pinks and gold. Gradually, the landscape came into view. Steven watched in wonder as a huge swathe of open countryside appeared out of the flat darkness. Countless green fields spread in all directions. Wooded hills formed a line with stretching to left and right from the hill beneath him, while across the valley, another line ran in parallel.

"That's the Cotswolds over there," Mindy said. "Lots of barrows. We did a trip to them back in the spring."

Below he could see what looked like a terrace with a high bank on the outside edge. Carol and Sean slithered down the slope and up onto this bank, then set off walking along its top. The couple from Worcester followed not far behind them. Steven watched the ambling pairs for a little while, then curiosity won out and he followed after them.

Heavy dew in the grass made the steep bank harder to climb than he had expected. Reaching the top, Steven could see another terrace below. These dramatic earthen constructions ran along the hillside, circling its considerable girth. Walking slowly on the slippery ground, he followed the high bank round, stopping frequently to gaze out at the vast rural landscape unveiling itself around him.

"Isn't there supposed to be a dawn chorus?" he asked on his return. He'd never heard one.

"We're too high up to hear it," Mindy said. "They'll be singing their little hearts out down in the trees. It's the only real downside of coming here."

"So what do you think?" Elspeth asked.

"Quite some view. What is this place? It doesn't look entirely natural," Steven asked.

"It's an Iron Age hill fort, but this top section was added later, for a mediaeval hunting lodge. There are a few information boards about if you have a look."

"Think how much work it would take to shift all that earth by hand," Mindy said.

"Picks made out of bone and antler, wooden shovels," Elspeth added. "Who today has the imagination to do anything on that scale, or to make something that would last as long?"

"Look!" Carol called to them.

Just visible above the distant hills in the south east a thin, brilliant band of golden light glowed. Steven looked for a few seconds, but his vision blurred and he had to turn away. Stood on the earthen embankment, they watched in silence as the sun cleared the horizon and rose majestically into the sky. Once it was fully visible, Elspeth started passing round cups of something warm, accompanied by small cakes.

"Will you let me know if you're doing anything else like this?" Vicky asked.

"Absolutely. Did you enjoy it then?"

"It's been wonderful."

"Hmm," the man at her side responded.

"Ignore his grumpiness. I think he enjoyed it really," the young woman added.

Steven saw the smiles flashing between them. They seemed an unlikely pair, but the connection they shared looked so strong, it almost seemed to make the air around them hum slightly. Exhausted as he was, and with eyes bleary from lack of sleep, he could see dancing spots of light circling most of his companions, flickering in different shades and with varying degrees of intensity.

"I'm going up to Birmingham next weekend, I don't know if you'd heard about it, but there's some sort of thing on at the Custard Factory," Vicky said.

"Discovering the forest," Mindy put in. "I'm going too. I heard about it at that moot the other week."

"I met Willow a couple of weeks ago. She seemed really interesting."

"I got that impression," Mindy responded.

"Ok, so maybe I'll see some of you there then? We need to get going. We haven't got over the festival last weekend yet."

"I'm getting too old to keep sitting up all night. You can drive," Dan said.

The woman chuckled at this. "Living dangerously!" Turning back to the rest of them she added, "I'll hopefully see you again then. Thanks for letting us come along."

As they all walked down the hill, the countryside came alive with colour. The rich greens of young brackens vied with soaring spikes of dark pink foxgloves, while birdsong filled the air. Steven felt elated, although his entire body ached from the cold and exertion. In the car park, he plucked up the courage to approach Mindy.

"This thing next weekend. Could I go with you?"

"Sure. I'm going in on the one o'clock train though. I don't like driving in Birmingham in the day." She grinned at him. "See you then I guess." She squeezed the top of his arm, and shot off before he even had time to think about it.

Chapter Four

Through the crush of the Pallasades and out into the public space beyond, Steven followed Mindy's slight form, trying not to lose her in the heaving crowd. The sheer swell of numbers disorientated him. Steven liked to think of himself as urban, but the enormous press of people here surprised him. His home town seemed small and provincial in retrospect, although it had been the entirety of his world for most of his life. Opportunities to travel had been few. Once outside the train station, they had a little more room to manoeuvre, and the noise lessened.

"I always feel a bit funny coming past here," Mindy said.

"Why?" Steven asked, knowing she had deliberately lured him into talking.

"I read a book once, right, and in it the church over there had been turned into a nightclub for supernatural beings."

"Right," he responded, eyeing up the uneven form of St Martin in the Bullring.

"Every time I come past, I wonder if this city has a secret life. You could be anyone here, anything."

"Would you want that?" he asked.

"What, a world with vampires and werewolves and stuff? I think so. I wonder if there was a bull ring here once, and if there were ever druids on Druids Heath."

"And did they ever make Custard at the Custard Factory?" Steven asked.

"They did, you know. So maybe all the other stuff is true as well. What do you think?"

"I don't know," Steven said, but he enjoyed thinking about it.

They hurried along the sides of streets heavy with traffic then at last plunged off the main road into a narrow, car-free street.

"This is it," Mindy said.

Steven caught sight of a giant statue, something like a man, but made out of all kinds of things. Mindy swept him through a low door, into a quiet space full of people. Having paid their entrance fee, they looked for seats. Steven scanned the room, and saw the woman he'd met in the Malverns sitting by herself. Mindy waved and went over, even though Steven had the impression she didn't know the other woman any better than he did. He followed, because that looked like the easiest option.

A middle-aged man presented himself at the front of the room and began talking about the event. Steven wasn't really listening. His attention wandered around the room in pursuit of a familiar face, but to little avail. Another man, one with a grey beard and a lulling voice talked for a while about the history of forests and woodlands. The room became warm and Steven slid into a restful state, as he tried to follow the unfamiliar descriptions of the history of British forests. There was a lot to take in but occasional words stood out for him. Aurochs. Small leaved lime. Pollards. Underwood.

Wild Boar. Mention of the creature whose image he had recently bought snapped him into paying closer attention to the descriptions of how forests may once have been. Try as he might, he found the man's droning voice hard to concentrate on. However, talk of a lost forest that had once covered the Midlands caught his imagination.

After a break, the next speaker was introduced as Willow Arden. As she came to the front of the room, she seemed nondescript. However, as soon as she began to speak, she had Steven's total attention.

"The forest may have gone, but the spirit of it remains. What has been lost can come again."

The voice; low, feminine and utterly compelling, stirred him from his previous stupor. Steven sat up, eyes opening, senses inexplicably alert. Then he saw her, truly. He guessed her to be about his height, with long shapely legs encased in black denim, and a close fitting black top with long sleeves. With her pale skin and dark hair, she looked stark somehow, but even from this distance he could see how her eyes flashed. In his first glance he took in the sharp angles of her face, the dark eyebrows and expressive mouth. She looked a lot like the woman from Neil's photo, and the face he had seen or imagined during the anti globalisation demonstration. He had seen those features – or something very much like them – in many of his dreams. She seemed important, and familiar. As she spoke, he focused on her words, hoping for insight.

"The woods are a dangerous place, full of mystery and perceived threat. Even now many people fear to enter them at night. They have been reputed to harbour not just thieves and outlaws, but also witches, fairies and the devil himself. Our medieval ancestors saw the wildwood as a place of spiritual as well as physical hazards and they are not the only ones of have equated order with goodness and chaos with evil." She paused, looking out at the audience, and for a moment it seemed to Steven that she stared him directly in the eyes. He quailed before her intensity, drawn to it, but terrified as well.

"Before humans came to these shores, the land was wooded and home to countless other beings. The history of people in this land is a history of tree felling and land clearance. We have taken far more than we needed. Once, the Forest of Arden stretched for many miles, but now only the ghost of it remains in small woods and coppices. Trees grow up that have never seen such woodland, and the sense of there ever having been a forest dwindles from year to year. How will you open your hearts to these stifled voices? How will you hear the cry of the dying forest, the echo of a vanishing echo? If you can hear the forest whisper to you, then you can be part of the process that makes it live again."

"Close your eyes," she demanded, her voice barely above a whisper. "Close your eyes and let my words carry you, down into the depths of the dark soil beneath, into the heart of the land where there is still memory, and the seeds of the forest lie still and buried, waiting to be found. For you are all seeds yourselves, all lying in secret places, waiting to be stirred into new life and new knowing."

Steven felt as though he was sinking, able to imagine the rich dark loam embracing him. Merely a seed that might never sprout, but which could lie dormant for countless years, waiting for the right conditions. Perhaps the time had come. He might be able to grow now.

"I am the spirit of the forest of Arden. I am the voice of the trees. I speak to you from the past, and I speak into your future, if you will take me into your heart. I am the green life of sap, springing up in this place of concrete and tarmac. I am the memory of buds and acorns, green shoots and the browning leaves of autumn. Listen to my call, hear my voice and come with me into the lost groves and glades where you might catch glimpse of red deer, or wild cattle. Follow me along the deer tracks to where the aurochs browse for their food and a thousand small birds sing from the high branches. I am the soul of Arden made flesh. I am the ancient wildwood and I will dance in your veins if you will but let me."

In his mind's eye, Steven could see very clearly the tangled trees and ancient giants of the wildwood. He seemed to float through these images, glimpsing flashes of movement from time to time, but not knowing what they meant. He could smell the living greenness of the air, and the slow ponderous existences of great oaks and limes. Carried by her sonorous voice and captivating words, he journeyed into the depths of his own mind, forgetting the hall and those who sat nearby him.

A hand on his arm jolted Steven into alertness.

"Wakey, wakey, time to go," Mindy announced.

Looking around, Steven saw that people were already leaving. He felt disorientated and not sure what had just happened to him. Swirling fragments of dreams still occupied his thoughts and he could hear a faint echo of that compelling voice in his head even above the hubbub in the room. The woman who had guided his dreaming remained invisible to his questing gaze. She had already left, he surmised, and the thought of having come so close to the person he'd been looking for without actually meeting her left him with a dull ache in his chest.

"Do you want to see if the Medicine Bar is open?" Vicky asked.

"Sure," Mindy replied.

Steven shrugged to himself and followed behind them, still scanning faces for the dark eyed woman.

"Have you seen the dragon?" Mindy asked, pointing upwards.

Tilting his head back, Steven saw a mass of claws and copper scales above him where a large dragon sculpture clung convincingly to the side of the building.

Sitting outside, with drinks in hand they began picking over the afternoon.

"I'm glad I came," Vicky said. "I feel like I've learned a lot."

"Me too," Mindy returned.

Steven just grunted an agreement, not feeling much inclined to talk abut his experiences.

"Do you think she meant it literally?" Mindy asked. "The woman at the end who kept saying about how she was the spirit of the forest."

"I doubt it," Vicky replied, gazing thoughtfully into the distance. "I don't claim to be any kind of expert, but I'm pretty sure it's what Druids do. They say 'I am' a lot. I think it's a technique they use for getting closer to whatever they're exploring. Does that make sense?"

"Like an empathy thing?" Mindy asked.

"I guess so," Vicky said.

Steven pricked up his ears at this. While he'd been immersed in the woman's talking, he'd never questioned what she said. It felt true. She sounded how he imagined the voice of a forest should – strong and certain, full of mystery and possibility.

"I'd like to think she was," he said.

Both women focused their full attention on him, making him feel distinctly uncomfortable. "You were saying before about werewolves and vampires…" he added uncertainly, looking to Mindy for support.

"Well, why not? Weird things happen," Vicky said. "And I can see what you mean, it's a lovely idea. The spirit of Arden in human form, teaching people how to care for the trees."

"We'd never know, would we?" Mindy put in. "I mean, you meet people all the time without knowing what they are, or who they are. So maybe she did mean it literally after all."

"I think sometimes that we choose our own reality," Vicky said. "That we see what we expect to see." She glanced down to her watch. "I'd best be off, Dan's cooking and I promised I'd be back for tea. I'll catch up with you another time, yes?"

"Be seeing you," Mindy said.

The remaining pair sat quietly, watching Vicky depart.

"She's an odd one," Mindy commented.

"What makes you say that?"

"Well for a start, her bloke's got to be like twenty years older than her, which is pretty weird if you ask me."

"I never thought age was all that important," Steven said. "So long as you get along together. Not that I'm any great expert."

"Are you single then?" Mindy asked.

"Yes." He looked up at the dragon again, not wanting to meet her gaze.

Taking the hint, Mindy changed the subject. "Come on then, let's have a nose round the bookshop and go find a train."

Steven thought the little complex was exactly how an urban environment ought to be – interesting and arty, with things going on, and water features, plants, and no cars. When they came out onto the main road and headed back towards New Street station, the noise, car fumes and run-down buildings came as a bit of a shock. Once, there had been forest here, he realised. Right now, the earth seemed distant and the lost trees hard to imagine. Maybe he could learn to at least imagine it, and he tried to picture what might have been there before the buildings. He did not glimpse the past, though. For a few moments he had an impression of flickering green energy, fragmenting the tarmac and clearing the way for an explosion of vegetative growth. The idea of it made him smile.

Chapter Five

"Are you doing anything now?" Mindy asked as they wandered slowly along the platform towards the exit.

"Not really," Steven said.

"I only live round the corner, if you want to swing in for a tea or a coffee or something."

"Ok."

The offer startled him, because there had never been one like it before in his life. Partly, he supposed, because he'd never previously spent time in the kinds of places where you might meet people. Or not the sort of people who might invite you home, at any rate. After school, most of his contact with people had been through miserable jobs where no one interesting stayed for very long.

Mindy took him to a flat in the basement of a large house. There wasn't much natural light, and the few rooms were rather messy, but he could tell she was proud of it.

"I only got it about six months ago. Took me ages to save up for a deposit. Before then I was still living with the parents – a major drag. Do you have your own place?"

"Yes."

"You don't say much, do you?"

"I'm sorry. A lot of the time I don't have much to say. You must find me rather dull."

"Oh. I thought you were just shy. You don't seem that dull to me." Mindy ceased talking for a little while as she ran water to put the kettle on. "So what sort of place do you have?" she enquired.

"I rent a flat."

"You don't sound like you're from round here. Near here maybe, but that's not a Bromsgrove accent, is it?"

"I didn't grow up here, no. I moved here a few weeks ago."

"Why?"

"I wanted to live somewhere different."

"So what was it?" Mindy asked as she sorted out clean mugs from her heavily laden draining board. "Relationship breakdown? New job?"

Steven sighed audibly. He had no idea how to answer this and wasn't entirely sure he wanted to say what had happened. He had no idea what anyone else would think of his life.

"Look, its ok, if you've got some big dark secret and you don't want to share it. All my friends tell me I'm far too nosey anyway, so don't pay any attention to whatever crap I come out with ok?"

"It's not that interesting," he offered.

"I'm interested in everything," Mindy said, a provocative smile playing across her face.

Steven considered the look n her face, and how alone he felt with everything. He wasn't used to sharing his experiences with other people. However, conversations with assorted professionals in recent months had been better than he'd dared to hope. He realised that h did want to tell her.

"My mother has been ill for a very long time. It got worse when my father left. I was fourteen then. I've cared for her ever since then. Then a couple of months ago she got more sick than I could manage. I had to give up. She's in a nursing home now. She needs more help than I could give her."

"Bloody hell," Mindy said. She gave Steven's shoulder a friendly squeeze, then passed him a mug.

"There was a lot to sort out. Legal stuff, medical stuff. She had quite a big house and I had to sell it to pay for all the costs but there was enough left to get me started renting a little place. I moved, I just wanted a fresh start."

He hadn't quite meant to say that much, but having started, the whole thing came tumbling out all too readily. It felt strange hearing himself describe what had happened in such a brief, superficial way.

"So all you've done since you were a kid is stay home and look after your mother?"

"I've always had part time jobs too, but basically, yes. I looked after her."

"Explains why you're so…" Mindy trailed off, looking distinctly awkward.

"What? Shy? Not good with people?"

"Yeah," Mindy said.

"Most likely," Steven agreed.

"So what's wrong with her?" Mindy asked.

"Depression, anorexia. I guess agoraphobia as she never went out if she could help it."

"And I thought my parents were bad."

"Are they?" Steven asked.

"Just middle class and neurotic. Nothing on this scale." She threw a pile of books and magazines onto the floor and gestured towards the exposed sofa seats.

Steven sat, gazing around him at the jumble of possessions – books, clothes, CDs and other assorted detritus. His own flat looked rather empty and unlived in by comparison.

"You've really been through the grinder, haven't you," Mindy said.

She covered his hand with her own, her skin slightly warmer than his. For a few moments, Steven stopped breathing. His entire body froze rigid and an icy shiver passed through the length of his frame. A roaring sound filled his ears, like flood in full torrent, or a hurricane, or a jet engine taking off. His thoughts blurred, overtaken by immediate sensation. Steven had no idea what was happening to him. It felt as though all control had been stripped from him and his limbs were directed by another. Heaviness and confusion filled him, but he had no means of regaining control.

Then Mindy was in his arms, as he pressed her back against the arm of her sofa. Her mouth yielded to his, tongue pressing into her heat, taking and tasting her. He had no conscious idea of what to do or how to do it, but his body had taken over, driven on by animal urges. She felt so warm, so soft, the sweetness of her overwhelmed him.

The zip on his jacket caught on her flimsy top, and when he pulled away and tried to untangle them he ended up pulling a thread loose. He fumbled, awkward and making things worse.

"Stop," she said softly.

There was a look on her face that he couldn't read. Something troubled, and it scared him to see it.

"Did I get something wrong?" he asked.

"It's not you," she said, pulling the unravelling threads of her top out of his fingers and snapping them to separate herself from him.

"I'm sorry about the top," he said, trying to work out what was wrong.

"It doesn't matter about the top," Mindy said. "Can you just… can you go, please? I shouldn't have done this, I'm sorry, it was a bad idea, I'm not…" she trailed off.

"Please tell me what I've done," he said.

"Please just go," she said, and her voice sounded panicky.

He rose awkwardly, knocking over his partially consumed cup of tea. She didn't seem to notice.

"I'll see you at the moot, yes?"

"Maybe, I don't know."

Feeling awkward and embarrassed he hurried out into the twilight.

Once he got home, Steven showered and put on something clean. After that he found it easier to think things through properly. He couldn't make much sense of what had happened between them. He didn't have her number, so he couldn't phone and apologise, but he wanted to say sorry for whatever had made her so suddenly uncomfortable. The memory of her mouth beneath his and the softness of her flesh sent him into a state of happy distraction, but the memory of her discomfort was like a punch in the gut. Steven felt he might easily sit on the side of his bed all night, contemplating everything that had happened. His first kiss, first caress, first taste of passion. He'd wondered before what all the fuss was about, watching supposedly erotic films late at night, but feeling nothing. Mindy had turned his world upside-down, filling it with wondrous possibilities. But then everything had gone weirdly wrong and he didn't know why.

Lying back on the bed, he wondered what it would be like to go further with her. The desire and the worry tangled together. He kept thinking about how she'd kissed him, and then about how distressed she'd looked. It made no sense. What was he missing?

In the morning, he ordered a bunch of flowers from the florists on the corner of his road. He wrote, 'you are beautiful," and set off with a spring in his step to go and look for a job. He'd been putting it off since arriving, but today the sun shone down and he had kissed a beautiful girl, and all things seemed possible. He stood outside the closed jobcentre, realising he had lost track of the days. Today was Sunday. Reading through everything in the window passed the time. He wasn't really qualified for anything they had on offer. By now, he supposed, the florist's van would have reached her flat. He hoped he'd got the number right. The ringing bell would draw her out, and then she would see the roses, and smile, and feel happy, and she would forgive him for not knowing what he was doing. He almost wished he could be there to see the look on her face, but he hadn't quite had the nerve to take the flowers round himself.

Armed with chocolates and a bottle of wine, Steven retraced his steps to Mindy's basement flat. The curtains were all drawn, even though it was only seven in the evening. His heart raced as he pressed the doorbell. He had no idea how she might react. Was it possible that she would she throw her arms round him right on the doorstep where anyone could see? Would she talk to him about what had happened and why she'd been upset? He wanted to understand.

There were no sounds audible from inside the flat. She didn't come to the door. Checking his watch, Steven decided to wait five minutes and try again, just in case she was in the shower, or something else like that. After ten minutes with still no sign of her, and he guessed she'd gone out with friends for the evening. He left the wine and chocolates by her door, tucked out of sight from the road. The gift would make her smile, he hoped and at least she would know he'd been thinking about her.

The next day, after applying for a few things in the job centre, he wandered round town and found a pretty little top to replace the one he'd accidentally ripped. It looked to be about Mindy's size.

"It's for my girlfriend," he told the cashier proudly, "but I'm not entirely sure what size she is."

"It can vary from one shop to another anyway," the girl replied with a smile. "Keep the receipt, and if it doesn't fit, you can swap it for another one."

"That's great, thanks."

He bought a card and a pen, then sat on a bench in the high-street and carefully wrote out a note.

Dear Mindy. This is to replace the top I ripped. I didn't mean to damage it. I hope this top will be ok, it's as similar as I could find. I have the receipt if the size is wrong. Here is my phone number if you want to call me. Could we meet up for a drink? I think I'm in love with you.
Steven.

He added his number to the bottom then sealed the card into its envelope. Going to Mindy's on the way home gave him a bit of a detour, but he didn't mind.

Knowing she would be at work, he didn't bother trying the doorbell, but left the card and parcel in the same place as he had the previous day's gifts. Those had gone, he noticed.

Chapter Six

Early in the afternoon, the rain began. Heavy clouds rolled in across the Worcestershire skies, blocking out the sun and destroying all suggestion of balmy summer. Steven stood at his window for a long time, watching the way the rain bounced on the pavement beneath, as a puddle grew around the blocked drain. He turned the television on for a while and listened to news of flood warnings. The phone hadn't rung yet, although he remained poised, ready to dash for the handset at the first sound. Surely she would call him today, having received the card and his number. He wondered if his offerings were still dry – the spot had been quite sheltered, but in this rain, water might easily collect there. If the card became too wet, she wouldn't be able to read what he had written. The idea worried him, but there wasn't much he could do about it.

Squatting down, he looked into the face of the wooden boar. Too close for his eyes to focus on it properly, it swam through his vision and almost seemed to move. Pulling his head back a little, he could see one eye, gazing back with an expression of challenge. Words from Saturday's strange lecture floated through his mind. *Reconnect with the forest.*

Discover the spirit of Arden. Find your own wild soul. The flat felt too small and oppressive.

Walk, said a voice that might have been his own, or the boar's, or even that of the spirit of Arden herself.

Steven pulled on his one waterproof coat, securing the hood around his head, then went out into the downpour. The streets were almost empty of pedestrians, but cars sped by, flinging water up at him. Soon his jeans were soaked through, but he ignored the cold and discomfort. He walked without thinking, not worrying about where he was going, just following what he assumed must be an instinct. So long as he kept moving, the chill from lashing wind and rain didn't get to him too much.

Soon all sense of time and distance vanished and walking became a compulsion he could not resist. Out beyond the boundaries of the town he went, following the A road as it plunged into open countryside. With the clouds low and dense, the light faded earlier than usual, although he had little sense of the time. Seeing a patch of woodland, he dashed across the main road, taking is chances with a fleeting break in the traffic. After climbing over a rickety wooden fence, he made his way in amongst the trees. Here the rain was much reduced, but he soon found that instead of continual small droplets, occasional large ones fell on him instead. Pushing back the hood of his coat, he stood listening to the sound of rain on leaves, and breathing in the damp, earthy smell of the woodland. When he walked, he did so without any real idea of where he wanted to go next. Being outside seemed more important than any thought of a destination.

He'd never been out in conditions like this before – not in a wild place. The most he had experienced of the elements involved dashing to and from work. It felt alien, but also intense and real in ways he wasn't used to.

The light faded away almost entirely. Steven realised he needed to turn back for home and that he was hopelessly lost, with no way of seeing the path. He stopped, gazing back into the damp and looming mass of trees that flanked the way he had come. There had been plenty of turnings he thought. How would he find the road again? Walking slowly, he tried not to succumb to rising panic. *The woods are a dangerous place, full of mystery and perceived threa*t. He could hear her words in his mind, all too clearly. In daylight the trees looked safe enough, but now they stood as darker shadows against the encroaching night and anything might lurk beneath them. Talk of wolves and wild boar seemed far less comfortable now that he walked alone in this muddy woodland. Ideas of ancient pagan deities tickled at his thoughts. It had been one thing talking about them in the warmth and light of an all too human pub. Now the idea of primal beings and old powers filled him with awe. What if he should chance upon such an entity? It seemed entirely possible out here, and terrifying.

Several times, he stumbled, his feet finding loose matter on the path, or skidding in the mud. He walked into a thorn, tangling himself in the sharp branches as he mistook the path's direction. The trees pressed in ever more closely and he felt increasingly vulnerable and lost. He stopped, feeling the cold dampness of his jeans more acutely than ever, as though all the heat in him was being sucked out into the rain. Panicking and flailing around blindly clearly wouldn't work. Sucking in a few deep breaths, Steven tried to think clearly. As he looked into what he first considered impenetrable gloom, he began to notice things. If he concentrated, he could make out some of the forms of trees. A faintly silver line ran between some of them, like a magical path. He blinked a few times, at first not quite believing it. Gradually he reasoned out what he had spotted – the puddles were thickest on the path, because there the ground had been eroded down to stones and clay. What little light remained, reflected down from the clouds and just made the route visible. He set off, following this faintly glimmering pathway. His feet found a harder surface beneath the layer of water, although from time to time the mud still caught him out.

Water soaked into his shoes, chilling his feet. The weight of it hung in his jeans, pulling him downwards with every step. Steven started to think he could feel the path not merely see it, as though the way forwards had a different resonance beneath his feet. The notion struck him as being irrational, but he couldn't shake it off. The land seemed to have its own language, and if he listened carefully, he could not only hear, but understand. Although he couldn't see the ground beneath his feet, he found no roots to trip him, and even in the worst of the mud he did not actually fall.

The woodland no longer felt like a place of danger. Instead, the trees seemed like friendly forms; companions in this strange night-time wandering rather than foes. Still the thought of wildwood and its more dangerous inhabitants reoccurred in his mind.

He doubted he would feel so at ease if the shadows really could harbour fierce creatures. Thinking back, he felt sure the first speaker at that talk had said something about big wildcats, and bears even, as well as the wolves living in the ancient forests. So far as he knew, he'd never been in mortal danger in his entire life. He supposed, according to the statistics he'd seen that getting into a car was about the most dangerous thing he did with any frequency. Everyone did that, so he didn't normally give it much thought. Perhaps it was the same if you lived alongside wolves and bears and things, he speculated. You got used to the fear. Given time, anything might seem normal.

He imagined it might be possible to walk through these woods and be taken back into the ancient lost forests. He could, even now be journeying away from the life he had known and into some kind of otherworld full of tall trees and primal dangers. The woodland seemed to go on forever, as it must have once done. How long had he been walking now? From the ache in his legs and the growing hunger in his guts, he thought it must be a long time. Everything he had been, with all the attendant grievances and limitations, he could consign to the past. He could start a new life. But as what? He had no skills to speak of, could not make a fire, did not know how to hunt, or build a shelter. How would he know what it might be safe to eat?

I can take care of sick people, he thought, but a treacherous voice in his head added, *so long as they aren't too sick.*

"I tried," he said aloud, making his confession to the silent trees. "I did everything I could. Most of my life I've just looked after her. I couldn't do it anymore." His own feeling of guilt threw up harsh accusations, whispering of cowardice and betrayal. Keeping her at home when he couldn't give her the care she needed would have been a worse sort of betrayal, surely?

At fifty, his mother already looked like a very old woman. Years of starving herself had sallowed her skin, and it hung slackly from her bones, making her seem barely alive. If there had ever been light in her eyes, he did not remember it. Some days, all she did was sit and stare out of the window, and cry. More times than he could count he had begged her to see a doctor, but she had always refused.

"You'll look after me. You won't leave me, will you Steven? Not you. You wouldn't do that to me as well."

The memory of her pleading stabbed him through all over again. The feeling that he had betrayed her wouldn't go away. She had been so weak in the end, so powerless. It had been surprisingly easy to get her taken into care, and at least now there would be trained people to look after her. Getting power of attorney had been gruelling, but in the end, social services had recommended it. That only came after a lot of hard conversations about why he hadn't done more and sooner, and the guilt from those exchanges had weighed heavily on him. Without a diagnosis, his mother did not legally count as a vulnerable adult, and without her cooperation, a diagnosis had not been possible. Only when she collapsed had it become feasible to call an ambulance. Everything else had followed from there.

He remembered the strange exhilaration of being alone for the first time. Alongside this, for the first time ever, he had been in control of his own life. The resentment in her eyes when he next saw her took all the pleasure from that brief triumph. *Does it make me a bad person if I'm glad about not having to be responsible for her anymore?* He asked, and not for the first time. Duty bound him to caring for her, but he felt that much of her illness had been self inflicted. Sometimes he thought that she had used her fragility to keep him prisoner, to stop him from leaving and making his own life. Had she been wrong in how she treated him? Had he been wrong to stay? He didn't know. Without the requirement to care for her, his life felt hollow. What point was there in his existence if he did nothing useful? What else was he good for?

"You are selfish and cruel, just like your father. Just like him. You're all the same."

No matter how far he ran, there could be no escaping from the words in his head.

Steven had the feeling that if she hadn't gone into care, he could not have continued as they were for much longer anyway. There had been times when he wondered if he was losing his mind – whatever he did proved wrong. Heating a room would be wasteful and stupid on one day, and not having a nice warm room ready for her would be a mistake on the next. He came to believe that the wrongness lay inside him, some inherent part of his nature that justified her responses. A thin strand of hope kept him going, and now, free from her influence he had the chance to rethink himself, untangling the mess of this relationship from his own true self. He hoped there would be something within him that he could like.

Stopping for a while, he leaned his back against the broad trunk of a tree. Droplets of water splashed down onto his face. Somewhere nearby, traffic hummed, proving that he hadn't wandered so very far from the world he knew after all. Steven did not yet feel ready to brave the lights and mayhem of normality. The trees around him felt like a sanctuary, and he had the suspicion that he would miss them once he ventured out. Still, he would have to go home eventually. The rain and cold were getting to him and he needed to sleep.

Closing his eyes, he saw the angular face of his inspiration. He still didn't know her name. The woman at the talk had been Willow Arden, but he didn't quite think she was really the woman he kept seeing in his dreams. She seemed more otherworldly. The raindrops trickling down his cheeks could be the touch of her fingers, he thought. Her face seemed full of life and passion, and perhaps compassion as well. He imagined that he could confess everything to such a woman – all his fears and failings would seem like nothing at all if he could only offer them up to her.

"Spirit of the forest," he whispered. "Let me find you."

He half-expected to hear her voice, but the only sounds were of wind, rain and rustling branches. The cold ate into him, more evident now that he had stopped walking. The tree at his back felt very real, just as real as the dripping rain on his sodden jeans, and the weariness in his limbs. The rest of his life resembled a dream, or perhaps a nightmare. None of it had ever been quite solid enough, just one insubstantial scene after another. He wondered if that was how being a zombie felt – not quite alive, but still moving somehow. Perhaps the world was full of zombies, but most of them didn't realise what had happened, he thought.

Suddenly, the wind abated, and the rain stopped. Large droplets still fell sporadically from the trees, but the sounds of the woodland changed. From nearby came an inhuman, wailing cry that chilled his heart and brought a cold sweat out along his back. Never before had he heard so haunted and unsettling a sound. It came again, but he could not tell the source. What creature could vocalise like that? He imagined supernatural beings stalking amongst the trees, howling in the aftermath of the storm. Steven didn't know whether he wanted to run, or to stay. Then his ears identified the sounds of a couple of individual cars and he realised there must be a road very close by. He set off as fast as he could, skidding over the mud and not looking back in the direction of the eerie sound. He felt as though eyes were on him, following his attempt at escaping. There was no saying what might happen if he looked back. The temptation to turn and surrender to his fear remained strong, certain there would be eyes glowing in the darkness.

Eventually, the path deposited him in a narrow lane and from there he picked up the main road. Car headlights dazzled him, seeming too bright and unnatural after his time beneath the trees. All those drivers speeding past – he wondered where they were going in such a hurry, shut up inside their little metal boxes, insulated from the night and from each other. He'd never much liked driving, even before his handful of minor accidents.

Steven's small, stark flat seemed remarkably cosy after his wanderings. The miracle of electric light, instant heat and boiling water for tea were not lost upon him. From the windowsill, his wooden boar watched with placid gaze as he cast off soaked clothes and drank scalding liquid. The wildwood did not afford such comforts and luxuries, he realised. Going back to primordial forest, if such a thing were possible, meant giving up all of this. There were quite a lot of things about civilization he rather liked. The softness of the mattress. The warmth of a duvet pulled over shivering limbs. How far was he supposed to go? How much should he be wiling to give up? What would his muse ask of him, if he could ever meet her in person?

Chapter Seven

Eager to see Mindy again, Steven arrived in the backroom of the pub before any of the others. He tucked himself away in a corner, where he could observe the rest of the room without drawing too much attention to himself. Swirling a glass of lemonade, he tried not to watch the clock. Time passed slowly. They were late, he realised. He knew some of them had lousy time keeping skills, but none of them arrived, and he wondered if he had the wrong day, or the wrong pub. He decided to give them half an hour, and if no-one showed by then, he would go home. After that, his attention fluctuated between the door and his rather battered watch.

Eventually, a group of them arrived together – both Johns, Elspeth, Neil, Diana and a woman he hadn't seen before. Their expressions were grim, and he wondered if they knew something he didn't. Conscious of Mindy's absence from their number, he experienced a rush of panic, imagining all kinds of horrible things that might have happened to her. Accident. Injury. Sudden death. Painful, lingering illness for which there was no known cure. The idea of anything tragic happening to her made him sick with apprehension. As they sat down at his table, the hollow feeling in Steven's stomach expanded a little further.

"Everything all right?" he asked nervously.

"No," Wiccan John declared. "No it isn't."

The silence hung heavy for a few seconds as he tried to find the courage to break it. "What's happened?" Steven asked, conscious of an atmosphere building.

"That's what we need to establish," Wiccan John replied. None of the other said a word, and Steven had the peculiar feeling this was all pre-arranged. He still had no idea what it meant, but it didn't feel good.

"Half an hour ago, I had Mindy on the phone in tears-" John began, but Steven interrupted.

"She's ok, isn't she? What's upset her?"

"She's a long way from ok. She says you've been harassing her, that you're acting like some kind of stalker."

"But..!" Steven began, hardly able to take this in. It seemed like a horrible joke and he struggled to believe what he'd just heard. "I didn't... I thought..." he stopped, lost for words. All eyes were on him, and he felt the accusation in those stares.

"So, are you denying it?" Diana asked, her tone measured and dangerous.

"I don't know what I'm supposed to have done wrong," he said, looking around for some clearer explanation.

"She said you've been acting really weird and that you frightened her," Wiccan John explained.

"When?"

"Last Saturday, after she went to that thing in Birmingham."

"I knew she was upset about something, but she wouldn't tell me what." he felt exposed. How could he defend himself when he didn't know what the problem was.

"Did she ask you to contact her?" Diana asked.

"Not exactly," Steven said. "But she gave me the impression it was ok. I gave her my phone number, she could have just rung me and said."

"You've been making her uncomfortable," Wiccan John reiterated. "She says you've been going round to her flat and leaving things on the doorstep, and that it's intimidating her. She feels very threatened," John added.

"I bought her flowers, wine, chocolates. And a new top, because I'd torn the one she was wearing," Steven said at a loss to see how any of this could have seemed threatening.

"Your tore her top?" Diana asked, anger creeping into her voice.

"I didn't mean to."

A leaden feeling had settled within him. Did Mindy really feel that way about what had happened? Why hadn't she said anything? At the time it had felt like there was a real chemistry between them, and she had certainly been the one making all the moves. He felt physically sick all of a sudden, his stomach churning threateningly as though it might empty itself at any moment.

Steven fought to gain some control over the rising panic, took a sip of lemonade but found the fizziness only made him feel worse. The rest of the moot waited in ominous silence, watching him, and Steven wanted nothing more than to get out of the pub and away from these people. He knew if he bolted, it would look like a confession of guilt, but what could he say to convince them that he hadn't meant any harm? He hadn't meant to upset her. It had never crossed his mind that his actions might have bothered her at all.

"She never told me," he said, clinging to this one line of defence. "Why didn't she tell me?"

"I asked her that," John returned. "She said she couldn't face it."

The unfamiliar woman cleared her throat. "Last time I checked, buying wine and flowers didn't count as an offence. If Mindy's chosen to take it that way, it's hardly his fault, especially if she's not said anything."

"She's very upset," John said.

"Yes, well perhaps she is," the woman returned. "That doesn't mean she's unequivocally in the right."

"We don't know you," Diana pointed out to Steven. "You've not been here long. For all we know, you could be the kind of guy who predates vulnerable women. The type who goes to moots looking for pickups."

"That's not me. I've never done anything like this before in my life," Steven said.

"Your word against hers again," the new woman pointed out.

"What am I supposed to say?" Steven asked in desperation. He looked at each of the faces in turn, but none of them seemed to offer anything by way of comfort or encouragement. "It doesn't matter what I say, does it? You've already made up your minds about me."

None of them spoke. Neil looked away, but Steven wasn't sure what that meant. He rose, unsteadily. "I might as well go. I didn't mean her any harm. I wanted to be nice to her. I got it wrong. I swear to you, she never said a thing to make me think she wasn't happy about what I was doing."

He squeezed between them and walked out. Another door in his life slammed shut. All his longing and desire for Mindy hadn't gone away, but with it came a horror of what he might have done. Had he really frightened her by bringing her gifts? Steven paused, gazing at his reflection in a darkened shop window. What he saw looked unremarkable enough. Not that broad, or tall, or strong. He was bigger than Mindy, but not intimidating, surely? His first impulse was to go round to her flat, bang on the door and demand an explanation, but after everything John had said, that didn't seem like such a good idea. She might see it as more harassment. The idea of seeing her, of talking to her and sorting things out drew him, but what could he say now? It sounded as though she wanted nothing more to do with him.

Sitting on his bed, Steven picked over everything he could recall of the previous Saturday. Mindy's invitation to go home with her for a drink. The way she had touched him, their closeness on the sofa. He didn't know much about how courting was supposed to work, but she seemed so open and encouraging, her smile full of wonderful suggestion. Thinking about the way she had moved when thy had kissed, he wondered if he had misunderstood everything. Perhaps what he'd taken for enthusiasm had been her trying to fight him off. Maybe she'd started it and changed her mind and he hadn't realised. At the time, the idea hadn't occurred to him, but now everything appeared in a different, darker light.

What have I done? He asked himself repeatedly. *Was I wrong?*

Could she have deliberately lied to John? But why do that? He didn't want to think she was that sort of person. Perhaps she regretted it and just wanted to get rid of him – that made a little bit of sense in relation to how she had acted at the time, but why hadn't she just told him to leave her alone? He had no idea what to think. She'd seemed such a nice girl, so generous and sensual, and he'd been flattered by her attention, but what if he'd got that wrong too? Conflicting answers raged in his brain, giving him no respite.

Steven clutched his head in his hands, feeling unable to cope with it all. The old voices were there: The ones that spoke of drink and pills, of late-night baths with razors, and the liberating potential of kitchen knives. They had been there for as long as he could remember, surfacing whenever things became too difficult, offering him escape, an easy way out of it all. He'd never entirely trusted them. He knew from experience that metal on flesh would bring pain long before it brought oblivion.

Why do you keep trying Steven?

No one wants you. No one ever wanted you. The world would be a better place if you weren't in it.

You don't do any good. You just hurt and harm the people who get closest to you. Do everyone a favour and open a vein.

Do us all a favour and get rid of yourself.

Walk in front of a bus.

Jump in a river.

Do it before you hurt anyone else. Before you do something worse. Protect them from you. It's the only worthwhile thing you'll ever do.

"Stop it!" he shouted aloud, flailing against the bed in a vain attempt to silence them. "Leave me alone. Just leave me alone."

They seemed so close, as though all of these voices came from people who were all lurking on the fringes of his mind, waiting to exploit another moment of weakness. There were plenty of times when he'd thought about going to a doctor. That, he'd always felt was what proved you were mad - if it got bad enough for it to seem like telling the medics was a good idea. There were plenty of days when he thought he was crazy, with his little voices. Still, they'd never told him to harm anyone else, only himself. It could be a one way ticket to a room with rubber wallpaper if he ever owned up. His mother's fear of what would happen if 'they' caught her had been with him his whole life.

Just like your mother.

He tried very hard not to listen, but it made little odds.

No one will love you.

He knew this voice better than any of the others. It came quiet and melancholy after the barrage of the rest, its message never changing.

"Why will no one ever love me?" he asked it.

Because you are too fat.

"How will I know when I am thin enough to deserve love?" he asked, intoning the words with ritual familiarity.

When your bones show through your skin. Ribs and pelvis. Hips and collar. Only then.

He had never attained that level of thinness. His mother had managed it years previously, birdlike and dangerously delicate. Taut skin stretched over perfect bones. Steven's body had refused to go the same way. Being too big was just a part of his wrongness. He could not replace his absent father, or ever achieve enough to liberate his mother from the demons of her depression. In the end, he had failed her.

No one will love you.

"I don't want this to be who I am!" he cried out. The voices on the edge of his awareness dissolved into laughter at this.

"If you come with me, I will teach you new ways of being crazy. Happy ways, terrible ways. There will be pain still, and loss and death, but there will also be beauty and laughter. Will you come with me?" This softly feminine voice did not seem to have come from inside his head. Steven looked around at his virtually empty flat. A long shadow passed across his window, throwing the wild boar sculpture into darkness.

"Who are you?" he whispered.

"Will you come with me? Will you give me everything that you are and could be?"

The other voices had fallen silent in face of this new speaker. He couldn't even feel their presence anymore. Should he fear whatever hushed them, or embrace it? Steven did not consider for long.

"Yes," he said.

The shadow passed, and orange streetlight filtered into his room once more, casting the boar in an eerie light. Its small piggy eyes seemed to be staring at him, but no further words came.

Chapter Eight

The local council's human resources office called him in for an interview a few days later. Steven had applied for so many jobs that he couldn't clearly remember what this one involved. Utterly unprepared, he tried not to sound as confused as he felt. Gradually, from the questions being asked, he pieced together that it was outside work, not clerical, that the pay wasn't very good, and that he had no relevant skills. He assumed he wouldn't be getting it, so was quite surprised when the officious sounding woman asked him how soon he could start.

"Tomorrow?" he tried, uncertainly. "I'm out of work at the moment."

"From the form you filled in, I see you've had a lot of short term and part time jobs. Why is that?"

"I was my mother's carer for a long time. She's in a home now."

The woman nodded, looking quite sympathetic. "I'll get all the relevant paperwork posted to you. You can start next Monday. See Marcy on the front desk, she can tell you where you need to go and who you'll be working for."

Surprised by this, he made his best attempt at enthusiastic noises and hurried from the building as soon as he could. At least having a job would mean something to do. There were a lot of hours he didn't know how to fill now he only had himself to please and freedom had not given him much pleasure. The idea of having something useful to do cheered him.

Not really thinking about where he was going as he left the council building, he took a wrong turn and ended up on an unfamiliar estate. It was a while before he noticed the mistake, and by that time it seemed to make as much sense to keep going forwards as to try and retrace his steps.

He didn't do it on purpose, he felt sure of that. His feet went of their own volition, even though he didn't consciously know the way. One road led into another and the occasional signposts didn't help much, until he saw one for the train station. He knew how to get home from there and headed off along the road indicated. After a while, it occurred to Steven that the houses looked vaguely familiar. He'd been down this road before, with its chestnut tree on the corner and tall, terraced houses. Then he stopped before a small gate, looking down at a flight of brick steps that led to Mindy's front door. The curtains were closed, and a milk bottle stood on the front door. She might be a matter of yards away, somewhere behind those walls. He wondered what she was doing, wearing, thinking. An ache welled up inside him, thinking that he had driven her away with his lack of understanding. Steven knew it probably wasn't a good idea to linger, but he wanted to see her, and couldn't quite pull himself away.

As he stood staring down, the front door opened, revealing a diminutive figure dressed in black. A small, pale hand reached out to lift the milk bottle. For some reason, she looked up then as though she felt his gaze upon her. Mindy gave a little cry of alarm and the bottle slipped from her fingers a she stood. The sound of it shattering seemed uncannily loud in Steven's ears. Glass and milk splattered around Mindy's feet, but she didn't look down. Her lips parted slightly and her eyes looked wide and frightened. Looking around, Steven had to admit the only possible source of this alarm was himself.

"What are you doing?" she challenged, her voice tremulous. "Why are you here? Are you stalking me?"

"I was just passing," he said, thinking how lame this excuse seemed. "I realised this was your road. Your house. I stopped, that's all. I didn't mean any harm."

"I'll call the police," she threatened. "You have to get away from me. You have to leave me alone."

"Please will you just talk to me," he begged. She looked so little and vulnerable, staring up at him, but at the same time the look in her eyes frightened him. He couldn't read that expression and just wanted the old, smiley Mindy back.

"There's nothing to say. Just leave me alone." She pulled her arms across her chest defensively.

"I didn't mean to upset you." He put a hand on the gate, and she jumped as though he'd struck her.

"Stay up there. Don't you dare come down here! I'll scream if you do."

"John said I'd scared you. I didn't mean to, honestly, Mindy."

"No? So what did you think you were doing?"

"I thought I was being romantic."

"What? What on earth made you think that was a good idea?"

"I thought you were flirting with me. You asked me to sit next to you. You even held my hand. You kissed me. Remember?"

"It didn't mean anything," she paled visibly and looked away from him.

"If I'd known, I'd have let you in peace," he said. "I'd never have done what I did if I thought you didn't want it."

"I didn't feel able to talk to you because you scared me. Happy now?"

"No... Mindy... I never meant... you didn't..." but he couldn't get the words in his head to come out intelligibly, and before he could explain, she retreated into the doorway.

"Stay the hell away from me," she said, and closed the door, leaving him with a clear memory of the hatred in her eyes.

For a while, he stayed, looking down at her door and trying to think. Her words had shocked him. They didn't tally at all with his own recollections and he felt as though the whole world was spinning dangerously out of control. She hadn't protested. She hadn't said a word. They were just gifts. Why would that scare her? He thought girls were supposed to like flowers.

The main door of the house opened, revealing a man with thinning hair and a dark expression. "What are you doing?" he demanded.

"I was just going," Steven mumbled.

"Stay away from my house, and my lodger," the man said. "I don't want to see you round here again. Understand?"

Saying nothing, Steven walked away.

As he trudged in the direction of home, Steven tried picturing Mindy's version of the story. He'd been alarming, pushy, and he'd read too much into what she'd done when it meant nothing to her. He thought they were getting together as a couple, that she liked him, fancied him. Apparently she hadn't felt any of those things so his trying to be romantic had come across as creepy and weird.

He compared the two versions – the one he recalled, and the one he imagined. They had a great deal in common, but there were a few critical differences. In his version she had been willing, encouraging him with touches and smiles until he succumbed to her charms. Something had gone wrong and he didn't know what, but it had clearly been a big deal for Mindy. He felt awful about upsetting her and wished there was something he could do, but clearly any attempts at fixing things were likely to just make things worse.

Just as he was rounding the corner towards his flat, a man in a long black trench-coat crossed the road, heading towards him. Steven picked up the movement in his peripheral vision, but paid little attention to it. Consequently, he didn't have time to see anything about who was striding towards him. The punch came out of nowhere, filling his mouth with the tang of blood and sending him sprawling across the tarmac, hitting his head hard on the ground and hurting his back as well. Lights danced before his eyes and for a while he thought he would pass out. A face danced before his eyes, out of focus.

"You stay the fuck away from her," a voice growled in his ear. "She's mine. Upset her again, and I'll kill you. Talk to her again and I'll beat you to a pulp. Touch her and I'll rip your fucking bollocks off. Got it?"

"Yes," Steven croaked through battered lips.

"Good."

The voice seemed familiar, but Steven couldn't place it. He didn't even try to get up, and so the other man got away without there being chance to look at him properly. When the pain in his head eased enough that he could move without feeling sick, he managed to roll onto his side. His back still hurt, but nothing seemed broken. He spat some of the blood out and made it onto his knees. People passed him on the pavement, but no one stopped to offer help or even ask if he was ok. Perhaps they hadn't seen him being attacked. Perhaps they thought he was a drunk, or a druggy. Maybe they just didn't care.

When he stood, the world swam and rolled a little, but he didn't fall. Tentatively, Steven made his way towards his own flat, and relative safety. Locking the door behind him, he sank down onto the cold tiles, then rested his head on the floor. The coolness helped, soothing him until he felt ready to move again.

In the bathroom, he splashed cold water onto his face. To his surprise, the mirror showed him were no marks left from the attack. Normally he bruised quite easily, but the punch hadn't raised so much as a red welt. His lips weren't swelling up even. Still he felt very rough, as though he'd been used as a punch-bag by someone who knew how to box.

Steven went back to bed, because he had nothing else to do. He flicked the television on and listened to the voices on a children's program, not really taking in their words. His head continued to thump and thrum, but he tried to ignore it and eventually he fell asleep. He awoke in darkness, cold and hungry, with the television still droning on in the background.

Chapter Nine

Water came in to fill up the hole slightly faster than he could get mud out of it. What had at first been a thick and claggy tangle of decaying leaves and other litter now emerged as a vile soup that fell all to readily off the trowel. Sweating in his waterproofs, filthy and exhausted, Steven felt calmer than he had for a long time. Clearing the drain had him in an almost euphoric state. Physical exertion often did that to him. He'd always loved working outside, mowing the lawn, or doing the other little jobs around his mother's house. Although he'd never been especially fit or strong, he could get most things done by slow attrition, and the drain job looked no different. Without the downpour it would have been easier.

There had been storms for days. Heavy rain fell for hours at a time, making huge puddles anywhere it could collect. Unblocking the drains would perhaps ease things a bit, and Steven knew Bromsgrove wasn't in any serious danger of flooding. Not like nearby Worcester. Today there were three of them out working on drains, in their high visibility coats, struggling against the downpour. Hardly anyone else had ventured out and he didn't blame them. It wasn't the weather for any sane person to expose themselves to if they could possibly help it.

He had the uncomfortable feeling that eyes watched him. Every now and then Steven looked up, glancing around as best he could, trying to find some reason for this suspicion. Water dripped into his eyes, blurring his vision. A woman with a small child hurried passed on the other pavement. A shop-worker gazed through glass, taking in the scene but not staying for long. Movement in his peripheral vision drew his attention. Nothing. Just the nagging feeling that he was being observed. *Jumpy* he told himself. Getting punched out in the street meant he wasn't paranoid - someone was out to get him. A friend of Mindy's. A boyfriend perhaps. He didn't really want to think about it anymore, so tried to concentrate on the oozing mud in the drain.

With the water flowing freely again, he set off looking for the next blockage. It wasn't long before he found it, down one of the smaller streets. He set to work quickly, wondering why there wasn't some kind of machine to do this job yet. Once he'd removed the plastic bottle jammed in the metal grill, it didn't take long. Straightening his back, he turned to face the shop on the opposite side of the road, and saw the display of tarot packs in the window. He stared for a while, trying to make out what they all were. He couldn't see much through the gloom in the shop, but there seemed to be clothes, books and all manner of things on its shelves. Making a mental note of the location, he resolved to come back as soon as he could. Finding it by chance like this had to be a good sign, he thought, and it was about time he had one of them. The rest of his life had gone so very wrong of late.

It occurred to him this was just the sort of place Mindy would shop in. She could wander down the street at any moment. He imagined her, in her long leather coat with her big black boots, and a black umbrella protecting her head. Would she recognise him in his council work clothes? Even after everything that had happened, he wanted to see her. Those pretty, dark ringed eyes of hers still cropped up in his thoughts all too frequently. The way she moved, the tones of her voice. Everything about her. But if she saw him, her sweet features would most likely cloud over with anger again, and he had no desire to see that. What would it take to persuade her to hear him out, to forgive him? He had made a mistake, he accepted that. He had moved too fast and got things wrong. If she gave him the chance, he would apologise and swear never to do it again, and perhaps that would improve things. She wouldn't smile at him or flirt with him again, he suspected, but at least if he could beg forgiveness, there would be less anger between them.

Realising he'd been stood dreaming for some time, Steven gathered up his tools and carried on with his job. Thus far there had been no two days the same. Working outside, fixing things as required, tidying up and generally making himself useful. It was easy enough work, and he liked it. Being out in the town, he realised he might see Mindy at any time. He had no idea what he would do or say if chance brought them into contact. Despite everything, he couldn't really believe she had gone from his life forever and remembered the girl at the demonstration who thought all things occurred for a reason. He didn't feel as though his relationship with Mindy had run its full course yet, but he would wait and see what happened rather than do anything.

Although the sign on the door said 'open', Steven couldn't see anyone in the shop. He stepped inside gingerly, feeling like a trespasser. Around him were countless shelves full of innumerable eye-catching things. A glass case sported delicate jewellery. One wall was dominated by clothes rails carrying fabrics in a rainbow of colours. There were racks of CDs, and displays of things whose nature and purpose he hadn't a clue about. Scanning through the numerous bookshelves, he found a bewildering array of titles, most of which meant nothing to him. Where on earth should he start?

As he studied the book spines, Steven felt the back of his neck prickle. It had been doing that a great deal of late, and he'd started trying to ignore it.

"Looking for anything in particular?" The woman's voice made him jump.

"Just browsing," he said hurriedly, not looking round. He felt like an interloper, and half expected the shop owner to throw him out. Now he knew he was being watched, and it didn't help his mood. Turning to leave, Steven stopped when the woman spoke again.

"I thought I recognised you."

He turned back then, getting a proper look at her solid form and weathered face. He nodded, recognising her too in that moment: The unfamiliar woman from the last moot.

"Steven, isn't it?"

"Yeah."

He cringed, expecting another tirade even though she'd not been all that harsh with him before.

"I'm Helen. I don't think we got off to a very good start."

"No. Thanks for what you said though, the other night."

"There's no need to thank me. I just tell it the way I see it."

"Nice meeting you again," he said. "I ought to be off."

"Were you looking for anything?" she persisted.

"Ideas maybe. I don't really know enough to know what I'm looking for."

"What interests you?"

"Trees I guess."

"Read any Glennie Kindred?" she gestured him towards a pile of slim volumes on the end of the counter.

Half an hour later, Steven left with half a dozen books, a card from the shop and an invitation to come back if he felt like it.

On Monday nights, a man called Peter ran meditation classes in the room above Helen's shop. Steven felt rather nervous about attending, in case he saw anyone from the moot, but he recognised no one. At first the sitting still and breathing deeply did nothing to calm him, but as the evening progressed he started getting into it, letting his mind wander as the man running the session spoke. The soothing tones of the guy's voice gradually began to have an effect, and Steven settled.

"Imagine yourself walking through a sunlit wood. It's a beautiful day and you feel at peace with the world. Everything is good. The trees are in full leaf, the air is full of bird song. You come to a clearing. Go into the clearing and sit down upon the soft grass. See what comes to you."

Steven found it very easy to picture. He could create vivid scenes in his imagination – a consequence of spending long hours with little else to do. Just as he wondered what he should do next, he heard a familiar voice.

"You again." She sounded pleased.

"Me again," he responded inside the daydream.

"You know, when you talk about this afterwards, Peter's going to tell you that you've just met your spirit guide. The others will have seen butterflies, blackbirds, a fox, a grass snake. One of them will have seen a unicorn as well I expect."

"Are you my spirit guide?"

She snorted at this, sitting down on the grass near him. "What do I look like to you?"

He looked, and saw something feminine, something with a face but it didn't form into anything coherent. "I don't know how to answer that."

"At least you're honest. So, what do you want?"

Steven thought about this. "I don't know that either."

"Well, that's the first problem identified then. Work out what you want."

Another voice cut through their conversation. "And when you're ready, let your attention return to this room, and open your eyes."

Startled, Steven looked around him, feeling a touch disorientated.

"Now," said Peter. "Whatever came to you in that glade was a special being, a spirit guide. Is anyone willing to share what they saw?"

"I saw a fox," said a rather pale woman on the far side of the room from Steven.

"A blackbird."

"A purple emperor butterfly."

"Some sort of snake, but it didn't seem dangerous."

A rather serious looking man in a black roll-neck top coughed self consciously. "Unicorn," he confessed.

"What about you Steven?" Peter asked him.

"Just the trees," Steven replied. He didn't feel ready to share. "I like trees," he added.

As they were leaving, Peter touched his arm and drew Steven aside.

"It takes some people a while to get to grips with meditating and visualisation, so don't worry if it doesn't all happen at once."

"It's ok, I enjoyed it."

"Good. That's good." Peter looked around, seeing the last of his other students disappearing down the stairs. "You have a very disturbed aura," he said.

"What does that mean?"

"It could mean a number of things, but you seem troubled, defensive. You might benefit from some chakra cleansing work."

"Maybe sometime," Steven said. He didn't much like the sound of any of it.

"Had a good evening?" Helen asked as he came down into the shop.

"Interesting. Apparently I need my chakras cleansing, whatever that means."

She raised her eyebrows at him, an impish expression on her face. "Oh dear," she said.

"So you don't believe in that?" he asked, very quietly so that the man upstairs wouldn't hear him.

"Not really," she said.

"But you believe in other stuff?"

"I don't do belief. I do first hand experience. As I see it, that's about the only thing you can trust."

"I guess so." Pondering her words, he said his goodbyes and set off for home.

What did he want? He thought of Mindy for a moment, then discarded the thought. There had to be something more than the unsettled mood she currently inspired in him.

Chapter Ten

A few hundred yards away from his flat, Steven once again had the perturbing impression that someone watched him. He turned, scanning the street. A couple of girls who looked about fourteen were sat on a wall, smoking and paying him no attention. Aside from that, there were a few cars. Catching a flicker of movement in his peripheral vision, he turned quickly. Nothing. Just a bird, or litter blowing in the wind, or some other equally innocent explanation.

While wandering around the farmer's market, he bought a loaf of fresh bread and some local apples. Being in amongst a crowd didn't help with his unease. He felt oddly vulnerable, constantly expecting to be attacked from behind. Steven knew he was being a bit paranoid, but that thought didn't keep the anxiety at bay. He dived into the relative quiet of the high-street bookshop, drifting from one section to another with no real intention of buying anything. Scanning the backs of the science fiction section, he jumped when an unexpected voice greeting him.

"Alright Steven?"

"Neil!" he said, overcome with relief at seeing a familiar face.

"How's it going?" Neil asked.

"Ok, you?"

Neil shrugged dismissively. "That moot stuff. Mindy. Not seen her since."

"Oh, right," Steven replied, uncertain how he felt about this.

"Not answering calls," Neil said. "Or John's."

"I hope she's ok," Steven said

"Sorry though. That was a shit night"

"Do you believe me?" Steven asked.

Neil pondered this for a while. "Different people see differently. Mindy's a bit haunted. Know what I mean? Can't help how she sees things."

Steven nodded. "Perhaps I should stay away from the moot anyway."

"Might be best. Busy?" Neil asked.

"Not right now."

"Going to a green fair in Redditch. Interested?"

"Ok. Let me drop this stuff home first."

Neil seemed to know his way round the buses. Steven followed in his wake, feeling disorientated by the unfamiliar surroundings.

"So how far away is Redditch then?" he asked after they'd been n the bus for what seemed like an age.

"We're in the middle of it already. Lots of trees."

Looking more carefully, Steven realised that there were indeed buildings tucked away amongst the greenery they were travelling through and that what he'd assumed was a wood, might well be a bit more urban.

"Town's a dump," Neil observed. "Trees are the best bit."

"You think all towns are dumps though."

Neil just grinned at this, but said nothing.

The Green Fair consisted of quite a few stalls in the town centre representing various environmental groups, along with an assortment of craft stalls. It wasn't as big an event as Steven had envisaged, but he didn't mind – a change of scenery and a way of passing the afternoon would suit him well enough. He browsed, not really intending to spend his money on anything.

A stall with paintings caught his eye. On one sizeable canvas, a woman nestled against a tree, her dark hair mingling with the bark, one slender arm stretched along a branch so that the two seemed connected. The face, in profile showed strong bones and dark eyes, half closed. There were pictures of landscapes, flowers, butterflies. In amongst the more conventional subjects he found butterflies with impossible gossamer wings and a dragon in water.

"Do you like that one?" the man selling them asked. "It's based on a Chinese dragon."

Steven smiled awkwardly. "It's good. Not that I know anything about art, but it looks good to me."

"Thanks."

Some of the framed pictures were stacked on the table, and Steven perused them. Dark eyes stared out at him from a face that seemed part tree, part human. He lifted the painting carefully.

"The Spirit of Arden," the man announced.

Steven felt a cool shiver pass through his body. The painted eyes gazed back at him, intense and demanding.

"Same model as the dryad painting over there," the man explained, gesturing to the picture Steven had already examined. He could see the similarity between the faces.

"There's probably a few others in there she's posed for. She's my favourite model," he finished, with a slight blush. "Not that I painted these. I can't do people. I sell work for a few friends."

Could there be two women out there with those irresistible eyes and striking features? Steven stared at the painting, absorbed by the image. Looking closely he could see the individual brush marks revealing how daubs of colour had formed that compelling visage. Having seen this image, he knew he needed it. Rare were the objects that caught his imagination. He lived with the bare necessities, but like the wild boar sculpture, this painting called to him. He had enough money to buy it, there being so few things he bothered to spend his small income on.

Carrying on around the fair, he paused at what appeared to be a ferret stall and stopped for a while to watch the pale creatures as they rolled and stretched inside their cage.

"Interested in ferrets at all?" a woman asked him.

"Not really." He supposed he probably shouldn't keep watching, taking up space, so moved on, and was quickly persuaded to buy fair trade coffee, and an environmentally friendly toilet cleaner. Soon he had his hands full. Steven found it hard to say no to these people – they seemed so sincere and determined.

Sat on a stripy blanket in a patch of shade, was a young woman with a small sign offering fortune telling. With her dark hair tied up in a scarf, and a brightly coloured dress, she looked like the kind of person who might frequent Helen's shop.

"Have your fortune told?" she asked, the soft bur in her voice suggesting she came from the southwest.

Steven sat down, parting with a few coins. The fortune teller produced a small bag and drew six stones from it, arranging them in a cross shape on the blanket. For a while she said nothing, her brow furrowed slightly in thought.

"There's something dark in your past, a trouble that still haunts you, and the ill will of another. Something twisted, deviant maybe. And your future, there's possibility and connection. That could mean love, not no in the usual sense I think. Not romantic love exactly, something else. I think you already know what you're looking for on that score." She looked at him thoughtfully then pointed to another symbol. "This one however means betrayal. Someone meaning to harm you."

"So what does the whole thing mean?" he asked.

"Is it the same person, or two people? I'm not sure. Someone you love and want to be closer to, someone who has cast a shadow on your life and will hurt and betray you. So maybe you can have what you want, but it'll come at a high price, or one aspect of your life is going to go really well, and another will go very badly. Sorry I'm being a bit vague. I'm really not sure how to read this."

"It makes some sense," he said. "Thanks. How do you do that?"

"These are runes. Viking symbols. They all have meaning, but… it is hard to explain. I use them to reach through to something else, and then the answers just come and I know what to say."

"Do you usually get it right then?"

"More often than not."

"So can you tell if someone's going to win the lottery, or what horse to bet on?" Steven asked.

"It doesn't work like that. It tells you what you most need to know."

"Interesting. Thanks."

She looked up at him again and he realised that her eyes were a remarkably dark shade of green.

"Don't let your emotions blind you to the flaws in others," she said.

"Bought lots?" Neil enquired as the bus pulled away.

Steven showed him the various bottles, and the painting. Neil pulled the frame out of the bag for a better look, staring intently at the face.

"Tree Woman," he said authoritatively. "Very good."

Steven resisted the temptation to ask if Neil recognised her. He thought the question would sound silly. But, if the image had been based on a model, then somewhere out there was a woman who looked at least a bit like this. He pondered the fortune teller's words. *Love, but not romantic love.* What did that mean? And who was going to betray him? He wasn't sure if he believed any of it, but the ideas circulated in his mind none the less.

"See you around," Neil said as they got off the bus.

"Thanks for this afternoon," Steven replied. "Let me know if there's anything else happening?"

"Will do."

There were a few unused picture hooks on the flat's blank walls. Steven put the painting where he could see it from his bed. The more time he spent gazing at the image, the more detail he saw – the leaves matted into her hair, the way the skin on her neck almost looked like bark. A buzz on his doorbell broke his trance. He pushed the button to release the front door, then went down to see who it was – he hadn't been expecting anyone. No one had ever visited his flat before, nor did he expect any deliveries. He assumed it was most likely a mistake, or kids messing about.

She stood silhouetted in the open doorway. All of a sudden, Steven's legs didn't feel quite equal to bearing his weight and he stumbled, his shoulder catching against the wall briefly. Mindy's eyes were reddened from tears. As he approached, she thrust a carrier bag towards him.

"Take it back. I don't want it."

He reached out and took the proffered bag, being careful to make sure his hand did not inadvertently brush against hers.

"Mindy?" he said in disbelief.

"I hate you," she said. "I hate everything about you. I don't ever want to see you again." Her words cut into him, but Steven said nothing.

"Everything's wrong," she continued, her voice plaintive. "I hate everything."

"I'll keep out of your way, I promise. I won't go to the moot again, or near your house."

"But you talked to Neil! And Helen said she'd seen you."

"I can't avoid everyone."

"No. You can't. It's not your fault," she said. "It's me. It's always me."

"I don't understand."

"Of course you don't. No one does." She sounded frantic, but he had no idea how to help her.

With no warning at all, she threw herself into his arms. Steven dropped the bag and froze, not knowing how to reconcile this with her previous words. She clung to him with what seemed like desperation. Then, like a figure in an impossible dream, she kissed him. He could taste her lipstick and a hint of tobacco smoke in her mouth as she crushed herself against him. The salt of her tears, and the scent of her perfume mingled together. He wrapped his arms round her, wanting to get passed all the anger and misunderstanding. Whatever he had done to upset her before, he wanted to make it better.

"I do fancy you," she said. "It's so difficult for me… my brain… everything… I panicked and I didn't want to and I couldn't make it stop."

Rather than risk doing the wrong thing, he simply held her and listened, waiting to see what would happen next. She remained in his arms for a long time, shaking uncontrollably. He tried to find soothing things to say, but the lump in his throat made speech difficult. Wanting to help her and having no idea what to do was painful.

Eventually, Mindy stepped away from him. "I'm going to get it right this time," she said. "I'm going to make everything better."

"I'm here if you want me, if you need me," he said.

"It's ok, I won't need you," she said with a smile.

He watched as she walked away, but she didn't turn back to wave at him. A feeling of foreboding swept through him, but he pushed it away as yet one more irrational fear.

The carrier bag contained the top he had bought for her. It smelled faintly of her flat, of incense, tobacco and something indefinable that might have been Mindy herself.

Chapter Eleven

Sitting on his bed, legs stretched out, back supported by the wall, Steven let his eyes drift out of focus. The more he stared at The Spirit of Arden, the more the picture seemed to shift and change, becoming many different faces, all strong boned and compelling. With every second that ticked by, the louder the alarm in his mind rang out, until he could not ignore it. Mindy had been utterly peculiar with him, and his sense of something being wrong refused to go away. He couldn't sit here and do nothing.

Go. Go now. There is still time.

She had perhaps a ten minute head start on him. Long enough that she would probably have made it home by now. Steven had the feeling that was where she had gone. Mindy was not a fast walker. Steven ran, his lungs aching after a few yards, unaccustomed to such demands even with the more physical day job. He refused to acknowledge the pain, even though his vision blurred slightly and he felt distinctly sick. After a couple of streets, he had to drop to walking pace, gasping for air like a fish out of water. As soon as he could, he ran again.

Steven banged frantically on Mindy's front door. He could see no sign of lights in her flat, and his knocking went unanswered. Gripped with apprehension, he pounded the wood until his fists hurt, but still she didn't respond. He half expected some bloke to leap out from behind her dustbin and knock him down, but no one did.

"Mindy, if you're in there, just shout through the door so I know you're ok. Talk to me! Please Mindy just talk to me."

Only silence came from the flat. Hearing footfalls on the concrete steps down from the street, he turned, and saw Heathen John.

"What the fuck are you doing here?" John asked him, his voice an irritable growl.

"She visited me, and she seemed very odd. I was worried about her, so I came over."

John pushed passed and banged on the door a few times himself. "Mindy, it's John. It's ok. Just open up and talk to me." When there was no reply, he turned to Steven. "See if anyone's about upstairs, and hurry."

Steven didn't stop to ask why John was there, he felt the danger too keenly to question it. He raced to the house's main door and banged for all he was worth. The owner arrived quickly enough.

"I thought I told you to keep away from my house," the man said when he recognised Steven.

"I'm sorry. I think something's up with Mindy. Please can you go down and check on her."

"Fine."

The door slammed in his face. Steven strained his ears, hoping for some proof that the man had indeed gone down to check. He went back to John.

"Well?"

"I told him. Hopefully he's gone."

"She phoned me," John said slowly. "I couldn't tell if she was laughing or crying. I thought she'd taken something, you know? She kept saying she was sorry, and then she said goodbye, and to tell everyone else she was sorry. She said to tell you she was sorry, that it wasn't your fault. I told her not to do anything stupid, but she hung up on me. I came over straight away."

"She came round to my flat, which was odd enough after what she's said about me. I got the feeling something was wrong, so that's why I came over," Steven returned. "I should never have let her go."

The door swung open. "If either of you knows any first aid, get in here now."

Steven took a step back - he had no idea how to do anything of that ilk. The look on the landlord's face left him fearful to think what might have happened. John hurried passed him and he followed, bracing himself for whatever he would see.

The bath water was crimson. Mindy's head hung over the back of the tub. Her eyes were closed, makeup streaked her pale cheeks. She looked lifeless.

"Steven, grab her wrists and lift them as high as you can," John ordered.

He followed the instruction, aware of the slipperiness of her skin, from the blood and water. He could smell the copper tang of blood rising up with the steam of the bath.

John worked around him, binding her mutilated wrists to staunch the blood as Steven hung on to Mindy's cold hands.

"She's not dead yet, Steven," he said grimly, "but its close. Another couple of minutes and she'd have been too far gone I think. She might make it."

Each minute drew out painfully. Steven tried not to look at the disturbingly red water, or the blood on his hands. He couldn't bear the sight of Mindy's face and eventually resorted to closing his eyes. The scream of the ambulance siren came as a blessed relief. Steven gladly relinquished his place to a nimble young man in green paramedic attire. They wheeled Mindy away and Steven slumped down onto the wet tiles. For a while, none of the three remaining men said anything.

"Shit," the landlord eventually said.

John washed his hands in the basin, his movements slow and repetitive. Looking down, Steven saw that his hands and clothing were smeared with blood. The sight of it horrified him, but he forced himself to stand and took his turn at the washbasin. Water flowed scarlet, vivid against the white enamel.

"I've got a bottle of whiskey upstairs," the landlord said. "I think we could all use a drink. My name's Ken by he way."

"Ken, that's a very fine offer. I'm John."

"Steven."

Ken's house looked as unlike Mindy's chaotic flat as Steven thought it was possible to get. Pale walls. Blonde floorboards. Minimalist furnishing and geometric modern art on the walls. Steven perched on the edge of a cream leather sofa, feeling rather awkward. The whiskey's warmth took the edge off the shaken state of his emotions. He didn't normally drink spirits - sweet alcopops had been his preference when he'd occasionally used alcohol to blot out the unhappiness in his life. He favoured sugary drinks, and the whiskey tasted rather peculiar to his unaccustomed palate.

"So how do you know her then?" Ken asked.

"We've been friends for a couple of years," John said.

"She seemed happy enough most of the time. Not that I saw her very often. You've got to wonder what would make a pretty girl like her do something like that," Ken observed, shooting a dark glance in Steven's direction.

"I don't know. I just wish she'd talked to someone," John replied.

Steven didn't say anything. He felt distinctly uncomfortable. Why had Mindy done such an awful thing? He went over everything he could remember of their exchange, realising just how odd she had been. Nothing in what he could remember explained her actions. He couldn't fathom what she might have been thinking.

"We ought to go," John said.

Steven looked up, hearing the 'we' and taking a moment to realise this meant him.

"Ok," he said cautiously. "Thanks for the drink."

Getting out of the house into the fresh air relieved him. He was still shaking slightly.

"I need to tell John and Elspeth what's happened. I can't do it over the phone," Heathen John said wearily. "Do you want to come along?"

"I thought I wasn't wanted."

"I don't know. This is such a mess. But you're right in the middle of it. I think you'd best come with me, if you're ok with that?"

Steven climbed into the passenger seat of John's car, and closed his eyes. "What if she dies?" he said.

"Don't," John replied. "Let's not think about that unless we have to, ok?"

Wiccan John and Elspeth lived in an old terraced house with a front garden full of catmint and lavender. Elspeth answered the knock, accompanied by a waft of cooking smells and the sound classical music. Her hands were stained and she looked flustered.

"Oh, hi John, come in. I'm stewing fruit so it's all a bit mad right now," she said. Then she caught sight of Steven and her expression darkened.

"I'm the bearer of bad news I'm afraid," Heathen John said.

She gave him a questioning look. Steven couldn't see much of what passed between them, but she nodded and allowed him into her home. Conscious that he wasn't entirely welcome, Steven tried not to make his presence felt too strongly. Elspeth gestured him towards a seat, then focused her full attention on his companion.

Sat on a cushion-bedecked sofa, Steven listened to John's recounting of the last hour or so. Hearing someone else explain it made it seem even more unreal as though he had never really been a part of it. A large orange cat climbed into his lap, digging its hefty claws into his leg. Elspeth covered her mouth with one hand, and sat in silence for a long time.

"I never thought she'd do anything like this," she said. "It's awful." She looked long and hard at Steven, her expression troubled. "And here you are again, right in the middle of things."

Before he could protest his innocence, John spoke again. "Much as I like Mindy, we have to consider the possibility that she isn't very stable," he said.

"What happens now?" Steven asked, realising that this reconsideration of Mindy's mental health could cast him in a very different light. He'd wondered if they would think he was somehow responsible for what Mindy had done to herself. The thought that he could be had been very much on his mind – although he could see nothing in his actions that might have set her off, the fear of guilt remained.

"We wait and see I suppose," Elspeth said. "Send her all the positive thoughts we can. I'll phone the others."

"I'll call the hospital, see if there's any news," John offered.

"I don't think there's much I can helpfully do," Steven said, "I'll leave you to it. Call me if anything happens."

"Sure," John said.

He suspected they were glad to be shot of him. Leaving the house, the cooler air cleared his head. With no one to keep up appearances for, he fell prey to terrible anxiety. Could he have prevented this afternoon's terrible event? He didn't know. She could die. It might be his fault. The longer he dwelled on that notion, the clearer it seemed to him that Mindy's actions must have stemmed from something he had said or done. That he could not identify the mistake did not reduce his certainty of its existence.

Steven dreamed that Mindy came to his house and thrust a tattered, bloodstained top into his hands.

"Leave me alone," she said. "I won't be responsible for what happens. It will all be your fault."

Then he was inside Mindy's flat. Hearing the sound of running water, he hurried towards the bathroom. Mindy lay, pale and naked, like some mermaid or siren, her dark hair fanned out around her, floating in the water. A large kitchen knife rested on the side of the bath. Steven took it, and with calm precision, slashed open each of her wrists in turn. Blood so dark it looked more black than crimson gushed from her veins. Without a word, she slipped beneath the water, her eyes staring up at him, accusing him. He dropped the knife, hearing it clatter on the floor. The bath overran with blood. It flooded the floor, washing over his feet in hideous, sticky waves. He could do nothing but stand there, passive witness to this vast outpouring of her life.

Waking, he scrambled frantically from the duvet, flicking on the light. Steven collapsed back into the bed, pulling the covers up tightly around him and trying to blot out those nightmare images. He saw himself cutting Mindy's wrists. The dream seemed far more vivid and substantial than his other memories. Half asleep and overwhelmed by panic, he had no idea which was the true memory, and which the fabrication. How could he have got into her flat? He didn't know. Why didn't she try to resist? He couldn't answer that either.

Just a nightmare, he told himself. The memory of her dying eyes, staring at him, remained. *Just a bad dream. It didn't happen that way.*

The phone rang, its sound demanding. Steven stared at the device, feeling his chest tighten. Knowing he should take the call, he approached, but could not bring himself to lift the receiver. The answering machine kicked in. It took him a moment to recognise the speaker as Wiccan John.

"Steven are you there? Please pick up the phone." The man's voice had a troubling quality that drove a stake of fear right through Steven's heart.

"I'm here," he said.

"Updates. They gave her blood. She's still with us, they don't know if she's taken damage to her brain or any other organs. It's going to take a while.

Steven clung to the receiver, and leaned against the wall. He didn't know whether to feel relieved or shattered by this.

"I thought you ought to know. Look, I need to make a few more calls. Will you be ok?"

"Yes," he responded. It was a lie, but he couldn't face saying anything else.

"You know where we are," John offered, and when Steven said nothing, he hung up.

He slumped, dropping to his knees and then doubling over. She might not recover. The prospect of waiting and not knowing wracked him until he felt like a thin shell wrapped around grief. Surely he could have done more? If he's not let her walk away, it wouldn't have come to this.

Follow her.

She showed you the way. It's what you've always wanted to do.

No more pain.

Familiar voices whispered to him of release. He could not help but hear their seductive promises. Blades would take away all feelings of guilt. There were scars on his left arm, self inflicted damage from his late teens. He touched the whitened flesh now, tracing the pattern of his own death wish. The knife hadn't been very sharp, and the shock of seeing blood stopped him before he did any lasting damage. It hurt, but with long sleeves to hide the cuts, that moment of desperation went unnoticed.

He had been very much alone then. Friendless, isolated, working antisocial hours with people he didn't like and spending the rest of his time caring for his invalid mother. There had been no light, no hope. Only the fear of pain had kept him from doing exactly what Mindy had done.

She had more courage than you.

She had friends who cared for her. Gentle, ordinary parents. Her own flat. Her own life. Mindy had youth and beauty and all the possibilities of life before her. From Steven's perspective, she seemed blessed, and he could not imagine what kind of distress could have driven her so far. It occurred to him that he knew little about her. There could be all kinds of demons lurking behind the facade. There had to be a reason, he decided, hoping with all his heart that it had not been of his making.

No tears came. The urge to weep filled him, but his eyes remained steadfastly dry. He couldn't really comprehend what was happening. People drifted out of his life to go their own way. They didn't die. He had never lost someone like this before. Fighting for breath and shaking out of control, Steven hugged his arms around his chest and rocked slowly back and forth. Mindy might die. He tried not to think about his own death, or the allure of opening a vein. Gradually, the malevolent voices on the periphery of his thoughts grew quiet.

Open the window.

He struggled to rise. Once he had managed the catch, fresh air washed into his flat, making him realise how close and stale the place had become. From a nearby tree came the sound of bird song, melodious and sweet. He could not see the singer, but remained transfixed by this unexpected beauty.

Mindy could die, but he'd got there in time. She was still breathing, and being looked after, and maybe he could hang on to that hope.

Chapter Twelve

Steven felt unsure of his place amongst the moot-goers. I didn't help that he'd never been to a ritual before and had no idea what to expect. After all the turmoil of recent weeks he felt odd about being asked to join in, but also grateful that they'd included him. He'd been afraid for a while that they would blame him for Mindy's actions – he blamed himself so it seemed only fair. Instead there had been regular email updates from Heathen John. John had made contact with Mindy's parents and while the message from them was to stay away, they also didn't want to alienate her friends. Steven was glad of the updates.

Heathen John gave him a lift to a carpark somewhere in the hills. He had a torch, but they didn't have to walk far, and Steven guessed this secluded spot in the trees was somewhere they had gathered before. He hadn't dressed up, not having anything special to wear, and was relieved to see John looked the same as he did for moots.

The torch light helped them find each other amongst the trees. Steven recognised most of the faces in the circle. Some of them were wearing fancy cloaks, but other than that they looked much as ever.

"Thank you for coming," Elspeth said to him.

"Thank you for letting me," he said, deeply moved by her unexpected welcome.

Steven realised that she would be the one holding the ritual. In the moots she hadn't seemed like much of a presence, but here in the wood, with a cloak around her shoulders she appeared to be a lot more powerful.

"If you have a lantern, put it down in front of you."

There were quite a few lanterns, but their light did not keep the darkness away.

Elspeth continued. "Take each other's hands, please. We make a circle of ourselves, a temple of our community. We make sacred space between us."

There followed a lot of unfamiliar things, but it all felt gentle and very safe. Steven wasn't sure any magic had happened, but he liked the way they'd come together and the care they were all expressing.

"We all come from different traditions so it doesn't make sense to try and do a spell together tonight. Instead, what I'd like to ask you to do, each of you in your own way, is to offer up prayers, spells, positive thoughts – whatever you can – for Mindy's healing and recovery. And if we all do that at the same time, so that our voices mingle?" Elspeth said.

Around the circle, voices rose. Steve could make out odd words, but not the sense of what anyone else was saying. He needed to be part of it, and added his own whispered hopes that Mindy would feel better, and that she would overcome whatever had brought her to such an awful state of mind. He hoped what they were doing could help her in some way.

When they finally fell silent again, Elspeth let the quietness settle between them before speaking again.

"I also think we should do something for us. We've all been affected by this, we're all shaken and grieving. We need to make room for that, too," Elspeth said.

"We howl," Diana replied.

They looked at each other. John and Elspeth nodded slowly. "Good choice," Elspeth said.

Steven glanced at the faces he could see around the circle, waiting to see what would happen. Leaning back in her wheelchair, Diana closed her eyes and released a muted sound of distress. In a moment, Carol took up the cry, then Heathen John's richer voice added anther layer of wounded expression. Others joined in. One by one, they howled, combining their keening voices together, letting the sound grow in volume. As their voices mingled, they stepped closer to each other, arms reaching around waists and shoulders for mutual support.

The wild unleashing of emotion around him tightened the lump in his throat. This spoke to the depths of his anguish, and he struggled to free himself into their communal grieving. His first attempt came as little more than an unhappy grunt, but Neil's hand gripped his shoulder, and then it poured out of him, rising up from his guts, full of disbelief and fear. He howled to the cloudy sky above. Howled to the wind and the earth. Those other voices matched his, sounding their sorrow.

Tears stung his eyes and made moist pathways down his cheeks. Steven tasted salt, and thought of Mindy's frantic kisses. *Why?* He asked himself, yet again. The memory of her, alive and warm in his arms, still seemed so fresh and vibrant. Even recalling the terrible sight of her in the bath couldn't drive off that feeling. *Had she really meant to do it? Was it just a cry for help gone tragically wrong? Could he have done anything that would have saved her from wanting to do that to herself? Had he got it wrong somehow? Was it all his fault?*

Keening and weeping, they clung to each other. Steven realised that whatever difficulties he had felt before, everything had changed. Sharing this intimacy of distress broke down all other barriers. They were kindred in suffering and tears; they shared in the same sorrow. For the first time in his life, he had a true sense of belonging. Tears ran freely down his cheeks, as he abandoned himself, letting out the turmoil of emotion he had carried within him in recent days. He would rather have been a pariah for the rest of his life, then had this experience of connection bought at such a devastating price.

Gradually, their cries melted away into quietness.

"Let us unmake our circle" Elspeth said.

She guided them though a reversal of the process that had started the ritual. Steven found is soothing after all of the emotions that had been poured into that space.

"We ask the trees to hold us, we ask the ground to hold us," Elspeth said when they were all holding hands again. "This temple is temporary, but we hold our community in our hearts as we leave this place."

There was a brief silence.

"Now we go back to my place and get medicinally pissed," Heath John said.

It wasn't the alcohol taking away the sharp edge of pain, Steven realised, but the company. They were in this together, all equally angry, confused and wounded by what had happened. During the evening, others dropped by – Helen, whose usually sharp tongue was curbed by the circumstances, and plenty of others he didn't recognise. They had a massive card to sign for her, and John was collecting cash for a gift which he would sort out with her parents.

"Are they Pagan friendly?" Helen asked, never one to pull punches.

"To be honest, I don't they were at all, not at first. They saw us part of the problem, part of the lifestyle that had got her into trouble," John said.

"I thought as much," said Helen.

"Well, they've come round a fair way, when I asked what we could send they softened up considerably. They're asking us not to visit but by the sounds of it, that's in her best interests. She's had a massive mental breakdown and it's going to take time for her to recover."

"Is she still in hospital?" Helen asked.

"And then she's being moved to a specialist psychiatric unit for a while," John said.

"If you need someone professional who can advocate for Paganism not being a mental illness, give me a shout," Helen said. "I know people."

"I'm hoping it won't come to that, but thanks," Heathen John said.

Sitting in the corner of an ancient sofa, Steven gazed at a photo on the wall. In it were a bunch of people he didn't recognise, and Mindy near the centre, staring out at him. Seeing her face made him want to cry. All he wanted was the chance to talk to her again, to make sense of what had happened between them, to make peace.

"I owe you an apology."

Steven looked up and saw that Diana had parked her chair directly in front of him.

"Sorry?" he questioned, thinking he must have misheard.

"Well, yes," she said. "It's a subject that really winds me up – rape and abuse. Did you know one in nine people report being abused as children?"

"I didn't."

"I could get on a soap box here, but I probably shouldn't. I'm not one of these women who thinks all men are potential rapists."

"I didn't know anyone thought that way."

"Then you've had a very sheltered life," Diana said.

"In some ways, yes."

"But, I wasn't going to talk gender politics. John told me what you did when you realised our Mindy might be in trouble. That matters. I never gave you a proper chance to explain your version of things, before, I made a lot of assumptions."

"I didn't really know how to explain," Steven confessed. "I thought things were ok. Maybe I overdid it, but I didn't really know what I was doing. I really thought she was ok with me. And I feel awful about it. I never wanted to hurt her. I just didn't know what I was doing."

"You surprise me," Diana said.

"What do you mean?" Steven asked.

"Well, you look the sort of man who probably attracts more than his share of women."

"Me?" He wondered if she was teasing him.

"You're being very modest."

"I am?"

"I'd have said."

"Oh." Steven considered this. He'd never thought himself especially attractive, and he'd never had the impression people of any gender found him appealing.

"I think that's one of the reasons I mistrusted you at first. I thought you could so easily take advantage of someone like Mindy."

Steven shook his head, struggling to get to grips with these suggestions.

"So, I judged you on appearances, and I shouldn't have done. I don't know you, and I shouldn't have made assumptions."

"Well, it was my word against hers and I can't blame you for siding with a friend."

"I wonder if that was such a good thing to have done. If we'd questioned her – perhaps it was the first sign that things weren't right. If she was disturbed, unhappy... if that was some kind of call for help. Perhaps someone could have spotted what was happening with her."

"I keep thinking that. What if I'd gone after her sooner? What if I hadn't let her go that afternoon?"

"You can go mad thinking like that," Diana said.

"Believe me, I know."

"So, am I forgiven?" she asked.

"Am I?" Steven returned.

"Something like this... it creates perspective. Life is all we have. People make mistakes... let's just try and put the past behind us and move on," Diana suggested.

"I don't know if I can, but you lot are all I have, the most I've ever had, and I don't want to lose that."

She smiled at him, the expression melancholy and full of understanding.

Sudden cramp woke Steven. He gripped his thigh, aware only of the sharp pain. Gradually it subsided, allowing him chance to notice how stiff he felt. He'd slept in the corner of Heathen John's ancient sofa.

Someone had covered him with a blanket. Looking around he found the room otherwise empty. The house seemed quiet and he had no idea what the time might be. His first response was to depart, leaving a note of some sort. Having unexpectedly stayed over in someone else's home seemed very awkward to Steven. He found the rather cluttered bathroom, splashed his face with cold water and rubbed the grit from his eyes.

A few children's toys were scattered around the edge of the bath. He hadn't noticed them on the previous evening. John appeared to live alone, but the assorted boats and fish made Steven wonder. As no one else seemed to be stirring, he examined the many small photos hung in frames on various walls in other rooms. There were quite a few images of the same blonde haired girl at different stages of growth. Of the girl's mother there were no obvious signs, and Steven wondered if this indicated estrangement.

It struck him then that he probably wasn't the only person with difficult things hidden away in the past. Mindy must have had her own demons. Perhaps everyone did. He'd always felt separate from other people, marked as different in ways he couldn't entirely identify. Never having been all that close to anyone, he had no insight into how those around him lived or felt. It occurred to him he might be more normal than not after all.

Heathen John came quietly down the stairs, still looking half asleep. "Do you want a tea or a coffee or some breakfast or something?"

"Tea would be great," Steven said.

John grunted an acknowledgement. Once in the kitchen, he set about loading the toaster with slices of brown bread. "You were dead to the world last night," he observed.

"I haven't been sleeping much. I guess it all caught up with me."

"Yeah."

"I didn't mean to impose."

"You're not, its fine. Knocking round the house on my own hasn't been any great joy."

Steven had nothing to say to that, so he kept quiet. John passed him a plate of hot buttered toast, with a generous helping of thick-cut marmalade. It tasted surprisingly bitter and far more interesting than the pots he bought.

"Elspeth's handiwork," John said, gesturing towards the neatly labelled pot. "She always makes more than she can use herself."

"Diana talked to me last night," Steven said, as the memory of their conversation returned to him.

"She's calmed down a bit," John observed.

"So I see."

"I think what happened… well, we've all had to look at things differently," John said,

"Yes. It's shaken me up too."

They talked for a little while, drinking tea and sharing their difficulty around accepting what Mindy had done. Neither man had any answers, but Steven found some comfort in being able to voice his thoughts.

Only later, when he was walking home, did Steven realise the implications of that morning's events. Without even thinking about it, he had accepted and consumed several pieces of toast in front of another person. His mind had been elsewhere, and he'd forgotten to be anxious. It had been fine. John had treated it all as perfectly normal and Steven found retrospectively that he felt entirely at ease with the experience. *What had he been afraid of?* He didn't really know, only that eating in the company of others seemed laden with an undefined menace. Eating had always been something to do privately, as though it was a shameful act. His mother treated food as a vice, and Steven had taken that idea to heart, relating to consumption not as essential to life but as an action he should feel guilty over.

Is this who I am? He asked himself. *Or is this something I've learned? Other people aren't like this. Maybe I'm not really like this either. So what else isn't really me?*

Revelation struck like a body blow. *I know what I want.*

"Good," a warmly feminine voice whispered across his thoughts.

Chapter Thirteen

Walking home from work in the drizzle, Steven had been drifting from one thought to another as the bus pulled in a hundred yards ahead of him. Several teenagers in school uniform disembarked, followed by an elderly man with two walking sticks. Then he saw a dark haired figure alight from the vehicle, her movements graceful. She turned towards him, as though she had sensed his gaze. Despite the distance between them, he felt the darkness of her eyes keenly. A playful smile darted across her lips, then she turned into the nearest side road and disappeared from view.

Steven stopped in his tracks, half certain he had recognised the woman from the painting, but disbelieving it could really be her. Having lived with her face on his wall for several weeks, he didn't really think she would step off a bus a few yards in front of him. On the other hand, how could he afford not to check? As the artist responsible for that painting lived somewhere in the area, the model could very well be local too. Steven set off at a jog, turning down the same side road just in time to see his quarry take a left some yards further on. She had quite a head start on him, and Steven kept running, trying to catch up sufficiently to get a closer look. No matter how fast he went, she remained ahead, even though when he did catch sight of her, she seemed to be walking.

Soon trickles of sweat were running down his back. Having spent most of the day hauling away rubbish that had been dumped on the outskirts of town, Steven knew he stank. Running after a woman, when he looked and smelled awful, probably wasn't the best plan ever, he thought, but he could hardly turn back now. He wondered what he would say if he did manage to catch up with her, but no words came to him. The odds were she would find his approach alarming, and think he meant to harm her. Remembering Mindy's panic, he slowed. That mistake he did not want to make again.

Ahead of him, the woman also slowed, and turned, watching him intently for a while. She appeared aware of his pursuit, but didn't seem to be alarmed, he thought. Too tired for further exertions, he followed at a walking pace, catching his breath. She didn't get any further ahead of him as they wove their way through a maze of roads and paths on a housing estate. He supposed if he called out to her, she might stop, but equally, she might think his intentions were unpleasant. There didn't seem to be any good way of making an approach. Disheartened, he considered giving up. The dark haired woman turned to her right, and he followed hurriedly after her. However, when he reached the same turning, he saw it led only to garages. A dead end. He thought for a moment that she had hidden inside one of the garages to get away from him, but felt sure she couldn't have had time. There was no other way out that he could see, and no-where else she could have gone.

Perplexed, he stood still for a long time. A small brown bird fluttered down and began pecking about on the tarmac just a few feet away, careless of his presence. Steven watched it for a while, wondering what it was, and where the woman had disappeared to. She couldn't have vanished into thin air. *If she was ever there at all,* suggested a treacherous voice in his head.

"I saw her," he whispered to the rapidly darkening day.

Above him heavy clouds were rolling in, and the gentle light rain was fast becoming unpleasantly heavy. He shivered.

The first moot without Mindy began as a sombre gathering. For a long while, no-one mentioned her outright, then Neil said "I miss her," and everyone agreed. After that the talk flowed a little more readily.

"So how do I learn more?" Steven asked. "I've been to a few meditation nights at Helen's shop, and I come along here, and I read things online, but I don't feel like I'm making much progress. So where do I go next?"

"There are courses you can pay for, but some of them are very expensive," Elspeth said.

"Do any of you teach?" he pressed.

The others all exchanged glances.

"Not really. And most of us haven't been formally taught. We just learn however we can and make it us as we go along," Heathen John said.

"You can get a lot out of books," Carol said. "That's mostly what I do, but then I'm into wicca and there are plenty of books on that."

"Are you the pagans?"

The unexpected interruption had them all looking round. The man who had spoken stood a short distance from their table, hands in pockets. His presence left Steven feeling ill at ease, but he couldn't have said why.

"We are," Wiccan John said carefully.

"Have a seat," Diana offered.

He sat, pulling his arms in close to his body. "So what's it all about then?" he asked.

"We were just talking about how people learn, whether you pay for courses, learn from books or make it up as you go along," Diana said pleasantly.

"And?"

"Everyone has to find their own way," Elspeth said. "Should we do introductions?" She went on to point out and name the people around the table.

"Hi," said the new man. "So what makes you think you're so special?"

"We don't," Diana said.

"We haven't made any such claims," Heathen John added, and Steven could hear the irritation in his voice. "We share some interests, we get together and talk about it, that's it. If you want to join us, fine, if you're here to criticise, we're not really interested."

"So what are you selling? Salvation? Power? Hope?"

"We're not selling anything," Diana returned.

"So why do you do this? Why don't you just face up to reality?"

"What makes you think we aren't?" Elspeth asked, an amused smile lifting the corners of her generous mouth.

"Religion's just crap, isn't it? All religion, it's just a way of burying your head in the sand, not facing up to things. You're all intellectually bankrupt. You're only fooling yourselves."

"So why are you here?" Diana asked. "Why bother coming along if that's what you think? Why not leave us to get on with it? We're not your problem, are we?"

"I thought you'd be different, but you're just the same as everyone else."

"We're only human," Elspeth said. "What did you expect? That we'd all be like some fantasy film or another?"

"If you want to know what we actually think, try listening rather than talking," Diana said.

The man rested his elbows on the table, hunching up. Steven tried to guess how old he was, but with a dense beard obscuring the lower half of his face, and large glasses exaggerating the size of his eyes, it wasn't easy to tell.

"Where were we?" Elspeth asked pleasantly.

"I have another question," Steven offered. "I was wondering if anyone else has experiences they can't explain. I worry that I'm going to sound crazy, but I see people sometimes and then they vanish."

"We were talking about this back at midsummer, weren't we," Elspeth said encouragingly.

"I feel things I can't explain," Carol said. "I think I pick up other people's feelings. Does that count?"

"The night Mindy ended up in hospital, Carol kept pacing round the house. I don't think she slept a wink all night, and we didn't know until the following day what had happened," her partner Sean added.

"Where do we draw the line between madness and vision?" Diana asked. "I wonder, there are so many people who are considered unbalanced because they see things no one else does, and hear voices. In older cultures, they would have been deemed holy, inspired."

"First Christianity demonised them, now the medical profession does," Elspeth returned.

"This is dangerous and stupid," the new man said loudly.

"And you'd be an expert, would you?" Heathen John asked.

For a moment they stared at each other, then the new man rose to his feet. "This is just a total waste of time," he said. He walked away.

"Well fuck you too," Heathen John said quietly.

"What was that about?" Steven asked.

"Just a weirdo," Diana said. "You get them now and then. I remember a guy a few years back who was prophesying that the witches and druids were going to start a war in Birmingham."

"Didn't even have the balls to offer a name," Heathen John muttered darkly. "Probably gets some perverse kick out of this kind of thing."

"Maybe he was hoping for naked dancing and virgin sacrifices," Wiccan John replied cheerfully.

"Not in this pub," Diana put in.

"Forget about him," Elspeth said. "He's not our problem. So where were we? The line between madness and vision. How do you determine between someone who needs medical intervention, and someone who is a visionary?"

"If they're dysfunctional," Carol said. "I studied psychology for a bit, and that's the critical thing apparently. More people than not have funny ideas, but so long as they can get on with their lives, there's no point treating it like illness. If they're dysfunctional, if they can't cope, they need help."

As Steven was pondering where this assessment left him, Diana cleared her throat.

"An it harm none, do what you will."

"That's about the size of it," Carol agreed.

Chapter Fourteen

I know what I want.

In the centre of the path, water had cut through the leaf litter, forming a stream that exposed the small stones and sandy soil beneath. Endless stair-rods of rain battered down. Steven could hear nothing beyond the sound of water drumming on his plastic hood. He didn't dare get the ordinance survey map out; the paper would saturate and ruin in seconds. Not really knowing where he wanted to go anyway, he headed up, thinking there would be less risk of floods on higher ground. His newly purchased walking boots chaffed his ankles, but they allowed him to get a grip on the mud.

Stopping to catch his breath, Steven looked around at the trees. There were quite striking differences between them, he noticed. He'd never really stopped and examined any trees properly before: They'd just been green and brown backgrounds to anything he happened to be doing outside. Blinking stray raindrops from his eyelashes, he saw the different tones and textures of the bark, the shapes of leaves, and the subtle variations in colour. Some stood straight, while others had been bowed or twisted by unknown forces. He could spot oak and holly now, but beyond that had no idea what any of them were.

Steven pushed the hood back from his coat, and at once the rain began to chill his scalp. His hair offered no protection against the downpour. Rain trickled down the back of his neck, into his face and eyes. However, he could hear properly without the hood in the way. Sounds of water in trees came to him, far clearer than before. Taking a deep breath, Steven felt the tension leave his shoulders. He hadn't even realised it was there. It felt as though a layer of grime had washed away, even though he hadn't appreciated he was filthy. The muck of urban life, of car fumes and air pollution might have explained some of it, but it felt less a bodily thing and more a mind issue. Out here, he could not hear the engines of cars above the sound of the rain. No shouting from the flat upstairs. No blaring of televisions or sound systems. No hum of fridges, or the ever-present buzz of other gadgets. No mobile phones. Steven rejoiced, silently.

He walked, letting the rhythms of it carry him outside himself. No one else had braved the deluge, and he travelled alone down broad, empty pathways. He remembered in early childhood, testing the backs of wardrobes, looking for a way to escape into another world. Later, when his father had gone and the responsibility of his mother fell onto his young shoulders, he delved into his own thoughts, finding a degree of comfort in solitude. He hadn't dreamed of anything otherworldly in those days, with hopes of escape into fantasy kingdoms long since shattered. Walking alone beneath these trees, Steven felt as though he had found the escape he'd longed for in that other life. Seeing the beauty around him, he felt he could be in any mythic forest. With the rain muting all other sounds, he could be part of a fairy tale. Fragments of half remembered stories fluttered in his mind. He'd been an avid reader once, a long time ago. Then there had been so much to do of late, and he hadn't been able tp spare the hours to lose himself in any kind of pretend. The real world had too tight a grip on him. Steven smiled to himself, because looking back at those years of being his mother's keeper, it didn't seem real at all. More like someone else's nightmare than anything he could have lived through himself.

Gradually, the rainstorm abated, and in its wake came brilliant sunshine. Water drops shimmered on leaves. Earthy scents rose from the sodden ground, along with the distinctive smell of damp leaves in the surrounding air. Steven pulled off his sodden raincoat and thrust it into his bag, glad to be rid of the thing. Sporadic bursts of bird song caught his attention but he scanned the nearby trees in vain for signs of the singers. Now that the rain had stopped, he could see everything with greater clarity.

For a moment he thought he could hear the sound of his own heart, beating loudly, but concentrating, he realised the pulse echoing in his ears did not originate inside him. With a hand against his chest, he could feel his heart pumping, and the other sound did not match it. Turning about, he tried to place where this curious noise came from. After a while, he picked a direction and followed it as best he could, cutting through undergrowth, with brambles tugging at his clothes. Where rain had collected on leaves it now fell upon him in great abundance. At the first opportunity, he picked up a path going his way. All the while, the pulse continued, varying occasionally in pace and rhythm.

The pulsing sound grew louder until Steven became sure it must be a drum. But who on earth would be out on a day like this, drumming in a wood? Enchanted by the peculiarity of it all, he followed the sound, until eventually the path brought him to a clearing. Stopping, he gazed at the scene, at first surprised by it, but slowly making sense of the image before him. A giant, dark head sprouted out of the ground, with leafy protrusions stretching out in several directions. He could make out closed eyes and a sizeable nose. The drummer sat to one side of this improbable head, resting her weight on one of its protruding parts. He wasn't certain if those were supposed to be tongues, moustaches, or something else entirely.

As far as he could tell, the drummer hadn't noticed him – she faced away, and had not turned, so Steven remained where he was, watching and listening. Her dark hair was probably shoulder length when loose, he guessed, but it had been caught up in a high pony-tail, leaving her lightly tanned shoulders bare. A light, strappy top clung to her torso, then her hips curved down into dark denim. On the ground at her side lay a bag, and a discarded coat. As she carried on, unaware of him, Steven wished he had something of his own to add. He had no drum with which to join in, and not much sense of rhythm anyway. He didn't know any suitable songs, nor did he feel equal to dancing. All he could do was remain on the edge of the glade, hoping not to disturb her.

Had his chance walk finally brought him to the person he'd been searching for? It seemed improbable, but everything about the scene before him was tinged with strangeness. As he gazed at the woman, he tried to decide if she could be the enigmatic being who haunted his dreams and meditations. Her figure looked about right, he thought: Tall, and neither bulky nor overtly delicate. The long hair looked about right, but unable to see her face, he couldn't be sure.

How long he stood there for, he could not have said. Eventually, she laid down her drum but remained where she sat. Steven couldn't quite bring himself to approach.

"I know you're there," she said softly, without turning to face him.

"I just stopped to listen," he said.

She laughed. "It's been such an odd day. I couldn't tell what sort of an audience I had. I thought you might be a spirit."

"Sorry, no."

She turned to face him then. Large, luminous blue eyes shone out dramatically. It took Steven a while to really see any other part of her face. Her bones were strong enough, her chin a narrow point, her mouth small and very mobile. This was not the woman from his painting, and yet he could see the forest in her gaze somehow.

"So, what do you want?" she asked casually.

The question caught him off guard and he stuttered awkwardly.

"I was just walking. I needed to get out, you know?"

"I know. Why do you think I'm here?" She set about putting her drum back in its case. "Rain tends to keep all the normal people away, which is nice. Some days it's just heaving with kids and townies up here."

"I've not been to this part of the wood before."

"No? Well, there's a visitor's centre not far away. Any time the weather's good, a whole load of people drive out of Birmingham to sit on the grass outside the centre. Most of them never make it as far as the trees. Beats the hell out of me."

Steven shrugged at this.

"I just like having the place to myself," she added.

"I can go. I don't want to disturb you."

She eyed him up for a moment before speaking. "You're ok. You're quiet enough, and you've got to be weird to be out in the woods in the rain."

He smiled at this. "So what is that you're sitting on?" he asked.

"It's part of the sculpture trail, the green man."

"The green man?" Steven asked, finding the name faintly familiar.

"You know, symbol of the wildwood, trees and nature and all that. Faces made out of leaves, or looking through leaves, or with leaves for hair. You must have seen them."

"No."

"Well, that's him," she said, gesturing at the head. Looking closer, he could see the details of leaves on the large sculpture. The face looked very male, and bore no resemblance to the image of a forest spirit that dwelled in his thoughts.

"They turn up everywhere," she added. "You'll be seeing them all the time now, you wait."

"Oh. Are there any green women?"

"Sure, you get tree women as well, and some don't really have a gender."

The spirit of Arden could be a green woman, he thought. A narrow face peering out from between the leaves. Images of a visage surrounded by bright green hair flashed through his thoughts.

"Well, I've got to be going. I promised I'd take my sons to the cinema this afternoon and I'll be late if I don't get a move on."

"Nice meeting you," Steven said.

Once she had gone, he stood in front of the wooden head for a while, studying its heavily lidded eyes. The face looked peaceful and benign. Nothing wild about it at all.

"You aren't the wildwood, are you? You're part way between there and us humans."

"Correct."

At the sound of this one word, Steven spun round, but the glade remained empty.

"Who's there?" he called out nervously.

A bird trilled from deep amongst the trees, but otherwise no answer came. Scanning the undergrowth and paths around this open space, he could see nothing. Steven wondered if he had been mistaken, hearing something else and mistaking it for a human voice. It had sounded like a word.

"I don't know how to find you," he said aloud. He waited, but the woods around him remained quiet this time. "You asked me what I want, and at the time I didn't know how to answer that. I've been thinking about it. I want to know who I am."

He'd almost expected she would speak to him then, her voice light on the breeze. Nothing happened. Sitting down on one of the green man's wooden protrusions, he thought about what he was doing. The woman who talked about trees. The model for the spirit of Arden. The figure who manifested in his dreams. They had collected into a single entity in his mind. Steven realised he'd started believing that by finding one of them, he would simultaneously find the others. Most likely there were at least two separate women, with a third he had imagined, based partly on the other two. Realisation that he had been fooling himself struck him hard, and he slumped. Another stupid idea.

Steven made his way out of the glade, not sure where he needed to go, and not entirely caring. The rhythm of walking had a soothing effect, and he needed that.

Chapter Fifteen

"I wonder how Vicky and Dan are doing," Elspeth said during a lull in the conversation.

"The couple from Worcester?" Sean asked. "There's been flooding down there."

"I'm sure she said she had a house by the river," Elspeth replied. "I hope they're ok."

"Have you heard from her?" Steven asked.

"She phoned me a few weeks after midsummer, but nothing since then."

"Climate change," Neil said. "Rain. Flooding. Climate change."

"Got to be," Heathen John agreed, returning to the table with drinks and crisps.

"Seeing the rivers flooding their banks, makes you remember how powerful nature is. We might think we control her, but we don't," Diana said.

"No doubt there will be more calls for flood protection. It won't help. The water has to go somewhere eventually," Heathen John added.

"Bloody stupid building on flood plains," Neil responded, helping himself to John's crisps.

"How do we relate to this spiritually?" Elspeth enquired of the entire moot.

As they contemplated this question, Steven felt an uneasy, prickling sensation along the back of his neck. He fought the urge to turn and look behind him at the rest of the room.

"I see it as the Goddess venting her fury. The more we damage her world, the more she will do this, until either we learn, or we perish," Diana said.

"Yes," Carol agreed.

"I saw something online about a ritual to change the weather," Heathen John said. "Felt wrong to me. This is happening for a reason, whether you call it the wrath of the gods, or climate change doesn't matter. We have to deal with it, not carry on as usual while trying to make the symptoms go away."

"Steven, you're being very quiet tonight. Any thoughts?" Wiccan John asked.

Steven shook his head by way of a response. He felt odd, as though he had unwelcome company.

"So are you just going to stand there glowering all night, or have you got something to say for yourself?" Heathen John asked, his expression visibly darkening.

Steven jumped slightly, thinking at first that the remark was meant for him.

"I'm just listening," said a voice from behind him.

Resisting the temptation to turn round and look, Steven scanned the faces of his companions, looking for clues. None of them looked too pleased. For a long time, the silence around the table held.

"So, keep talking," the man at Steven's back said.

No one said anything for quite a while until the man Steven couldn't see spoke again.

"I'm all ears. I want to hear how you're going to explain everything away as divine intervention or some other crap."

Elspeth stood, her expression formidable. "If you have nothing positive to contribute, kindly go somewhere else."

"So you can't take having your pathetic ideas challenged."

"You aren't offering a challenge. You're just rubbishing anything you hear," Elspeth answered levelly. "It's not the same thing."

Steven stood too, then turned to face the intruder. He had no idea what he was doing, it felt alarmingly like he'd lost control of himself. He had a height advantage of a couple of inches over the nuisance guy. Remaining still, he stared, hoping he looked more intimidating than he felt.

"Is that the best you can do?" the man asked, with a sneer.

"No. I'm just getting started," Steven said, his blood racing. His body felt strangely full all of a sudden, as though his skin had stretched slightly to accommodate something extra. Light headed he had no idea what to make of any of this, but had no desire to resist. He heard words issuing authoritatively from his own mouth.

"Go away."

What exactly he'd done, he couldn't say, but the man before him took a step back, appearing to shrink slightly. For a few seconds, he had the bizarre impression of another set of features looking out through the unremarkable face before him. This other visage had a cruel slant to it and Steven shivered. As the man left, Steven dropped down into his seat, shaken. His body felt like his own again, but so weightless it might float from the chair.

"Nice one," Neil said.

Normal conversation resumed almost at once, but Steven remained quiet, thrown by what had just happened. Apparently no one else had noticed anything out of the ordinary. Did that mean he was imagining things, or had they just not seen what was going on? *What on earth had it that been about?* The second face seemed familiar. When he placed it, the shock made him spill his beer. Surely that had been the man who told him to keep away from Mindy.

This is madness, he told himself. *You must have imagined it. Don't think about it. You're over-reacting. You're out of control.*

"All right, Steven?" Heathen John asked from the other side of the small table.

"I don't know. Maybe I'm coming down with something. I don't feel so good to be honest. I might go out and get some air." He rose to leave.

"Me too," Neil said.

"Bugger it," said Elspeth. "Let's just all go and have a wander shall we? I don't know about anybody else, but that asshole wrecked the mood for me."

Steven wanted desperately to be on his own, to think and clear his head a little. There was no getting away without seeming rude, or lying, and he didn't feel up to that. He walked at the back, keeping apart from the various conversations going on around him. Memories of Mindy filled his thoughts. He still couldn't reconcile himself to her absence. It seemed as though she should be there, walking next to him, with everything forgiven and them friends again. He felt sure she would love the barely inhabited streets under orange lights. Even though he'd not known her long, the ache of her not being there had a powerful influence. Odd, he thought, considering he had spent all his life with his mother, and parting from her still felt like a guilty relief.

When at last they went their separate ways, Steven couldn't face going back to his flat. Nervous energy coursed through him, and his thoughts whirled constantly. He set off with quiet determination, knowing where he needed to be.

At this late hour, the cemetery lay quiet and untroubled by the living. So many dead people. So much grief. He could feel it pressing down on him with an endless weight of tears. He sat down on the edge of the path and wondered what on earth he was doing here.

"I wish we'd sorted things out," he said. "I wish we'd talked, properly. I never meant you any harm. I hope you knew that. What was going on with you? What was so bad that you had to cut yourself up like that?"

He thought about his mother then, and her prolonged attempt at staving herself to death. A slow suicide she hadn't quite managed yet, but which had robbed her existence of all real life and colour for so many years. What had it achieved? The sheer pointlessness of it all staggered him. And then his own life, bound to his mother's by some feeling of duty and by endless guilt. All those wasted years and aborted dreams.

"What were you so afraid of that made killing yourself seem like a better option?" he asked the night. "And what about this other stuff? The guy who threatened me. I thought I saw him again tonight, looking out through someone else's eyes. How mental is that? But what if that was real? Who is he Mindy? There's no one else I can ask. No one I can take this to. This is the last thing you need right now with everything you're going through."

Speaking his thoughts, he rambled from one topic to another, searching for the faintest hint of explanation or comfort, but finding nothing. Mindy was in some hospital and in no state to deal with any of this. He had started seeing things he could not explain. There were no pleasant explanations in either case. He had a nagging feeling of wrongness.

"What if it wasn't a suicide attempt," he said aloud. The temperature around him seemed to plummet. Steven became conscious of just how dark the cemetery was, and how quiet. There were no sounds of distant traffic. All around him lay row upon row of the dead. Every late-night horror movie he had ever seen came back to him in a rush, and with it a panic that blotted out everything else. He ran, skidding over loose gravel in his race to get back to the gate, to streetlights and signs of the living.

In his hurry to escape from his fears, he almost ran into the man. Slowing at the last moment, Steven realised how ridiculous he must look, fleeing a graveyard in the dead of night as though a horde of demons were after him.

"Sorry mate," he said, trying to dodge out of the way.

The man leered at him, a dangerous smile twisting his face unpleasantly. "I wouldn't go out on my own at night if I were you."

The implied threat made him stop dead a pace or two beyond the man. Although he felt threatened, running for it no longer seemed like the best choice. Steven turned, trying to think of something to say. He had no response to offer but needed to know if it had been a passing malice, or if this man meant him harm. When he turned, the street past the graveyard appeared entirely empty. Orange streetlights bathed the pavement, offering nowhere to hide. Steven stood unmoving for several minutes, looking around him. It couldn't have been a trick of the light. There had been a man. He had spoken. Either he had vanished into thin air, or Steven had imagined the entire incident.

Shaken, he turned for home, wanting to be in a familiar place with solid walls around him. But if he had hallucinated the whole thing, he realised it could happen again anywhere. And if it had been real, what protection could his flat offer against a man who vanished at will?

Chapter Sixteen

Steven knew he had a paranoid streak in his nature. If he walked past a group of teenage girls and they giggled, he tended to feel like they were laughing at him. He assumed others would blame him for anything that went awry, and expected official bodies and institutions to threaten his autonomy. Intellectually, he understood what was going on in his head, but that had no effect on immediate emotional responses. Having spent so much of his young life afraid – of mistakes, abandonment and authority, he defaulted to fearful responses before he had time to think about it.

For a few days, he overcompensated by ignoring his gut feelings. *Paranoia* he whispered to himself every time anxiety flashed through him. There had been a figure stood in the doorway of a nearby block of flats that morning – and perhaps that person had been watching him, but it didn't mean anything. The prickly feeling of being observed did not necessarily mean there was someone tracking his every move. He could have imagined the sound of footsteps following him down an empty street after work.

Paranoid, he told himself, looking out of the window and seeing someone on the far side of the road looking up towards him. The phantom watcher always appeared too far away for clear identification. Steven tried to laugh at himself, but the feeling of insecurity grew deeper every day, as though this exposed feeling was building towards a crisis.

He went to a workshop in the room over Helen's shop. 'Understanding your soul' sounded like it might prove useful, and it beat sitting in his flat watching television. Settled out of the way at the back of the room, he listened at first with interest, and then with growing frustration. According to the speaker, he had planned this life in absolute detail, whilst in heaven between incarnations. Steven hated the notion. His life seemed miserable enough without having to accept the idea that he had somehow chosen to have it like this. He considered leaving, but being so far from the door, he couldn't depart without drawing considerable attention to himself.

The speaker – a cheerful woman with a large bun of grey hair and a purple trouser suit – talked of spirit guides. She enthused about angels and animal friends, guides, guardians and other benevolent entities.

"The universe is full of unconditional love," she announced. "All you have to do is open your heart to it, and your soul will fill up with joy."

At her words, Steven felt himself shutting down even further. Unconditional love? He'd seen precious little of that, and remained unconvinced of its existence. The woman before him seemed so certain that everything out there was warm, friendly, loving and good. Steven remembered holding Mindy's wrists, trying to stop her precious blood from ebbing away. Where was universal goodness then?

"Everything happens for a reason," the speaker continued. "Things that seem to hurt us are friends in disguise, teaching us and helping us to understand our soul's plan for this lifetime."

Steven shook his head, unable to reconcile this idea with his own experiences. He accepted that pain and hardship could be teachers, but the idea of some good intention behind all the things that went wrong struck him as horrible. Better by far to believe that there was nothing personal in it. He'd been striving for a while to accept that the unhappiness in his life might have been bad luck and nothing personal. Now apparently it was there to help him and that felt decidedly worse. He couldn't accept that.

"Whenever we feel sad or alone, we should pray for guidance, and open our souls to the good angels who watch over us and keep us from harm."

And where was Mindy's good angel? As others had intervened with questions during the talk, Steven raised his hand.

"Yes?" she speaker asked.

"So there are only good spirits out there trying to help us?"

"That's right."

"You don't believe in anything malevolent, in evil, in bad spirits or anything like that?"

"The only evil in this life comes from our own fear, our unwillingness to accept the love of the universe."

"A friend of mine tried to kill herself not so long ago. Where was her good angel then?"

"If it was in her soul's plan to try, but then fail to commit suicide then we must trust that there was a good reason. Her life was a gift, a thing of beauty and wonder, and no doubt she has taught any people valuable lessons."

"So you're saying it's ok for a person to kill themselves? That fits in with your idea of universal, unconditional love?" Steven could feel anger boiling within him. The woman seemed so smug and certain.

For a while, she didn't answer, but the benevolent smile left her face, and a troubled expression replaced it.

"You are clearly in pain. You need to understand how this sadness fits in with your own soul plan. Sometimes the hardest lessons to learn are the ones that are most driven by love."

"I'm sorry," Steven said, rising to his feet. "I don't think being here is part of my soul's plan after all."

With all eyes upon him, he walked the length of the room and escaped through the door. While he hadn't enjoyed being the centre of attention, he felt better for being out of the talk and away from a world view that filled him with anger and uncertainty.

"Is it half time already?" Helen asked pleasantly as he reached the bottom of the stairs.

"No. I couldn't take any more of it."

"Such is."

"It's just so... smug. All that certainty that everything out there is good and lovely and it all happens for a reason."

"And you don't believe that?" Helen enquired.

"Do you?" he counter questioned.

"I see no evidence of it."

"I was starting to feel like some kind of lone freak up there," Steven said.

"It's new age stuff. Fluffy. It's all about feeling warm and fuzzy and good about yourself," Helen said quietly.

"But their money is as good as anyone else's and I have bills to pay."

"So there are other ways?" Steven said.

"Lots of other ways," Helen reassured him.

"Can I ask you something?"

"You can ask. Whether I'm willing or able to answer is a whole different matter."

"Do you believe there are both good and bad spirits?"

Helen thought about this for a moment. "I think good and bad are rather subjective ideas. It depends a lot on your own perspective. But I see no reason why spirits shouldn't be diverse."

"Thanks. I thought so too. Mind if I browse the books?"

"Be my guest."

After ten minutes of leafing through various publications, Steven still hadn't found what he needed. He'd skimmed through more than a dozen books, looking for references to harmful spirits.

"Any joy?" Helen asked, returning from the back of the shop with yet another mug of coffee. She appeared to subsist on the stuff.

"No."

"If you tell me what you're looking for, I might be able to help."

"It's hard to explain," Steven said although it was more the case that he didn't want to try.

"You'll have to do better than that," Helen replied

"I can't. And I want to be gone before that lot upstairs emerge."

"Understandable. Why don't you come back tomorrow and I'll see if I can help," she said. "From the look of you, it's serious."

"I don't know. Maybe I'm just going crazy."

"Hmm."

Hearing sounds of mass movement from above, he hurried from the shop and set off for home at a jog. All the outdoors labouring had done wonders for his fitness levels, he realised. He'd never been healthier of body. Unfortunately, he didn't think the same could be said for his mind. Hardly a day passed without a moment or two of serious paranoia. He frequently had the impression of being followed or observed without catching sight of anyone who could be doing that to him. As a consequence, he no longer knew if he could trust his perceptions. Steven didn't dare tell anyone for fear they would think him mad. For that matter, he wasn't convinced he wanted anyone believing him either, given he didn't quite believe himself.

Not feeling confident he was doing the right thing, he went back to the shop after work the following day. While Steven feared ridicule and rejection, he also felt a deep need to share the disturbing ideas that had formed in his mind. He came to the conclusion it would be better to test them and be laughed at than to carry on in this state of desperate uncertainty.

When he arrived at Helen's shop, the window had a closed sign in it, but he could see the owner inside, and tapped lightly on the glass. Once she saw him, she came to let him in.

"I had a feeling you'd come back," she said. "There's obviously something bothering you."

"You'll think I'm nuts," he said.

"I get to hear a lot of crazy things in this line of work. If you can shock me, I'll give you any book you like for free. How's that for an offer?"

She grinned, and Steven relaxed a little. Helen didn't look like the sort of woman who would make a bet like that unless she felt certain of winning it.

"Come out the back, we can sit down, have a coffee and you can tell me what's on your mind."

"That's very kind of you," he said as they walked through to the little room under the stairs. She shrugged in response to his words. "I wouldn't be too sure of that." Helen put the kettle on and pointed him in the direction of a chair. "So, what is it?"

"Mindy," he said, taking a deep breath. "What if it wasn't attempted suicide?"

"Well, it could easily have been an accident. She looked the type to self harm, and she did wear gloves all the time, which is common in people who have self-harming scars. I've run into that enough times."

"I hadn't thought of that, but it wasn't what I meant."

"Go on." Helen stared at him intensely.

"I think something happened to her that made her do this. I don't know what."

"Is this why you were asking about harmful spirits?" Helen asked.

"Yes," Steven admitted.

"Is this pure intuition, or do you have something more concrete to base that on."

"You don't think I'm mad?" he asked.

"Maybe you are, I don't know. That's not the point. I want to know why you're thinking this way."

"I saw her that day, just before… before she…" He paused to draw a breath. Helen didn't need him to explain that bit. "She visited me and she seemed very odd and out of control. I thought something was wrong, but I didn't think she'd harm herself. Once she'd gone I had this strong feeling she was in trouble, so I went after her. She'd called John, and he turned up about the time I did. I don't know what she'd said to him exactly."

"Do you think she was using drugs?" Helen asked.

"Possible. I've got no idea. There's a lot I didn't know about her."

"Much as I hate stereotyping people, it wouldn't shock me to learn she'd been using something to alter her state of mind. Some people get into real trouble with that, they can't handle what it does to them. You can get acid flashbacks any time, I gather, so you can never be sure what's real."

"I have days like that," Steven admitted.

"Are you an acid user?"

"I've never taken any drugs at all," Steven said, somewhat defensively. "It's just that I've had a lot of things happen that didn't seem real, or that seemed real at first and then didn't."

"Well, drugs only work because they plug in to your existing brain chemistry, so you could get the same effects without taking anything much."

"How?"

"Sleep deprivation, drumming, dancing, all the shamanic stuff, prolonged pain or physical exertion, bondage, mild flagellation… all sorts of ways to alter your perceptions."

"I had no idea."

"But we're getting off track here. What do you think was going on with Mindy?"

"There's this man. I've seen him a couple of times, but I'm not sure if I'm just imagining him. That's not a good start, is it?" Steven said.

"Go on."

"He threatened me and told me to get away from her. If he's real in any sense, I've no idea who he is. Maybe she was in some kind of trouble. I don't know."

"How very peculiar. Why do you think you've imagined him? From what you've said he sounds real enough. A boyfriend perhaps."

"Because on a couple of occasions he's disappeared into thin air. I said you'd think I was nuts."

"I'm not shocked, you don't get the book. Puzzled maybe. Could he have been a dealer perhaps? Someone she owed money to?"

"I don't think so." Steven took a deep breath before offering his final insight. "I once saw him looking at me out of someone else's face."

"You're serious?"

"Utterly. I saw him just for a moment, in anther guy's face. Either I'm going mad, or it really happened and I don't know what to believe."

Helen stared at him for a long time. Steven held eye contact with her, willing her to take him seriously. For the first time he realised just how much he needed someone to share this with. It was too crazy to deal with alone.

"So, which book do you want?" she asked finally.

"Do you think it's real then?"

"Your experiences are real to you, I accept that, but beyond that? Hard to say. If Mindy has been troubled by a malevolent spirit then there are things we can do. Protective magic to help her stay safe as she recovers. Leave that one with me."

"Thank you," Steven said. "That's a huge weight off my mind. I had no idea what to do. I keep seeing him, or at least I think I do, but I'm never sure."

"And you think he's some sort of spirit?"

Steven hesitated, trying to decide what he thought. "Yes," he eventually said.

Helen nodded. "And you think he caused Mindy to try and kill herself, or even that he tried to take her life?"

"I know how mad this sounds, but I think he had a hand in it. She seemed scared and like she was trying to stop something."

"I'm not judging just yet. I want to be clear about what you think is going on. So, why are you seeing this man?"

"I feel like he wants me for something, but I don't know what."

"Do you think he wants to harm you?"

"I'm trying to find another explanation, but I keep coming back to that."

"Why?"

"I don't know. Maybe this is just what he does."

"And you're sure you aren't just imagining it? This isn't guilt, or a reaction to Mindy's actions, or some kind of self indulgence?"

"No. At least I hope not. How can I tell? That's the thing. I know what I've seen, but I don't know if I can trust that, or if there's something going badly wrong with me. It's scaring me," Steven said.

Helen blew out slowly through hr lips. "Has anything like this ever happened to you before?"

"No, not before all this started."

"And have you seen other things you couldn't explain?"

Steven smiled. "A couple of things, but nothing else as sinister as this man."

"I've got to ask Steven - have you any history of mental illness. You, or any of your immediate family."

He sighed, reluctant to say but knowing that if he kept anything back, he'd be limiting her scope for helping him. "My mother's anorexic. She's not ben well for a long time. She collapsed last year, and… well, she's in residential care now. Probably will be for the rest of her life. Psychiatric care. But the rest of my family are ok as far as I know. I don't know about myself. I've no idea how much of what I think is normal."

"Oh, I suspect most of us would look a little crazy if examined too closely," Helen said cheerfully. "We all have our moments - that's a big part of the fun with being Pagan."

"So it's not just me then?"

"Course not. Although don't imagine for a moment this means every Pagan you run into will be happy to hear about it. Plenty of them only believe what they experience for themselves. I'm more like that than not. There's always a few people who go round spouting about how they're being psychically attacked by their enemies. Most people tend to assume they're putting it on to try and make themselves look important. It's not a clever way to go."

"I haven't talked to anyone else about this."

"Very wise. I wouldn't go blurting this around unless you want a reputation for being a complete nutbar."

"Thanks."

Helen chuckled. "I try to tell it like it is."

"What do I do now?"

"What do you want to do?" she asked.

"No idea. I suppose more than anything else I want to know if what I'm seeing is real, or if I'm going round the bend."

"Understandable." Helen shook her head and looked thoughtful for a while. Having nothing more to add, Steven waited to see if she would come up with anything else.

"This really isn't my area of expertise. While there are things I can do, I'm not sure how useful they would be to you. And to be honest if there's anything in this at all I'm not sure I want to be involved."

"I wouldn't want to be involved either, given the choice," Steven said.

"Then you're smarter than many. Every so often I get some kid in here asking how to summon up demons. Bloody idiots."

"What do you tell them?"

"To piss off."

Steven nodded at this, moderately amused. Helen was quite a formidable woman and he could picture her intimidating teenagers all too easily. He suspected she probably enjoyed that sort of thing.

"Look, there are people. Not that I know any of them well. Some of them are probably a bit unhinged, but there are people who talk about this kind of thing. Now the risk is you end up with some reinforced, shared hallucination with someone crazier than you are."

"But there might be someone out there who can help me?" He asked, trying not to hope.

"It's possible. I'm not making any promises though."

"Is there someone you could put me in touch with?" Steven pressed.

"Give me a couple of days. I'll see what I can do."

"Thanks Helen. I really appreciate it."

"You might not. Let's see how it goes, all right? And let me know if anything changes."

Chapter Seventeen

Within a day, Helen had a contact for him. He didn't ask how she knew the woman, but accepted the information with true gratitude.

On the telephone, Cerridwen Riversong sounded fairly normal. Aside from her name, and the inevitable direction of their conversation, Steven thought she seemed nice, and no more crazy than anyone else he'd encountered. Not, he decided, that this was necessarily much to go on given his background. They went over the basics of what had happened and he answered her numerous questions as best he could.

"I want to meet you in person first, somewhere neutral. I need to get a sense of your energies before I can commit to working with you," she said.

"Ok. Where do you want to meet?"

"Come and walk round Cannon Hill Park with me."

"Sure."

"I don't charge for what I do. This is a calling, not a profession. I don't mind gifts, but I don't accept money."

"Understood."

After the weeks of rain, that Saturday afternoon turned out to be scorching hot, without the faintest trace of cloud in the sky. Steven tried to find some shade, but at two in the afternoon, there wasn't much to be enjoyed. He waited exactly where he'd been told to, trying to spot Cerridwen. The one thing he hadn't thought to ask for was a description of her. From everything Helen had said, he supposed that she would be rather theatrically dressed, and would stand out from the crowd.

A woman with dreadlocks and a brightly coloured stripy dress sat down at a nearby picnic table and pulled out a book. For a moment he wondered if this might be her, but she seemed intent on reading and oblivious to everyone else. He wondered if he should go up and ask anyway. A young goth stopped to feed the ducks, but having done this, kept walking.

"Nice afternoon, isn't it?"

Steven turned, not having heard the woman approach him. In his first glance he took in a black dress with long sleeves, and curly reddish hair framing a weary looking face. She had a pierced eyebrow, he noted, but otherwise looked fairly conventional. He didn't recognise the voice, but hearing someone on the phone could be deceptive.

"A bit hot for me," he said carefully.

"I think you might be Steven, yes? You have a troubled aura," she said.

"I'm Steven. Are you Cerridwen then?"

"Indeed. Shall we walk?"

She set off at a gentle pace, moving from one patch of shade to the next. Steven expected more questions, but his companion remained quiet, so he went along with that, not really knowing what to say. When she stopped to sit on the grass, he did the same, keeping several feet of space between them.

"Good," she said. "Any questions?"

"Do you think you can help me?"

"Possible. We'll have to suck it and see."

"But you're willing to try?" he asked, needing to be clear.

"Yes. You seem genuine. When do you want to start?"

"Whenever suits you." he felt nervous, now that something might be going to happen. What had he let himself in for? Torn between the fear of disappointment, and the fear of experiencing something unequivocally real, he had no idea what to do.

"Now's good for me," she said. "Or should I give you enough time to lose your nerve?"

"Now's good," Steven said, not sure that if he walked away he'd manage to come back.

Out here, in the blazing sun, surrounded by noisy children and tired-looking parents, his fears seemed a little foolish. The ominous man of his late night wanderings and all his jumble of feelings about Mindy nearly dying didn't belong in this place or time. More than ever, they seemed like phantasms, and proof of his failing wits. He followed Cerridwen, doubting himself all the way.

Her home turned out to be a narrow place in a long terrace. From the outside, it looked all too normal, but once she opened the door, Steven could smell something so inviting that most of his worries eased. Once inside, the scent intensified. Some of it came from the drying herbs hanging from countless hooks in the ceiling. The walls were painted in dark colours and curtains covered the windows, giving the place a cave-like feel. After the heat outside, the cool air felt wonderful.

"Do you need anything?" she asked. "A drink, the toilet? Best attend to that first."

"I could use a glass of water, thanks."

Without a word, she vanished off through her tiny living room to the kitchen beyond, returning with cold water to slake his thirst. Looking around, Steven noticed a picture on the wall depicting a beautiful woman with a crown of leaves in her hair. He stared, open mouthed.

"I see you've found Hazel," Cerridwen said.

Steven gazed at the luminous green eyes and the last of his doubts vanished. He had the feeling that her presence in this house must be a good sign; proof that he had made the right decision. Maybe he did have a guardian angel watching over him after all, he thought. But his angel was all earth and woodland with shades of light and dark, not some airy fairy fluffy thing.

"Did you paint this?" he asked.

"Oh no. A local chap. Henry Marsden. I bought it a couple of years ago. I wish I could paint that well but I can only do abstract work."

"Oh," Steven said, somewhat lost.

"If you're ready, we could make a start."

"What do I have to do?"

"Follow me."

He hadn't expected to go upstairs, but followed without question. The back room had evidently been dedicated to magical practise. Looking around, Steven took in the circle painted onto the wooden floor, and the innumerable symbols around it. An altar, resplendent with huge candles and other paraphernalia dominated one wall. He hesitated on the threshold, unsure as to whether he should go in. The room had an atmosphere all its own – an echo perhaps of things enacted here.

"Come in," she said softly.

With her explicit permission, it seemed easier to cross the boundary.

"What do I have to do?" he asked.

"Did Helen tell you much about me?"

"Only that she thought you might be able to help," he said tactfully. Helen had made a few choice comments that he didn't feel inclined to repeat.

"I work as an oracle," Cerridwen explained. "I may be able to help you find answers. I'll go into a deep trance state. All you have to do is ask me questions. Make the questions as clear and precise as you can."

"How many questions can I ask?"

"As many as you need to. If I get too tired and lose focus before you're finished then you'll just have to put up with it. So, think carefully about what you want to ask."

"And I can ask about anything?"

"Past, present, future, are all as one," she said.

"Ok."

"Sit down over there on the cushions. Do not move or speak until invited to. I will need a little time to prepare and it's very important that you don't disturb me."

Steven settled himself on the pile of cushions in the corner of the room. He felt comfortable enough. Cerridwen walked the circumference of her circle, a constant flow of indecipherable words humming in the air as she went. She lit candles, made gestures. It looked quite theatrical, but with every new component she added to the ritual, Steven felt the air buzz more intensely with energy. He wondered if there was something happening in the room, or if his own nerves were the source of this impression. Then she pulled off the black dress and sat naked in the centre of the circle, her eyes closed. Steven couldn't help but stare at her small, pert breasts and the curve of her stomach down to her all too visible crotch. As his mother's carer, he'd seen her wasted body more times than he wanted to number and there had been nothing erotic in the experience. Otherwise, Mindy had provided his only in-person experience of women. Lean, firm and full of life, Cerridwen's body had a distinct beauty of its own, and he could not take his eyes from her. The sight almost made him forget why he was there.

The heavy eyelids lifted, and her gaze blazed out at him. "Speak," she instructed; her voice low, and strangely heavy.

"I want to know why Mindy tried to kill herself," he said.

Before him, Cerridwen drew a deep breath and turned her head slowly, eyes closed in an uncanny search.

"She had so much fear and pain inside her. At first she just wanted the physical pain to blot out everything else. Just a few cuts. A little blood. A small release to make it all bearable again. She had done it before. But why keep suffering? Why live with it any longer? She could make it go away."

When the voice that didn't sound like Cerridwen's died away, he ventured another question. "What was she afraid of?"

"She was afraid to live, and afraid to die. Afraid of feeling and not feeling. Afraid of things she had done, and things that had once been done to her. All her soul was riddled with it, like a cancer eating her essence away. She suffered alone."

"Was there anyone else involved in her seeking death?"

"Her death was entirely of her making, she called it to her."

Steven hesitated. The answers seemed full of riddles. He considered the idea that it was all make-believe - that this woman before him had no real insight, and simply saying what she thought he wanted to hear. He tried another line of questioning.

"The man who attacked me. Is he connected to Mindy?"

"Yes."

"Is he connected to her suffering?"

"He is her death."

"Why can I see him?"

"He wants you."

"What will he do to me?"

"He will become your death."

"Do you mean he will try and kill me?"

"He will become your death."

Cerridwen's head dropped low on her bosom and for a long time, neither of them said anything.

"Steven?" the voice came as a faint and distant wisp of sound, desperately pleading in tones he thought he knew.

"Mindy?" He rose, not thinking of anything but that voice and the possibility of some connection.

Cerridwen's head shot up, and her eyes opened wide. A vicious smile contorted her face and she hissed at him.

"I wouldn't go out on my own at night if I were you," she said.

Steven pressed back against the wall, staring at the face in front of him and wishing he had some means of defending himself. Gradually, Cerridwen's expression softened, and she lay back, her hair tumbling over the edge of her carefully painted circle. Having no idea if this was normal, Steven remained where he was, trying to contain his own panic. He no longer felt safe here; uncertain if he could even trust the apparently hard wall at his back. Visions of hands emerging from the plaster to grip his throat made him lean forwards. Cerridwen's words continued to replay themselves in his mind, all sense lost in the repetitions.

She sat abruptly, reaching for her dress and tugging it back over her head.

"Did you get what you wanted?" she enquired in her normal voice.

"I don't know. It was pretty confusing. What did you mean about -?"

She cut him short. "I can't help you with the interpretation. You have to make your own sense of what I said."

"Oh."

"You look shaken. Was it bad news then?"

"For a while there, you sounded like someone else."

"That can happen. Many different voices speak through me. I have little sense of it while it's happening. I am just the vessel through which the mystery flows."

"Doesn't it frighten you?"

"Why should it? This is what I am."

"Just one more question. That artist you mentioned, Henry Marsden. Do you know how I can get in touch with him?"

"He used to sell his paintings through a shop on the Selly Oak High Street. I can't remember the name of the place, but if it's still open, they might be able to tell you."

"Thanks. I'll come back with a gift some other time, ok? What should I bring?"

"Whatever makes sense to you."

Steven left as quickly as he could; glad to be out in the sunlight again, with the cars, the large advertising boards, the kids on bikes. In the sun he felt safer, and with the hubbub of normal life around him the fear he had felt faded a little. He had been looking for an experience to bring everything into focus, but once again it came down to either trusting what he had perceived, or believing that his mind was on the blink. If he had cracked up, then the world remained a coherent, rational place where everything made sense. If he was sane, then for his experiences to be at all valid, the rest of the world must be inherently crazy. Neither option looked good.

He walked towards the main Selly Oak thoroughfare, and the prospect of finding Henry Marsden. Chasing a woman whose face he liked seemed sensible compared to everything else happening to him.

Chapter Eighteen

The day's intense heat remained punishing. From Cerridwen's house to Selly Oak's main road, and from the small gallery there onwards, Steven trudged, his head aching from the temperature and brightness. The tarmac seemed to throb with an excess of sunlight, and the inescapable flavour of car fumes sickened him. He walked, because it seemed so much better than being still. As though he could run away from the events of the previous hours and pretend they'd never happened. A mad chase in a different direction to distract himself from ideas he couldn't yet handle.

There were more trees around him once he escaped from the main road. The directions he'd been given took him back towards King's Norton station, but he had no real idea where he was. He'd lingered in the shop for quite a while, looking at the three Henry Marsden paintings they had on display. Beautiful pieces, full of trees and strange, barely human figures. The images soothed him, blotting out the fear and uncertainty for a while. He couldn't stay with them, but searching out the artist offered a degree of escape.

Knocking at the door, he tried to work out what he could possibly say that wouldn't make him sound like a stalker. A small man in his late middle years answered.

"Yes?" he enquired.

"Are you Henry Marsden?"

"Yes."

"I bought a painting from you," Steven said, blurting out the first thing that came into his head. "Well, not from you directly, but from a friend of yours."

"Some problem with it?" the man asked. "Or did you want another one?"

"I need to find the woman who modelled for it."

"Why?"

Steven looked around in hope of finding some inspiration. Nothing came. "I really want to meet her," he said.

"And do you think she will want to meet you?" The man sounded unconvinced.

"I don't know."

"If you've developed a crush on a picture, then you probably just need to get out more. She won't want to know."

"It's not like that."

"No?"

"It's about the Spirit of Arden. I need to talk to her about that."

"And you imagine she can tell you something meaningful?" Marsden sounded unpleasantly amused by the thought.

"I don't know."

"Willow's just a model. She's a nice enough girl, she takes her clothes off for art, and she has a beautiful body. She isn't the spirit of Arden, all she did was pose for me."

Steven hung his head slightly, feeling utterly foolish.

"I'm flattered that my work has affected you so much," Henry Marsden continued. "But I don't think there's much I can do to help you."

"I'm sorry to have disturbed you," Steven said. "Thanks for talking to me. I appreciate it." He turned to go.

"Wait a moment."

Looking back he saw the door remained slightly open but the artist had vanished from view.

"Here." Marsden thrust a small green card into his hand. "Her phone number. Talk to her if you must. She might meet you, if you ask her nicely. She has a lot of admirers I believe."

"Thank you."

"I have a photographic memory. If anything happens to her, I'll be able to describe you in perfect detail," the artist said calmly.

"I just want to talk to her," Steven said, alarmed by the remark.

"Good."

Disorientated in the maze of streets, Steven struggled on in the heat for some time before he found the railway line again. Affected by the soaring temperatures and the claustrophobic press of people, he could hardly think. Nothing felt real anymore. The peculiar events of the early afternoon and the sound of Cerridwen's voice all blended into an uncomfortable mess of feelings and impressions. *What of it was real?* Always it came back to that one, frustrating question for which there never seemed to be a good enough answer. He clung to the small green card as though it could protect him. His sweat impregnated the substance of it, obliging him to hold it more carefully so that he would not moisten it too thoroughly and smear the ink. Through it all, the train rattled and the urban landscape rumbled passed his window. *So many houses.* Beyond the windows were hundreds, thousands of people, all going about their lives oblivious to each other. Did the magic of existence really mean anything to any of them? Looking around the half-full train, Steven wondered how many of his other fellow travellers doubted their perceptions or saw impossible things. They all looked normal and unconcerned, lost in newspapers, iPods or just staring out of the window. He felt utterly alone.

Then later in his flat, he stared at the rumpled card for a long time before working up the confidence to do anything with it.

Willow
Experienced and Professional Life Model
0777919778

There were no details. He could divine nothing from these scant facts that helped him in the slightest, but still he sat and stared, looking for inspiration and courage somewhere between the lines. Realising it was almost nine in the evening, Steven thought it would have to be now, or wait until the next day and a more sociable hour. With trembling hands, he made the call, waiting nervously as the ringing tone echoed in his ears.

"Willow speaking."

In those two words, he heard so many things. Warmth and seduction. Beauty. Confidence. Playfulness. He could hardly think for the intensity of impression.

"Hi," he began nervously. "I got your number from Henry Marsden. You model for him."

"That's right. So, do you want to book me?"

"Book you?"

"To pose for you."

"Oh. Sorry. Umm…" he paused. What on earth could he say? "I know this is going to sound odd, but I just wanted to meet you in person."

"Right." Did he imagine it, or had a cold edge crept into her voice?

"I didn't think you would, but I wanted to ask. I've got one of the pictures you modelled for – *The Spirit of Arden*. And when I spoke to Henry Marsden, he said of course you aren't the Spirit of Arden, but I wanted to meet you all the same." Steven knew he was flailing about helplessly and decided it might be better to stop talking.

"It's the Spirit of Arden that interests you then?" Her voice had changed again, becoming lower, conspiratorial.

"Yes."

"Mmm. And Marsden told you I am not the Spirit of Arden?" She chuckled lightly to herself at this. "Mind you, he's a funny old sod is Marsden. But that's partly why I like him."

Thoughts wheeled chaotically through Steven's head, but he could find nothing to say.

"Why do you want to meet me?" she asked; the playfulness back in her voice.

"I'm not sure. Curiosity. A gut feeling. I can't really explain, it just feels like the right thing to do."

"That's a more original answer than I usually hear. Ok. I'll meet you somewhere."

"I don't live in Birmingham, but I don't mind coming into the city if that would suit you."

"It should be somewhere public, but not too dull. Do you know the canals?"

"Not really."

"I know the perfect place," she said. "You'll love it. It's how a city ought to be."

After the call, Steven cradled the receiver in his hands until the machine started bleeping at him. He recounted her few words to him, absorbed by memories of the rich tones of her voice and the way she had moved him. Willow had spoken to him and it seemed as wondrous and unreal as most of his recent experiences. Looking up at the picture on his wall, Steven grinned to himself, feeling giddy, foolish and happy. The sound of her voice had banished all the shadows from the early part of the afternoon. It felt as though sunlight emanated from inside him, lighting his flat and keeping all darkness at bay. There would be no room for unsettling men and grim threats tonight at least. In just a few days time, he would meet the focus of his obsession in person. Trying to imagine how the encounter would play out, Steven wondered how he would keep from being an inarticulate bag of nerves. What on earth would he say to her? He had images of just sitting at her feet, looking up adoringly and listening to whatever she said, but had the feeling that might not work as a strategy.

He wondered why she had agreed to his request. What could possibly be in it for her? He supposed he must have sounded rather silly. Any sensible person would have brushed him off, not agreed to a date. *Was it a date?* He thought not. Best not to assume anything. She must be a little crazy herself, to agree to such a meeting.

Chapter Nineteen

Walking along the canal-side, Steven could feel the upbeat energy of the evening as people started to come out and enjoy the fading sunlight. Pubs and cafes sprawled onto the pathways with tables and chairs, suggesting bohemian delights. His feelings were mingled apprehension and excitement, but caught on the buzz of the cheerful people around him, his confidence grew. Simply being here would be an experience, no matter how it worked out.

There hadn't been much of a summer, until now at least. The return of the sun lent buoyancy to the Gas Street basin area. There were flowers everywhere, brightly painted narrowboats tied up alongside the walkways and the sound of happy people all around him. Steven hadn't explored this part of Birmingham before, but took to it at once. It felt lively, permissive and utterly careless of whatever he did. Beautiful women in delicate, revealing summer attire caught his eye, as did some of the men with their open collars and figure hugging shirts. In a place like this, who would even notice his looking at them, much less care? Until Mindy, no-one had ever shown the slightest interest in him and consequently Steven had never had chance to explore his own desires and interests. All people seemed a touch alien to him – fascinating and unobtainable. He liked to look, but it had a lot in common with his habit of reading menus from fast food outlets he never expected to use.

Approaching the unfamiliar bar where they had agreed to meet, Steven scanned the faces of people at tables, wondering if he would recognise Willow and half afraid of some crushing disappointment. He had such high expectations of her, but what would happen if she didn't live up to them? He knew the evening might be one huge anti-climax. Marsden's less than complimentary words returned to him. *Willow's just a model.* As though the rest of her identity had no importance. Having a beautiful face did not mean she would turn out to be interesting, or insightful – he knew that. Then he had to worry what she would think of him – he had so little to offer, and supposed she would find him boring. What could he say to interest her? He knew so little, had done nothing of interest with his life. For a moment, he considered turning around and going home.

A tall man left the one of outside tables, heading for the bar. His movement caught Steven's eye, although there was nothing distinctive about the man. Once he had absented himself however, Steven could see an all too familiar profile that had previously been obscured from his view. She sat alone at a small table, gazing out at the water, a thoughtful expression on her face. Most of her long dark hair was currently pinned up at the back of her head, but strands of it fell loose, framing her face. An ache gripped Steven; he thought it might be longing, nostalgia, or but he couldn't say why the sight of her affected him so deeply. As though sensing his gaze, she turned and a fleeting smile touched her lips. For a foolish moment, he thought she had recognised him. Determined not to let his nerves make a fool of him, Steven approached.

Recognition seemed to shine in those large, dark green eyes, even though they had not met before, not in person. The face before him was utterly familiar. He had seen her before, countless times both waking and in dreams.

"Willow," he said.

"Yes. And you must be Steven. I think I have seen you before." She scrutinised him. "I wonder," she added, but what precisely she wondered, she did not reveal.

"Was that you at the Custard Factory, talking about the lost forest?"

Her eyes sparkled. "Ah. So you were there. And where else might I have seen you?"

Steven's mouth went very dry. He recalled his numerous visions of this woman, but hardly felt he could even tell her that she had appeared in his pathworkings.

"I've been to a few other things," he said, knowing he sounded pathetic. "Can I get you a drink?" he asked quickly, feeling more at ease as he diverted the conversation away from his innermost thoughts.

"By all means."

She made him talk. Steven had no idea what it was about her that broke down his defences, but all those closely guarded secrets from his recent past came out, fragmented and hesitant. He'd wanted to learn more about her but she evaded his clumsy attempts at questions, and set upon him with skill, teasing out all kinds of personal details he had never meant to share. His absent father, his difficult mother, his loneliness and lack of direction came pouring out at an embarrassing speed. None of his troubled history seemed to bother her, and she even appeared interested in his words.

As they talked, a lone fact took prominence in his mind. She wasn't beautiful. The more he looked at Willow, the more evident this became. Her eyes were a little too big for her face, while there was something birdlike about her nose. She had pale skin, not Mindy's exquisite alabaster, but flesh that looked a touch unhealthy – more like his own. Her teeth were slightly uneven, her ears a little too short for her face, her jaw a fraction too long. Examining her features individually, each one appeared flawed to him. And yet the whole combined into something compelling. The more he watched, the harder it became to take his eyes off her. The way she moved, the little expressions that shifted her features, all enchanted him. She appeared older than he had been expecting as well. Steven had imagined her as an early twenty-something – nearer Mindy's age. The woman before him could have been anywhere between thirty and fifty. He couldn't tell. Gradually it dawned on him that what enthralled him about this woman wasn't her physical appearance, but the personality shining through it.

"Does the lost forest call to you?"

"Yes," he said. "I went walking a few weeks back, in the rain, amongst the trees. It felt so timeless, like being in another world. I never feel like I fit in here. I don't know what to say to people, or what to do with myself. It's different with trees, none of that matters."

"Exactly."

"I feel so wrong most of the time."

"Maybe you aren't wrong. Had you considered that the rest of the world might be horribly out of kilter, and you the only true thing in it?"

Steven couldn't help but laugh aloud at this. "No. I never thought of that. That's quite a funny idea."

"No, you wouldn't imagine that for a moment, would you?"

"How did you… the forest… how did you find it?" he asked.

"It was always here. Lost from sight, but not truly gone. I see it. The ghosts of long dead trees. I can look at an ordinary street, and see the forest trying to push back through. I hear the baying of wolves in the darkness."

"For real?" he asked.

"Yes," she said. "And you believe me." It wasn't a question.

"Yes."

"So what is it that you see? I think there must be something you've witnessed that sets you apart a little, or you wouldn't be so ready to believe me."

"You," Steven whispered, as she drew his final secret from him.

"And now you have an interesting puzzle. Because whatever you have seen, it can't really be me, can it? Just a dream or a fantasy in your head." Her tone remained level, revealing nothing of her thoughts. Steven had the feeling she was testing him rather than offering disbelief, but he didn't attempt to answer the question. After a few seconds of silence, she spoke again.

"Is the idea of the lost forest just a fantasy to you? A place to escape from this 'real world' where you manifestly don't fit in?"

"Maybe," he shrugged. "Does that matter?"

"It might be the most important thing."

"I don't like most people," he admitted. "I don't understand most of them. I feel like an outsider. I like the idea of a clean, green world that hasn't been mucked up by people."

"Interesting. And do you want to be all powerful in this make believe world of yours? Do you want to be in charge? Is it some kind of self indulgent ego trip?"

"When I think about the forest, I think about being a small sapling in amongst the bigger trees. Or a squirrel in the branches. A little bird. Something like that."

A small, but knowing smile illuminated her face for a few seconds. Much to Steven's surprise, he realised he was enjoying the interrogation. No one had ever pushed him to think so deeply before and he liked where this had taken him.

"Are you catching a train?" she asked.

"Yes."

"Then you'd best get a move on, the last one heading your way leaves in half an hour."

"I'd lost track of the time."

"I often have that effect on people," she said. "I have a bus to catch, so I should make a move too. Well, it's been interesting meeting you, Steven."

"Can we do this again sometime?"

"No," she said, and disappointment settled heavily in his stomach. "Not this. Something else perhaps. We'll see. I might just give you a call one of these days."

"That would be great."

She touched her hand to his cheek, and the flush of warmth from her skin permeated his entire being.

"No wonder the boar chose you," she said. Before he could come up with any kind of reply, she turned away, long, smooth strides carrying her through the crowd.

For a long while afterwards, he could still feel the tingle of her fingers on his cheek. All the way home, Steven racked his brains, trying to remember if he had mentioned the boar to her and inclined to think he hadn't. What did she mean; that the boar had chosen him? That didn't make a great deal of sense. Strange and compelling as she was, Willow had not disappointed him in any way. He wished he'd managed to learn more about her, and looking back over their long conversation he could see all too clearly how she had evaded his questions and side-tracked him by enquiring about his own background. There wasn't much he knew now that he hadn't previously been aware of. Willow had revealed little of herself – he had no clue where she lived, if she lived with anyone, where she came from, and what aside from trees mattered to her. How on earth had they managed to spend so much time talking about him? Retrospectively, Steven felt unnerved by the disappearance of his normal reserve. However, she hadn't seemed at all perturbed by his confessions, so perhaps it hadn't been such a bad thing to be so open. He hoped she would call, but resolved not to pester her any further if she didn't.

Chapter Twenty

Several days prior to the fortnightly moot, Wiccan John phoned Steven to alert him to the change of venue.

"After that idiot turning up twice, Elspeth really didn't fancy a third."

"I don't blame her," Steven said.

The new venue was outside the town centre and a slightly longer walk for Steven, but he didn't really mind. He'd grown accustomed to long walks. The place seemed quiet enough and, with the anti-smoking laws having recently gone through, he didn't even have to contend with the haze of tobacco fug. When he arrived, he found Diana and Carol were already there, and deep in conversation. Carol's husband Sean looked to be exiled from the debate and seemed relieved when he saw Steven enter the room.

"How's it going?" he asked as Steven took a seat near him.

"Pretty good. You?"

"Lousy day at work, but otherwise ok," Sean said.

"New pub seems alright," Steven observed, looking round.

"Well..." Sean's expression darkened somewhat. "It's not the first time we've had to move. All it takes are one or two nutters to wreck everything."

"What happened before?"

"A couple of Christian evangelicals gave the landlord a hard time about our being there."

"Is that legal? I thought there were laws against religious intolerance," Steven said.

"Not back then there weren't. This was a few years ago. And mostly the laws are work related anyway."

"I didn't realise," Steven said.

"Things are better than they used to be. It's ok to be out as a Pagan these days, you aren't likely to lose your job for it, or have social services knocking on your door."

"Did that really happen?" Steven was taken aback.

"Don't you remember all the fuss about the children taken into care, whose parents were supposedly witches?"

Steven shook his head.

"No one ever really found out what happened there, but it made a lot of Pagan people very nervous at the time. I was in my teens then, but it was pretty scary. My parents always told me to say I was C of E, is anyone asked." Sean laughed at this recollection.

"So your parents are Pagan too?"

"Wiccans, both of them. I grew up with it."

"Hi," Neil said, announcing his presence as he pulled up a chair.

Then Heathen John, Wiccan John and Elspeth all turned up together, making it impossible to continue the conversation.

"Hello Steven," Helen said as she slid into the seat next to him. "How are things? Any progress?"

Before he could answer, she was inundated with greetings from the others, some warmer than others, Steven noted. He guessed Helen and Elspeth didn't really get on.

"Well?" Helen pressed, once she no longer had everyone's attention focused on her.

"I saw Cerridwen," Steven admitted. "It was a bit disturbing to be honest."

"But was it useful?"

"Well, possibly. I'm still getting to grips with what she said."

"She's got a good reputation," Helen said. "I don't have much time for people who play at magic, or do it for money, but Cerridwen might just be the real thing."

"Thanks. I'm glad I went, just not sure what to make of it all."

Around them, the table fell quiet, and Steven looked up to see what was going on.

"There's no easy way of saying this," Elspeth began. At once, the moot became utterly still. "Things haven't been easy lately, what with Mindy, and the hassle we've had, and I've had a few personal difficulties too, which I won't go into. I just don't feel like I can keep doing this. I don't have the time, or the energy, or the emotional commitment to keep this moot running. I'm sorry folks. If anyone else wants a go, they'd be very welcome."

The gathering remained silent. Steven looked around, hoping to see someone else ready to step forwards. All of the others seemed to be looking at their hands or their drinks. Surely they weren't just going to let it go?

"You've done a really great job these last few years Elspeth. I'm sure I speak for all of us in thanking you for everything you've done," Heathen John said. There were murmurs of agreement.

"I can't do it," Helen said. "I'm lucky if I make one moot in three. If I had the time I'd offer to take it on, but that's a non-starter."

"I don't want the additional responsibility," Diana replied from across the table. "I'm bearing up ok at the moment, but there's no guarantees that'll continue to be the case."

Other mutterings of 'too busy' fluttered around the table. None of them seemed willing to take over.

"So this is it then," Heathen John said. "It's been good. Hopefully we can all stay in touch."

"Hang on a minute," Steven heard himself saying. "What exactly does it take to run this thing?"

Elspeth looked surprised by the question. "You have to be here for pretty much every moot, and if you're away, you have to make sure someone else is here instead. That's the main thing. Beyond that, advertising it, keeping up the listing in *Pagan Dawn*, making your telephone number and email address available for people to contact you, fending off occasional weirdoes, running events – whatever you want to make of it really."

"I don't want to see this moot fold," Steven said. "It's a big part of my life. It matters to me." He looked around the table, wondering if he could take the next step, and whether the others would accept his doing so. "I'm up for trying to keep it going, if the rest of you are ok with that?"

Neil grinned. "Cool."

Much to Steven's surprise, no one else took issue with his suggestion. He had no idea if he would be equal to the job, but as it appeared to be him or nothing, there didn't seem to be anything to lose.

"I've never run anything at all before in my life," he pointed out. "And I know bugger all about Paganism."

"You'll get help if you ask for it," Helen said.

"Well, I hadn't expected that to happen," he said in lowered tones once things settled down again.

"Life would be very dull if we could see everything before it hit us," Helen said. "So, are you more or less crazy than you were last time we talked?"

"Both, possibly."

Steven walked home in a state of flux, shifting between wild excitement at what he had done, and fear that it would all go horribly wrong. Could he really take the moot on and make it work? Elspeth hadn't made it sound too difficult, but what did he know? He couldn't have stood by and watch it disintegrate. Still it amazed him that the others had accepted his offer. They all knew so much more than he did – how could he possibly have wound up in charge?

Stopping to tie up a loose shoelace, he realised there was someone else on foot not far behind him. There had been so many such moments of late that he tried to push it from his mind. Forcing himself not to look back, Steven resumed walking, conscious now of the steady sound of feet on tarmac. He wanted to check behind him, but resisted the temptation to turn round and have a look. Most likely the person following him was just someone else on their way home from the pub. However, when the sound accelerated he succumbed and glanced back over his shoulder. He caught a glimpse of a long coat, short, spiky hair and wild eyes of the man racing towards him. The situation seemed decidedly unfriendly. Not stopping to think, he set off at a run, glad he hadn't consumed much alcohol during the evening. There had been a few items in the local news about muggings and he didn't want to be the next victim.

The orange streetlights distorted everything slightly, making it hard to judge distances. Steven didn't see the shallow hole in the pavement. He felt a nasty jar in his joints when the ground wasn't quite where he expected it to be. Then the slow motion of falling as his ankle buckled under him, hands flailing, scraping on the hard ground as his sudden descent sent him sprawling across the tarmac. Pain seared his awareness, shooting hot and fiery from toes to shins. He wondered if he had broken a bone. As he tried to get to his knees, a sharp blow to the side knocked all the air from him. For a moment Steven lay still, too stunned to move or think. A second blow sent the adrenaline running in his veins, his head suddenly very clear. Steven knew that his pursuer had caught him and meant to harm him. Face down on the pavement, with nothing to defend himself, he expected the worst.

"My wallet's in my back pocket," he said. "Take it. I don't have a mobile phone or anything else like that."

A hard boot connected with his thigh, distracting him from all thoughts of speech. Once again he tried to get to his feet, but his attacker pushed him roughly down.

"What do you want?" Steven shouted.

This time he rolled and managed to get his shoulders off the ground before the next blow came. He ducked, and it skimmed his jaw, barely grazing him. The man squatted down in front of him so that they were eye to eye.

"I told you not to go out on your own," he said.

"What do you want?" Steven said, his anger muting both the fear and the pain he felt.

"You."

The answer seemed bizarre, and Steven could only attach one meaning to it. "Are you going to try and rape me?" he asked, trying to buy time in the hopes someone would see them.

The man laughed at his question. "I want a lot more of you than that."

With time to look and think a little, Steven felt fairly sure he recognised his assailant. A cold dread seeped through him, chilling his blood. "So I get something like what you did with Mindy?"

"Yes." The 's' drew out into an exaggerated hiss, full of menace.

"I don't want to play," Steven said through gritted teeth. "Leave me alone."

"Never."

Staring into the pale face with its mad-looking eyes, Steven digested the admission that this being had driven Mindy to attempt suicide. He shuddered as a wave of pure rage passed through him. The pain in his sides and ankle didn't seem to matter anymore. He hadn't been imagining things. Mindy had been pushed to self-destruction. The thought of that blossoming young life, so close to being cut short, focused his anger to dangerous precision. He pushed himself up off the ground and at the same time lashed out, aiming his fist towards the gloating face. It felt like thumping a wall, but his hand passed through the man, and then there was no one there at all. He staggered, almost losing his balance. Now his fist hurt as well, and the pain seemed real enough, but what had he hit? Where was it? Steven swore under his breath. The last of his doubts evaporated – whatever he was up against, it seemed real to him. It might well have caused deaths already. He had no intention of being the next victim.

Looking around, he could see no one in any direction. The streets remained empty of moving traffic, and in the orange light, nothing seemed real. The adrenaline rush began to wear off, making him more conscious of his painfully twisted ankle and bruised ribs.

"I'm not afraid of you," he said aloud to the silent street.

When he tried to sleep, the pains from his various minor injuries became more apparent, and kept him from rest. Steven had considered calling the police, but the peculiar melting away of his assailant made that difficult. The bruises all looked real enough though.

I'm never far from you. Just beyond the door, outside the window. Waiting. Sooner or later you'll let me in.

"I don't think so," Steven said aloud, trying not to listen to the voice in his head. He knew hearing voices wasn't a good thing, especially not malevolent ones, but they had been a part of his life for a long time now. He had thought he could cope with them.

You're sick in the head Steven. Sick, sick, sick. Tell the doctors about me. Get some pills to shut me up. Get a diagnosis and a label. Paranoid delusions? You know you're paranoid. Obsessed head fuck. Sick and paranoid.

"Go away." He rolled over, pulling the covers up around his head as though a layer of fabric might keep the voice from tormenting him further.

You can't hide under the covers. I am not the sort of monster that vanishes if you pretend it isn't there. I'm inside you. You cannot escape from me.

Steven tried ignoring the voice. It needled him with sharp, unpleasant comments, picking at his insecurities with surgical precision. To distract himself, he tried thinking about moments when he had felt strong, and good about life. Moonlight on water in a rain-soaked wood. Willow's dark green eyes. Helen's unconventional support and ideas. Her shop, with its distinctive smells. Eating with Heathen John and not even thinking about it. Willow's occasional, secretive smiles. He wrapped these memories around him, finding warmth and comfort in revisiting them. There were people in his life for whom he truly cared. People who treated him kindly and with respect. He imagined them stood around him, a circle of goodwill and companionship. The poisoned voice spoke no more.

As he drifted towards sleep, he had the feeling that he wasn't alone. This presence brought no threat with it, rather it offered comfort.

"Help if you need it," a voice whispered to him from the dreaming borderlands.

Steven had the impression of there being a shape in the bed beside him. Close enough that he could feel it, yet not actually touching. He did not reach out, or open his eyes, happy to accept the impression of comfort without questioning the source. Knowing that he could sleep safely, Steven surrendered to the encroaching darkness, the skin on his cheek tingling slightly where Willow had touched not so many days before.

Chapter Twenty-One

Returning from shopping, Steven heard his phone ringing before he made it into the flat. His heart accelerated. Normally the sound caused him mild irritation at best – the majority of calls he had were from people trying to sell him things. This one felt different even before he made it to the receiver.

"Hello Steven," Willow said.

For a moment, his mind went blank and he couldn't think of anything to say. "Hi," he stammered.

"And how are you today?"

"I'm fine," he said. "You?"

"I've just come back from seeing Marsden. He mentioned you. I don't think he trusts your motives you know. I think he suspects you of trying to get into my knickers, and there's a delightful irony there after all, given that he usually wants me to sit naked. He's quite a lecherous old goat, bless him."

"Oh," Steven said finding he couldn't help but picture this.

"Am I embarrassing you?" Willow asked.

"No, no. Not at all," Steven replied, glad she couldn't see his crimson cheeks.

"Hmm."

"So, how can I help?" he asked, keen to steer the conversation towards safer waters.

"Are you free today?"

"Yes."

"Good. Go in to town and catch the two o'clock bus to Alvechurch."

"And then?"

"Oh, I don't want to spoil anything by telling you. Wait and see."

"Ok," he said. He felt oddly safe with Willow, even though she was decidedly strange. Or perhaps, he reflected, because of that.

The bus stank of warm people, the air thick from being breathed too often. Steven pressed as close to the window as he could, hankering after space and coolness. Every few minutes the bus stopped to pick up or put down travellers, but Steven tried his best not to pay much attention to the tight press of noisy strangers. The man sitting next to him stood up to leave, soon to be replaced by another person in similarly worn jeans. Steven didn't even look round, not interested in who sat next to him.

At first he though the driver must have some air conditioning on. The oppressive atmosphere eased a little and the temperature dropped to a pleasanter level. Breathing deeply, Steven realised he could smell something fresh – like woodland after a downpour. He savoured the taste of it, his thoughts lost in the associations this unexpected aroma brought. Then the passenger next to him rested her head against his shoulder and he jumped, shocked by the unexpected contact.

"I suppose they're better than cars, but I never did much like buses," Willow remarked, sitting up straight again.

Steven laughed aloud, realising who had taken him by surprise.

"Do you live in Bromsgrove then?" he asked.

"Maybe."

With Willow next to him, his feelings of claustrophobia receded and the journey seemed to pass far more rapidly. They didn't talk – between the rumbling of the bus and the conversations of other people, it required too much effort. Steven enjoyed her silent companionship. Although they were no longer touching, he felt intensely aware of her presence, their proximity so intimate that his skin prickled with it.

The bus dropped them in the middle of Alvechurch – a small town he hadn't visited before. It seemed a nice enough place, but there was nothing to render it particularly interesting and he wondered why Willow had chosen it as their destination.

"Where now?" he asked.

She looked around as though trying to get her bearings. "This way I think."

Soon they were out of the town centre and walking through a moderately affluent housing estate. Steven heard the distinctive cacophony of a train passing nearby. The road narrowed, climbing steeply towards a bridge, and crossing the railway. They left the road and made their way down to the canal. Steven supposed it must feed into the extensive Birmingham network of waterways.

"I'm guessing you like water then?" he asked.

"Very much so. I prefer natural rivers, but canals are better than nothing."

They walked along the towpath in amicable silence. There were blackberries in the hedgerow beside them, and Steven picked a few, surprised to find them ripe so early in the season.

"Do you want one?" he asked, offering her a shining berry. Willow took the sun-warmed fruit from his fingers.

There were ducks on the water, shy moorhens and occasional coots. Narrowboats hired by holiday makers passed from time to time, their engine noise shattering the stillness of the hot afternoon. Steven rejoiced in the open space, in the vast stretch of sky above him and the freedom of being out walking. Every so often he risked a glance at his companion, still struggling to believe she was here with him. They carried on along the towpath, and she started to talk.

"I'm going to tell you some things about me. What you do with this is up to you. I won't tell you what to do, ok?"

"Sounds fine to me," said Steven.

"Some years ago, I decided to embody the spirit of the lost forest. The spirit of Arden."

"You can just choose to do that?" Steven asked.

"Basically yes. I decided I wanted to dedicate my life to the forest, and to bringing it into as many people's consciousness as I could. I dedicated myself to making the forest real again."

"Wow," said Steven. "You can do that?"

"Essentially, yes. It took time to learn how to do it well, how to communicate with people, how to bring the forest through myself so that others could see it. You see that in me, don't you."

"Yes," Steven said, overcome with a feeling of wonder.

"It's the forest that draws you, I'm just enabling that. What you have to work out is how you want to relate to the forest and what you want to do."

"I just have to choose?" Steven asked.

"That's how it starts," Willow said. "And you keep choosing, one way or another."

"Thank you," he said even though he wasn't really clear how any of this could work.

Without explanation, she led him down a steep path away from the canal side and into a field. In the welcome shade of a giant oak, she stopped and turned, her arms open as though offering an embrace to some unseen being.

"Here we are," she said.

Looking at the ancient tree, Steven knew exactly why she had brought him here.

"Let's sit," she said.

Cool from the tree shade, the grass felt luscious as Steven twirled its long leaves between his fingers.

"This oak is more than four hundred years old," Willow told him.

"That's old."

"Not really, not for an oak tree. It could live more than twice as long again." She paused, giving him time to absorb this. "Four hundred years ago, it sprouted from an acorn. When there would have been far more trees here. Before the canal was dug. Before the trains, and the cars and aeroplanes. It remembers quieter times. A whole different world."

Her voice hushed to little more than a whisper. "If you listen, you might hear it."

Steven could hear the wind rustling leaves above him. He tuned out the modern sounds, the hum of cars and the distant rattle of a train. The tree said nothing at all, but its quietness consumed him none the less. There seemed to be truth in that silence, if only he could reach through to it somehow. After a while he stopped trying. It didn't seem important. The longer he sat, aware but not able to grasp the things he intuited were there, the more comfortable he became with this. What did he need ultimate truth for, anyway? Perhaps it was enough just to be and feel.

"Lie down," she said, her voice as whispery as the wind stirred leaves.

Steven lay back, and she took his head between her hands, holding the weight of it. With his eyes closed, Steven felt as though he was floating.

"Feel your own roots in the soil," she said. "Your deep, deep roots going down into the ground, and into the past, holding you firm. Nothing can harm you here. You are safe. And feel the sky caressing you, nourishing you with light, with air. Let go. Let go of everything and I will take you on a journey. Come with me, Steven. Follow me beneath the tree shade, down the ancient pathways, and into the forest."

Willow's voice carried him, just as it had done the first time he encountered her. Following her took no effort. The forest came to greet him. He felt it in the soil beneath him, rising around him and claiming his awareness. He could picture himself all too easily, in verdant wildwood, far from human invasions. The imagined scene became increasingly real, until he lost all sense of his reclining body.

Following a straight, narrow track, he travelled beneath the leafy canopy, his senses overwhelmed by sight and smell, by the sounds of life, the feel of the pleasantly cool air on his skin. Willow guided him down into the roots, amongst the tiniest living things and the decay of old leaf litter. He climbed the vast, uneven terrain of bark in the company of ants, then fluttered into awareness as a small bird who fed upon the insects. Life and death played out their eternal dramas around him. Creation and destruction twined together like the ivy around the oak.

So many kinds of existence. But no story. The idea had never crossed his mind before, but now he saw it all too clearly. He could empathise somewhat with all these countless lives, and felt sure they had dramas of their own, but not any emotional language he could understand. He couldn't turn these experiences into any kind of narrative, as he had with previous meditations. Nothing here offered a reflection of his waking life.

A boar ran alongside him. Steven felt the rhythm of its trotters pounding into the leaf litter. The creature seemed oblivious to him, snorting occasionally as it ran. Steven moved with it, catching glimpses of its rough brown coat, the glint of light on tusks, powerful muscles moving beneath the skin. He ran with it, letting the animal's pace become his own. Feet biting into the soft ground. Snout tasting the air. The transition came easily, so simple that Steven barely noticed it. He ran within the boar's skin, feeling the shape of it, the raw strength and instinct. Rooting beneath a tree. Gulping down a mouthful of something and then moving on. Everything in the moment. Nothing but immediacy and need. No dwelling on the past or fretting about the future. He knew those existed. The boar had wisdom, knowledge and needs, but the creature's relationship with time was entirely different from his own.

The boar slowed, ambling along the narrow forest ways, pausing now and then to scent the ground, or take a bite at anything edible. There were young piglets nearby, and a sow, although none were visible, the feel of them carried on the air. He would fight, kill or be killed as was called for in protecting them. The sheer strength of this body overpowered him: The force in it and the wildness, the absence of rules. This boar knew no restraint, only its drives and inclinations and the exhilarating rush of life swallowed down from one great bite to the next. The realness of it shocked Steven, but he had no time to think about what that meant.

He felt the ground shudder, as towering creatures crossed the path a short distance before him. Vast expanses of slowly moving animal, with long horns that seemed in danger of catching on the trees. They crushed saplings before them, pausing sporadically to tear off and chew up smaller branches. Steven in his boar skin could hear the low rumbles of their voices, but the sense remained beyond him. It seemed a companionable sound, a gradually shifting community conversing as it travelled. Perhaps there were stories here after all, once he began looking for them. After the massive beasts had gone, he looked down at their hoof-marks, wondering at the sheer size of them.

The boar carried him deeper amongst the trees, where trunks pressed tighter together and the light became a dark green. Only in its absence did he realise how the birdsong had been ever present before. In this darker, denser region, nothing sang or stirred aside from the sounds his own movement created. The boar he had become seemed to know its path all too well, and carried him on with absolute certainty, even though Steven could see little sign of an actual path.

Did this forest have a centre? He had the feeling it did, and that the boar was taking him towards its secret heart. The way grew ever more tangled, until he had to push through gaps between twisted trunks, squeeze beneath fallen logs and scrabble through the pits made by roots torn from the earth when the trees had fallen. He wondered if they were going somewhere that had its own kinds of meaning. *Back to the quest for truth?* He asked himself. It seemed too simple. There could not possibly be a host of answers waiting for him in the middle of this dream of a forest.

"Come back to me Steven, back along the boar path and back to yourself."

The wild pig sped up, as though hearing the command but determined not to comply with it. Steven had no idea which impulse to follow – this blind run into ever thicker undergrowth, or the call to return? Could he choose to stay, or to leave? Did he want to? What would happen if he chose not to go back? Things seemed so much simpler here. The boar raced onwards, and he had no idea how to make it stop.

"Listen to my voice Steven. Wherever you have gone, you need to come back now."

The sound of Willow's voice seemed such a fragile, far away thing. He tried to follow it, but the running boar gave him no time to think. He could not turn round, or stop even, and had no voice with which to call out for help. The boar carried him away.

They came into a clearing, in the centre of which stood a pair of standing stones, capped by a third. Spiral patterns covered every part of the construct. The gap between these sculpted stones was big enough to permit a man, or a boar even, to pass through. Held firmly within the boar, Steven circled the stones cautiously. They looked much the same from every angle, but there was a faint glow to that central gap, and looking through it from either side, he could see nothing. The sight of it both frightened and excited him. Here after all was the centre of the forest. He felt it. The place called to him, offering wonder and mystery beyond all imaginings if he dared to step through. He knew that the boar meant to carry him across into whatever lay beyond.

"Enough," The Spirit of Arden said softly. He had not heard her approach, but she stood beside him all the same. Her single word sent a strange tremor through him, unsettling every part of his being. Then he no longer wore the boar form. The transformation shocked him and standing as a man again felt peculiar indeed.

"What happened?" he asked.

"The boar took you. I'm sorry I didn't stop him before."

"Why?"

"You aren't ready," she said.

"Why?" he persisted, realising how childlike he sounded.

"I didn't mean you to come this far today, but the boar is strong, and he likes you."

"He would have kept me safe."

"He would have kept you." She placed her hand lightly on his shoulder, drawing his attention to her face, and away from the mysterious stones. "This is not the true forest," she said. "They cut my forest down a long time ago. This is just the ghost of the memory of a dream. Nothing more."

"It isn't real then?"

"It's very real, and it will steal your soul if it can. This is a hungry place, beautiful, but full of its own dangers. It isn't a good idea to stay here too long."

"What will happen?"

"You will forget yourself. You had already started to become the boar. Eventually you would have forgotten your other self, your other body."

"Would that be so bad? I'm not that great in my other body. I feel much more alive here."

She shook her head sadly. "And what will happen to your physical body, if you choose to stay in this dream of a forest? You will slip into a coma and you will die. You won't be the first to dream themselves to death either. Take your insight, your knowledge of the boar and go back to your life, and live it with all the passion you have. You can make that other life mean more to you. There can be wonder and beauty, if you are open and let it in."

Steven had no idea how to answer this, so when The Spirit of Arden took his hand and started walking, he followed obediently. Surprisingly, the way back seemed easy, with a clear path to follow. After everything she had said, he thought the place might fight to keep them, but it did not. They stopped in a clearing.

"You are close enough to yourself now," she said. "Wake, and return to your body, remember everything. Your friend won't be there when you wake, for I told her to go home. She has given you everything she can, the rest is up to you now."

He'd never seen such an odd expression on her face before. Then it struck him – this being in his trance was not Willow. She'd brought him to this place, but she was as human as he was. What he'd met here and in his dreams was not the human model and activist. In this place, he'd met something of the forest, something ancient and powerful, wearing a face he knew. He'd found what he'd truly been seeking, or at least he'd started on the right path at last.

"Go well," she said, and compelled by her voice, he went back to himself.

Chapter Twenty-Two

Steven awoke in the twilight, his back damp from the grass and his limbs stiff from lying in one position for too long. Sitting up, he looked around for Willow, but saw no sign of her. He called her name, but knew in his heart that she'd gone.

It's ok, he told himself. *You knew she wouldn't be here. You were told. Calm down.* Alone in the darkness, he didn't feel entirely confident despite all the clear messages in his trance. There seemed to be nothing he could do but try and find his way back while trying to make sense of things.

Her phone buzzed ineffectively until a computerised voice cut in to tell him that the person he was trying to call could answer right now. He hung up and decided to let it go. Mostly, he wanted the reassurance that Willow was well. He hoped she was just busy. Aside from Henry Marsden, Steven didn't know anyone who had any direct connection with Willow. Neil had apparently seen her around, but they weren't on speaking terms. He had no way of finding out where she was or if anything had happened to her.

They hadn't spent much time together, but everything he had seen of her in person seemed to correspond with the figure who haunted his dreams and meditations. Willow was Arden, but Arden was more than Willow, he felt. He'd thought at length about her words on the way to the tree, about how she sought to embody the spirit of Arden. Her silence now, and the message in his trance meant that he might not see her again. She'd come into his life for a reason and, job done, had moved on to other things.

The idea of having lost her proved painful to think about, so he pushed it to the back of his mind and steadfastly ignored it. Realising he had no scope for contacting her disturbed Steven, leaving him feeling hollow. No amount of ignoring his apprehension could demolish the feeling. He had no idea what to do next or what any of the cryptic things he'd ben told really meant for him.

When the telephone rang, he leapt for it. "Willow?"

"Sorry, I think I may have the wrong number." He didn't recognise the male voice that responded.

"My mistake, I was expecting a call," Steven lied awkwardly.

"Is this the right phone number for the Bromsgrove moot?"

"It is," he said. Steven had forgotten his details were on all the moot information now.

"I'm pretty new to Paganism. I just wondered what it's all about really, and whether I could just come along."

"Its nature-based spirituality is the short answer, and you'd be very welcome to come along," Steven said.

They spent a while discussing the details, and he came away from the call almost euphoric. Steven realised he could really do this: He could take the moot and keep it going. Talking to a complete novice made him realise what a huge journey he had made in the preceding few months. Leaning on a windowsill, he gazed out at the darkened streets, smiling to himself at all the recent changes in his life. It would all turn out ok, he decided. Willow had been a gift. She would get in touch when she felt like it, or she wouldn't and either way he felt grateful for the experience. He'd figure out what to take from it, and what to do next. He hadn't lost The Spirit of Arden.

On the far side of the street, a figure emerged from a patch of deep shadow. Steven had no idea how long the man might have been there. At this distance, he could make out little more than a shock of spiked up hair, and a long trench coat. In a flash of all too familiar paranoia, he wondered if he was being stalked, and spied upon. The figure could have been that of his ominous man, but plenty of the goth kids dressed that way so he couldn't be certain. Two instinctive responses dragged him in different directions – hide, or chase? He could pull down the blind, shutting out the night and the figure. Or, he could run out there and turn the tables on the unsettling presence, assuming it was him. Steven had a brief vision of finding some lone, punk youth and getting his nose bloodied for his efforts. The longer he procrastinated, the less chance there would be of finding the suspicious lurker.

He could still feel the boar, strong and certain inside him. No need to think, only to feel and do, to follow nature and act. He made for the door.

The boar thundered inside him as he ran, pushing him forwards and providing wild energy for the hunt. Nothing in the unfolding events seemed entirely real, and the sense of tusks and fury remained strong, keeping him from thinking better of the attempt. At first, he could see no sign of the troublesome figure, but followed the road with an uncanny feeling of certainty. Then he saw the man, walking at a fair pace, yellowy tones of streetlights catching on the spiked hair, and reflecting occasionally off the sleek leather coat. If he heard Steven's approaching gallop, he showed no signs of concern.

The boar wanted to charge, to run down this offender and trample it underfoot, breaking bones and turning flesh to pulp. Steven fought for control, not wanting to throw himself into the back of a stranger, fearing he had the wrong man. In his struggle with the boar, he briefly lost all control over his feet, and staggered, toppling into a nearby garden hedge. A large and startled pigeon flew out from amidst the plant life, squawking its surprise. The sound drew the leather coated man's attention, and he turned. As Steven regained his feet and some of his dignity, he saw the gaunt, ashen face and fiery eyes.

Should have charged while we had the advantage he felt the boar thinking.

The all-too familiar man smiled, his thin lips drawing back unpleasantly to reveal even, pearly teeth. His nostrils flared as he breathed, creases forming and vanishing over his brow and a nervous tick playing freely in one eyelid. He looked insane. Steven had a brief flash of vision, seeing himself as others might. Dishevelled, climbing out of a hedge. Of the pair of them, the other man probably looked the crazier, but not by much.

"You," the other man hissed.

"Well spotted," Steven said.

The boar seemed to be immune to fear, and feeling its presence still strong within him, Steven's usual nervousness could not get a hold. The ominous man seemed slighter than he remembered – proving to be a far less imposing figure. Unbalanced. Overconfident. The boar saw its opportunity and charged. Steven's shoulder slammed into the man's chest, the force of it throwing them both to the ground. Being on top, Steven had the advantage, but his opponent's hands struggled for his wind pipe and the fight began in earnest.

Steven had no time to think. He surrendered control of himself, letting the boar vent its fury. There were occasional moments of clarity, brought on by pain, but the rest blurred into movement and hatred. The boar wanted to gouge and gore, sinking lethal tusks into soft flesh, tearing out the guts and making blood run freely. Steven's body lacked the natural weapons to bring death about, but his jaw ached from the boar's ferocious inclinations. It wanted tusks, and Steven felt he might sprout them from his face if this carried on much longer. He couldn't entirely be certain who was fighting whom anymore, much less who had the advantage. The tang of blood filled his mouth, but he couldn't tell where it had come from.

"You can't kill me," the man beneath him grunted.

"I'll settle for making you go away," Steven managed to respond.

"I can't."

"Can't, or won't?"

The man leered up at him, a disconcerting smile on his angular face. "See you around," he said, and as the final word escaped his lips, he ceased to be.

Steven crashed down onto the pavement. The blow knocked the last of the boar out of him, leaving him alone and winded. He felt empty, sore and ravaged, trying not to think how he must look. Fortunately it was late, there weren't many cars about, and at present, no pedestrians either. Hauling himself up, Steven checked himself over. Everything hurt, and he had a few nasty scrapes from the uncanny man's boots, but nothing serious.

"What on earth am I doing?" he asked the night sky.

There had been no man. No fight. You fell down, kicked and beat the pavement in a moment of delusion. You have completely lost the plot. Mental. Loopy.

"He is real," Steven muttered to himself, limping in the direction of home. "He's real. It's all real. Or real enough."

He wished for Willow's presence. She seemed detached from the rest of reality, but unconcerned by what others considered normal. Someone like Cerridwen Riversong would be welcome company. Anyone who would give his version of events consideration and not dismiss him as barking mad. With someone else to believe the story, he might just be able to accept it himself. Steven thought of the moot, only a few days away now. *Likeminded people.* Could he tell them what he'd been through, or were they too normal to cope? Would they look at him with disbelief in their eyes if he told the story of this bizarre day? He had the feeling Mindy would have believed him. But then, if he guessed right she knew all about the ominous man, but had never risked saying anything.

How could he get rid of this being? He tried to remember what Cerridwen had said from the depths of her trance. None of it had made much sense to him, and the precise words evaded his attempts at recollecting them. Words about death. *You can't kill me.* Why not? Steven wondered. If the man wasn't real of course that would make perfect sense. You couldn't kill something that only lived in your mind, after all.

With the door safely locked and the blinds pulled down, Steven felt a little more secure. The familiarity of his flat created at least an illusion of everything around him being solid and dependable. He tried to call Willow again, but her phone went straight to answering machine. He left a message then tried to get Helen. She didn't answer either and at that point he gave up. More than anything else, he needed to hear a friendly voice, but couldn't think of a decent excuse for calling any of the other people he knew.

Chapter Twenty-Three

Having made a point of turning up early to the moot, Steven found he had a long time alone in which to sip at the new brand of cider, and think too much. Three days had passed since his fight, and during that time he had turned up for work, and otherwise had no contact with anyone. He'd been tempted to drop round to Helen's shop, but couldn't work out what to say to her. There had been no word from Willow and he didn't know what to think about that. Still he hadn't quite plucked up the nerve to visit Marsden or try and get his phone number. Given the man's previous response, he'd half expected a knock on the door from the police and awkward questions about the missing woman. He hoped she was alright and that there was a perfectly sensible explanation.

The new man, Lou, turned up bang on eight o'clock, his nervous glance around the sparsely inhabited room making him all too obvious. Steven waved.

"Are you the guy I talked to on the phone?"

"If you're Lou, then that's a yes."

Steven had a good ten minutes to fill the newcomer in on what the moot got up to, and who the regulars were. Explaining it all gave him a feeling of wisdom he'd never had before: As though he had become someone whose insights and actions mattered. Lou appeared to hang on his every word, asking intelligent questions and occasionally offering small details about himself.

"I went to a lecture ages ago, this woman called Raven Olivia? Don't know if you know her?"

"No idea," Steven admitted.

"Anyway, a lot of what she said made sense to me. About seeing the wonder around us, the miracle in every breath, that sort of thing. It stayed with me. I've been moving about a lot with my job, so I've not had chance to meet that many people."

"Are you likely to be in the area long?"

"No idea to be honest," Lou said.

"What do you do?" Steven asked.

"Surveying."

"What, as in market research?" Steven asked.

"Land surveying. For building companies."

As the rest of the moot rolled in – all of them late to varying degrees, Steven made the introductions. Neil turned out to have heard of Raven Olivia and professed to be quite a fan. For a while, Steven sat in the middle of it all, listening to the various conversations around him but not following any of it. He liked having the hubbub of social activity surrounding him like this. *My moot.* Every time he remembered, the thought of it made him smile. Now it was his responsibility to look after the group, to nurture and protect it. From across the table, Elspeth caught his eye and smiled encouragingly. He was glad she had come along, having feared she might stay away. Her presence encouraged him considerably.

Steven knew it was just a dream from the beginning. Usually such insight would cause the whole scenario to unravel around him, but this time the action played out, and his knowledge of its unreality didn't seem to make any odds. He hadn't dreamed anything in quite a few nights that he could remember. Most of his sleeping experiences where wispy, insubstantial things, leaving him with a few hazy impressions at best. Every so often, one would come that invoked all his senses. This dream was one of the unusual ones. He could feel the earth, solid beneath his feet as he ran, and each footfall brought jarring awareness to his ankles and knees. The brambles tearing at his skin felt all too substantial, as did the low branches whipping his face from time to time. The dense woodland around him looked solid enough and had yet to melt into something else. He even had to breathe, and when he sucked in air, he could taste the green dampness of trees.

With the inexplicable certainty of dreaming, he knew this was only the edge of the forest. The path didn't go into the centre, although if he could find one that did he might be safe. Something chased him. He couldn't see it when he glanced behind him, nor could he hear it. The feeling of being pursued kept him running. Not knowing what raced after him fed his fear, making the unseen monster on his heels seem terrible. He struggled to run, each step harder than the one before it, as though the air had turned into honey and he could no longer push through. The danger behind him closed in, lifting the hairs on the back of his neck, and making him sick with apprehension. He knew it was getting closer, but couldn't turn to see it.

The middle of the forest would be safe, that seemed evident. However, he had no idea why this might be so. The only visible path kept to the perimeters, so he struck out through the undergrowth in a final attempt at escaping his pursuer.

"You can't run from me forever." The voice came from behind him, but it didn't sound like anything. There were just words in his awareness.

Although he could think for himself, Steven didn't seem to have much control over his body, which continued trying to force its way through the many saplings growing together in a thicket.

"As you cannot escape me, you should let me take you. It will hurt less if you give up."

These words sent a fresh wash of panic through him. Then a bright, clear voice came to him from somewhere ahead. "You don't have to give up."

The statement gave him courage and he kept going.

"You can fight until your last breath if you want to."

He knew that voice. It wasn't Willow, but the spirit who shone out through her eyes sometimes. He ran harder, finding the threat at his back less pressing than the sense of where he needed to be.

"This way," she called.

"It is easier to surrender," said the voice at his back.

For an immeasurable stretch of time he continued, unable to catch up with the spirit, but also remaining just beyond the reach of his pursuer. It felt as though he wasn't really moving at all, even though his feet still appeared to be running.

"Choose how to submit to him, and you won't be ruled by him," she called out.

"Give up and you won't be tied to following her for the rest of your life," the voice behind offered, and Steven knew what to trust, and who to trust. He felt no doubt.

The trees closed in around him, their branches weaving a cage from which he could not escape. Alone now, he watched the trunks pressing ever closer about him.

A hungry place the spirit said, her words floating up from the depths of a forgotten memory.

Steven awoke to find that every part of him ached and that he was lying on the floor next to the bed. Evidently, he had fallen out of it during the night. The duvet tangled about him, unpleasantly hot. Lying on the floor a few inches from his face, the boar statue stared back at him, its expression as challenging as ever. Steven locked gazes with it for a while, trying to make sense of his half-remembered dream. His alarm buzzed loudly, disrupting his thoughts and reminding him of the job he should be going to. Even if he did hurt all over, he still had to show up and do his bit.

Standing under the shower, he examined the rapidly healing bruises from his recent fight. None of them looked too bad now. However, the stiffness in his limbs did not surrender beneath the flow of hot water, and his calves ached especially badly. Steven considered how much he felt as though he had spent the night running.

Pulling a partially rotted mattress from a ditch, Steven wished he'd had a better night. Today's duties were more arduous than usual, and his weary body was not co-operating. On the other end of the mattress, his fellow worker Kevin swore and swatted a wasp away.

"I hate this pissing job," he announced.

Steven nodded a response but didn't waste breath trying to reply.

"I always think I'm going to find a body one of these days. My girlfriend says I watch too many crime programs. But it could happen. You lift the mattress up, or the fridge or whatever it is, and there it is. Dead. I reckon bones wouldn't be too bad, but a full on rotting corpse has got to be really gross. Have you ever seen a dead person?"

"I don't think so," Steven said.

"Me neither."

Steven only half listened to Kevin's chatter. No matter what he did, or how mundane his environment, the boar remained on the edge of his thoughts, nudging at him, pressing to be let back in. Steven had no idea what would happen if he acquiesced. There were plants under the debris, he realised. Anaemic from lying in darkness too long, they straggled across the ground, refusing to give up on life.

Something had died around here. The smell of it reached him, tugging at his guts. Rank, sickly, and laden with decay, he recognised the stench instinctively. Kevin didn't appear to have noticed yet. Cold sweat formed in Steven's hands, making it harder to handle the broken flower pots he'd been hauling over to their trailer. The more he tried not to think of what they might find, the more images borrowed from zombie horror films returned to him. Maggoty flesh still impossibly alive, reaching for the living with murderous intent.

"Bollocks!" Kevin protested, backing away from the last few things in the rubbish pile.

"What?" Steven ventured a little closer.

"No idea. Dead, whatever it is. Shit. I knew this was going to happen. What did I tell you?"

The smell had grown worse, and Steven moved to be upwind of whatever had died. He made his way over to Kevin, cautiously looking for the corpse. It turned out to be a small, pathetic heap of fur, not really identifiable as anything.

"Might have been a cat," Kevin suggested. "I don't want to move the stinking thing."

"I'll do it," Steven said.

He took a few steps forward, breathing through his mouth so that the smell didn't get to him. The dead animal looked pitiful; a forlorn and empty shell slowly returning to the earth. Morbid fascination kept him staring at it for a while. He tugged on the roll of carpet beneath it, and the body rolled, landing on the ground. The underside of the creature had partially rotted, showing flashes of white bone. Just as he turned his attention back towards the other junk still to be shifted, Steven had the feeling of being watched. He looked up. Stood a few feet from him, on the other side of the cat, was the uncanny man. His trench-coat flapped slightly in a breeze the mortal watching him could not feel. Unmoving, the man stared down at the cat, then raised his eyes to meet Steven's gaze.

Making an involuntary noise of alarm, Steven leapt backwards. The ominous man smiled at him.

"What's up with you?" Kevin asked.

He realised then that Kevin couldn't see the third person stood beside the fly-tipped rubbish. It made the figure seem less threatening, he discovered.

"Cramp I think," he said quickly. "Better now."

"Bastard when that happens," Kevin agreed cheerfully. "I'll tell Sam we found a body. She'll have a fit."

When he looked again, the figure had gone. Rather than throw the dead animal in with the human waste, Steven scraped a shallow hole in the ground and buried it there. Kevin watched, somewhat amused, but not saying much. Once he had tamped the earth down over the small body, Steven felt better about it. He supposed it probably didn't make much odds to the dead creature either way. They did have people who dealt with roadkill, but it seemed easier to just bury this poor departed thing. He wasn't sure if the roadkill guys would come out for something dead in a fly tip.

As they packed up, he wondered if the discovery of the little corpse held any deeper significance. The brief manifestation of the entity haunting him made him question what he'd found. Was it a threat? Or something more complicated.

"Have a tea break," Kevin suggested. "You're as white as a sheet."

"If this was a film, the cat would come back to life and eat our faces or something," Steven said, trying to lighten things up.

"Too right. Dead things really creep me out," Kevin agreed.

Steven wondered what his companion would think if he'd seen the unnatural man standing over the dead cat a few minutes before.

Chapter Twenty-Four

A week passed with no word from Willow, then a second. Steven did not keep trying to call her. Worried about her, he set off into Birmingham one Saturday morning in late August. All Steven could think of doing was paying a visit to Henry Marsden. A plan he felt might have looked more promising had he kept Marsden's address. He tried to find his way from Kings Norton Station, but with no success. The route he had taken the previous time had involved too many wrong turns for him to easily recall the way. Tired with the wasted effort, he then attempted to make his way back to the main road through Selly Oak, but having started in the wrong direction it took him more than an hour. The traffic noise wore on his nerves and he regretted coming out.

The art shop had a large 'we have moved' sign hanging on the door. Looking closer, Steven noticed a map for their new location, in Halesowen. He didn't know Birmingham all that well, and had never ventured that far so he had no idea how to get there. They had a phone number, but he had no means of recording it and knew he wouldn't remember. In desperation, he bought a notepad and pen from a nearby newsagent, and jotted it down. Hopefully they could give him a number for Marsden, and Marsden could tell him if Willow was ok.

Then Steven remembered he had promised Cerridwen Riversong a gift in return for the bizarre few hours he had spent in her company. He spent another hour trying to find her house, and eventually had to ask for directions. The rows of near identical terraces gave him a feeling akin to claustrophobia. Eventually he located her house, and knocked lightly on the door. There was no response. It occurred to him that she would be a good person to talk to abut his recent experience, but fate had sent her elsewhere this afternoon and cast him adrift him without guidance. He left his small offering on her doorstep, resigned to just catching a train and going home. He'd been carrying it about for too long, keeping the box of handmade soaps in his bag with the intention of dropping in next time he was in the area. He felt badly about not doing it sooner.

All around him, people were eating on the street or ducking into cafes and fast food joints. Steven's stomach rumbled. Breakfast had been a long time ago, and light. Eating in the street had been one of the big taboos growing up. He remembered countless times when his mother had shared her criticism with him, damning as vulgar and ignorant the people brazen enough to consume food stood up where everyone else could see them. It disgusted her, but fascinated his child self. Greasy chips eaten from newspapers. Limp burgers in dry baps. Rustling plastic covering pies, crisps, chocolate. Forbidden vices all.

"It's bad for you," she had said innumerable times. "Eating standing up will make you sick. You'll make a mess of your clothes. And anyway, it's too expensive. I don't have money to waste on junk like that."

She'd been so adept at feeding his guilt, he realised. Her own food anxieties had become his as well.

"You had breakfast didn't you? You can't be hungry already. You're just greedy. You'll end up fat and no one will love you then. Do you want to be fat? Do you want to be repellent?"

He had always seemed too fat, in his own eyes. When he looked in the mirror, he never much liked what he saw. He had questioned the reality of everything else lately, why not challenge these firmly held beliefs as well? Whenever he thought about food, he could hear her voice all too clearly.

"You're not hungry, you're just making a fuss again. You always make such a fuss about everything and I really can't be bothered with it."

Years of her words came back to him in ugly fragments. Words that had taught him to fear food, and feel ashamed of his perfectly natural hunger. In his teens, when her increasing illness had allowed him a little freedom, Steven had watched others eating fast food in public, but had never dared to try it for himself. Observing them as they fed calorie laden edibles between their lips had seemed voyeuristic at the time. Pornographic even. There was something communal about shared eating, he realised. It was more than just nourishing the body. But his mother hadn't been very good at connecting with others. Perhaps it was part of the same problem. He still had a lot to figure out and today did not feel like the time to try and face that particular demon. He bought bottled water, but did not go any further.

The train rattled him back towards home, and Steven found himself thinking about his mother and wondering how she'd got to be so anxious about food.

Having some distance from her had given him a little clarity. It didn't seem likely that she'd got that way on her own. He wondered how many of the cruel lines she'd trotted out where things someone else had once said to her. Then it struck him that she might – in a really unhealthy kind of way – have been trying to protect him. If she had been taught that her whole value as a person depended on being skinny, maybe in trying to make him thin she's been trying to take care of him. The thought felt deeply peculiar. He wondered if this was what people meant when they talked about ancestral trauma.

Eventually, he got through to the art shop, now relocated to Halesowen. They furnished him with Henry Marsden's number, and he dialled it at once. The wait seemed interminable, but at last a rather weary sounding woman picked up.

"Hello?"

"Is this the right number for Henry Marsden?" Steven asked, fearing the shop had made a mistake.

"Who's calling?"

"My name's Steven, I just wanted to ask him about a mutual friend."

"Oh. So you haven't heard?" the woman said.

"Heard what?" Steven asked.

"Henry had a stroke a couple of weeks ago. He's back from hospital now, but he still can't talk and he's rather confused."

"I'm so sorry," Steven said, genuinely shocked by the news. "Is he going to be ok?"

"Hard to say. He's made some progress but it was severe. Do you want me to pass on a message?"

"He doesn't know me all that well, I doubt he'll remember me to be honest," Steven said. "But I do hope he gets better."

"Well, we haven't quite given up hope yet. He's a tough old thing. He might be bloody minded enough to pull through this."

"I hope so."

"It just came out of nowhere, the woman continued. "One day he was fine and the next... this. He's not that old really. The doctors say he must have had high blood pressure for some time. I told him to get himself checked out, but he never paid any attention to me."

Steven made sympathetic noises, and was relieved when the woman finally ended the conversation. He supposed she must be under a lot of strain but he had no idea what to say to her. He guessed Willow had known about this and been affected by it. As someone peripheral in her life he did not feel entitled to her attention, and knew he could not offer her meaningful support.

Steven sat on his bed, staring at the Spirit of Arden painting and hoping for inspiration. Nothing came to him. A gut feeling told him that there was an answer to all of this, but he couldn't put it together yet.

As the evening proved warm and pleasant. Steven went out. He had nowhere to go, but found his way to the local graveyard There were other people drifting along the narrow sandy pathways, passing the rows of small plaques, urns and flowers. The atmosphere felt more peaceful than melancholy. Being so close to the dead made him think of Mindy and how close she had come to joining them. He'd not heard much about her lately, just enough to be hopeful that she might yet make a full recovery.

Looking around, he half expected to see the ominous man watching him from some shadowy corner. *Who are you?* he asked silently. *What are you? And what do you want with me?* He had no answers, but supposed there must be some. Then a thought crossed his mind, and he stopped breathing for a few moments, stunned by the implications of his idea. If those meditations had a reality of their own, then maybe he needed to go back into the forest to properly understand things.

Lying flat on his back, Steven shifted on the bed until he felt comfortable. He had meditated on his own a few times, but this felt different. Closing his eyes, Steven tried to remember what Willow had said about the forest. Gradually, pictures formed in his mind, of stately oaks and slender birches, dappled patterns of light and shadow. Squirrels chattered in the branches overhead, and nearby a woodpecker tapped loudly in its hunt for food. It didn't feel as real as it had before, and he was unable to manifest himself into this idyllic scene. With no real sense of a body, he drifted, and the forest changed around him. It seemed quiet and unthreatening. Steven had no sense of the boar. This looked like the forest he had seen before, but it wasn't what he needed to find.

Steven wondered if he was just remembering and imagining rather than connecting to the place he had seen in other journeys. In his previous visits, Willow, or perhaps the spirit of Arden had guided him, and she had a magic all her own. With her, anything might be possible, but alone he feared he lacked whatever it took. After resting for a few moments he tried again, concentrating on the feel of the forest rather than its immediate visual impact. This time he had a stronger impression of it. However, he felt like he was on the outside of an onion, knowing there were layers to contend with but having no idea how to penetrate them.

Concentrating, Steven tried to will himself deeper in. He could feel the possibility, like a taste in the back of his mouth. Foliage closed in around him. He had images of brambles and tangled thickets, impenetrable barriers of prickles and intense growth. However, the harder he tried to push through, the more difficult it became to hold any image of the forest in his mind. After what felt like a very long time, he gave up and rolled over, burying his head in the pillow for a while. There had to be a way of doing this. When the idea first struck him, it had seemed so easy, but now his head ached from trying. After his ineffective efforts, he felt too tired to think anymore. He couldn't quite sleep, but drifted along the edges of unconsciousness, chasing after partially formed ideas that all failed to resolve into anything coherent.

Chapter Twenty-Five

"I brought you some incense, and a scented candle," Steven announced somewhat awkwardly as Cerridwen opened the door to him. Although he had already left a small gift on her doorstep, there had been nothing to indicate the sender.

"Come in," she said.

They hadn't spoken much on the phone, but she had been willing to see him again, for which Steven was grateful. He'd gone to some effort with the incense, managing to buy grains of frankincense, rather than mere joss-sticks, and hoped it would suffice.

"Have a seat," Cerridwen said, pointing towards her cushion bedecked chairs. "So, let's go over this slowly. What exactly is it you want me to do?"

"I'm not sure. There's something I've been trying to do by meditating, but I can't do it on my own. Last time I did it I had help, but I can't contact the woman who worked with me then, and was wondering if you would be willing to have a go. I need someone to guide me."

"I've little experience of putting other people into trances. I'm not sure I can do what you're asking."

"But would you have try?"

"Talk me through what you want to do," Cerridwen said. "I'm not making any promises until I understand what you need."

"A while ago I was taken on a very intense journey. I suppose you could call it a pathworking, but it was far more real than anything I've done on my own. I travelled through a forest, to the centre. On my own, I can go to the forest, but I can't go any deeper."

"And why do you need to go deeper?"

"I met... guides? I don't know what to call them, but it was a profound experience and I really need to take it further." He hoped the Spirit of Arden would forgive him for describing her thus, but he couldn't face trying to explain the full extent of his connection with her.

"And the person who helped you before is no longer available? What happened there?"

"She had some personal stuff going on and I don't want to impose on her," he said, hoping this partial honesty would be enough.

"Hmm. What do you want from this journey? Don't talk to me about the details, tell me what your deeper need is."

"Insight I suppose. I've spent most of my life not really knowing what I wanted, who I ought to be, how I should live. I realise I don't have much idea who I am and I want to change that. This previous pathworking stirred something in me. It's not easy to explain because I'm following a hunch as much as anything else. One of the reasons I got back in touch with you is I'm fairly sure if you think I'm wasting my time, you'll tell me."

She smiled at this. "I would."

"Am I?"

"I think not. There is a true spiritual quest at the heart of what you want to do, and I respect that. So what you want is something like a guided meditation and help to keep focused on your intentions."

"That sounds about right, yes."

"I can do that."

"Now?"

"If you want. You may as well use the floor."

Lying flat on his back, Steven closed his eyes while Cerridwen made her preparations around him. He breathed deeply, trying to relax. The mix of hope and fear engendered by the prospect before him, made it hard to be calm.

"Breathe slowly and deeply," Cerridwen said. "Let your breath become the focus of your awareness. Listen to my voice, and be guided by me, and forget all else. Just my voice and the slow rhythm of your breathing. Rest, and let your mind travel freely, Steven."

Her tone remained low and compelling. Steven found it easy enough to be directed by her.

"I want you to imagine that you are walking in your forest, surrounded by luscious undergrowth."

With an external voice to keep his attention focused, the journey seemed easier by far and he plunged deep into the forest as she commanded. He walked, aware of his feet and the solidity of ground beneath him. All around, the trees teemed with life and noise, some of it friendly, some less so. Out there beyond the limits of his sight, the boar waited for him. He hoped it would not seek him out, having no idea how to deal with the creature's intentions just yet. The idea of the boar drew him, speaking to him on a deep, wordless level. It also frightened him, offering a loss of control that he didn't like the look of. What if it took him over, or carried him further than he could cope with going?

"Journey deep into the forest Steven. Listen to your heart and be guided by it. Let the things you truly need come to you."

Cerridwen's voice sounded distant now, but her words affected him. He could feel a subtle tug pulling him onwards. Paths twisted and turned in all directions, but the mysterious centre of the forest called to him and Steven had no doubts over which way to go. Trees blurred around him, green smears on the peripheries of his vision as he accelerated wildly. He had no form or feet now, only a desire for movement that carried him at extraordinary speed. On the brink of his awareness, Cerridwen's low voice urged him onwards, telling him that he knew the way to find what he needed most.

The thunder of running came from somewhere away to his right. Steven could feel it echoing through him, and tried to accelerate and escape. No matter how fast he went, he could sense this determined pursuer gaining on him. It had to be the boar hunting for him. Steven had no idea what it wanted, but decided it would be better not to find out just yet. From the sounds of its crashing through the forest and the uncomfortable feeling seeping through him, the boar did not come across as being benevolent. Rather than being caught by it, he had to reach the centre of the forest and find Arden. Nothing else mattered to him and he focused all of his intent on this single goal.

The boar hit him squarely in the side, knocking him to the ground. Tusks pressed against his flesh. In the pain of it, Steven was surprised by the vividness of his impressions: The boar's assault felt as uncomfortable as real pressure on his physical self might. Looking up, Steven met the powerful creature's familiar gaze. Unlike the wooden sculpture, this boar presented not merely the look of challenge but real danger. It opened its mouth, showing yellowish teeth, its breath smelling earthy as the heat of it covered his face. From this angle, the creature seemed a lot bigger than he had imagined, with its gaping maw a vast expanse.

There could be no escape from those jaws. Slowly, the great mouth descended, bringing darkness and crunching. Vast flat teeth ground his essence, tearing him apart and breaking him down into the smallest fragments. Even in the midst of this violence, Steven remained aware, feeling himself being consumed. No matter what he did, he could not free himself from the giant boar's hungry jaws as it snapped the bones of his dreaming self. By slow degrees, the boar ate him. The experience of being chewed defied words. He had the feeling it hadn't taken him simply as food, but for some other, less obvious reason. The process seemed weirdly tender, even in the midst of all his suffering. It destroyed him out of kindness, chewed with compassion, swallowed with the deepest of affection.

Consumed, he could think of little beyond the boar. Splintered and pulped, he lost all sense of his own shape and sensations. Then, going down in the darkness, he travelled inside the creature, moving through the endless twists and turns of its inner passageways. Steven disintegrated entirely, losing himself to the spirit that had taken him. Surrounded, and overwhelmed, he found peace.

"Damn. I knew something like this was going to happen. Come on Steven, wherever you've gone, you need to come back now. Listen to my voice. Focus on my voice and come back to yourself, become aware of your body again. You've done enough for one day. Come on. Listen to me. Follow the sound of my voice. Remember yourself lying on the floor. Remember the weight of your body and how it feels to be inside your skin."

The words came to Steven, and gradually he picked up some sense of their meaning. Cerridwen was calling him home. At first he had no idea how to move or follow her orders. The idea of a body took him a while to grasp, the notion of movement followed a little while after. Even then, she seemed distant, and he could not work out how to escape from inside the boar. The more he listened to her, the clearer her words became. Rising like a swimmer in deep water, he became aware of light, and lessening pressure.

"Come back Steven. Wherever you have gone, its time now for you to return. Listen to my voice, follow the sound of my words. I call your spirit back to your flesh."

He broke through, struggling for breath, his head pounding and limbs sluggish. It took him a great deal of effort to sit upright. Next to him Cerridwen sighed with audible relief. For a while, neither said anything as they both recovered from their efforts.

"Did you find what you needed?" she asked.

"No. I was closer though."

"I'm sorry it didn't work," she said.

"It worked at first and then it all got out of control."

"Do you want to tell me about it?"

"I was eaten by a boar," he said.

Cerridwen smiled. "Now, I'm not an expert on this sort of thing, but my understanding is that it is a powerful, significant thing to be eaten by a spirit."

"This is normal?" Steven asked.

"Not normal, but common for people drawn to such work. Being dismembered so as to be made anew is a rite of passage for some."

"Thank you for telling me this," Steven said. "I thought I'd messed up."

"Not at all. Now, you're going to need to take things gently for a few days. Sleep as much as you need to, drink plenty of water. Phone me if you need to."

He thanked her again.

The trouble was, even though he had come back to himself, Steven still felt the boar around him, holding and digesting him. He felt detached from his surroundings and even from his body.

"Do you want to try this again?" Cerridwen asked.

"I think so. When?"

"Early next Saturday afternoon is good for me. I have a couple of hours free then. But only if you feel ready."

"I can do that."

Cerridwen nodded. "I think you might be a natural at this," she said. "It's not an easy path, but if it chooses you, there isn't much you can do about it."

"How do you tell if it's chosen you?" Steven asked.

"The spirits give you no peace until you accept them."

"Then what happens?"

"Anything. We can talk about this another time. I'll make you some sugary tea. I always find that helps."

Grateful, he closed his eyes and leaned against the nearby chair. He could smell the boar. Cerridwen's sugar laden tea grounded him a little, but he remained inside the boar, and nothing else felt entirely real to him.

"Earth to Steven. Come in, Steven!"

Realising he had been staring into space, Steven turned. "What?" he asked Kevin.

"I asked if you wanted to stop for a bit. I reckon we're due a break."

"Oh, yeah. Whatever."

Concentrating hadn't been easy. Steven didn't know what had happened to Sunday, and work seemed to be passing in a daze. Chunks of the day were missing from his memory. He'd been emptying bins.

"Good weekend then?" Kevin asked.

"What?"

"Looks to me like you've got the mother of all hangovers there. So I take it you had a good weekend, yes?"

"Oh, yeah," Steven said, his sluggish thoughts managing to conclude that agreeing would probably get Kevin off his case.

"Didn't have you down as a party animal."

Steven tried his best to smile at this.

"They say it's the quiet ones you have to watch though, don't they?" Kevin added.

Steven found himself wondering who 'they' were, but didn't argue.

"I'll grab the flasks from the van then, shall I?"

"Sure, thanks" Steven said.

He went back to studying the ground. It had all kinds of tiny contours, and he could see a few ants scurrying about. Anymore demanding mental activity than this made his headache. Steven could see everything around him well enough, but it seemed to be behind a layer of something. *Through the boar,* he suspected. The feeling of having been eaten remained with him. At first he had assumed it would wear off as time passed, or that he would feel better for sleeping. Two days on and he was still inside the boar, still wandering lost in its inner ways, and unable to engage fully with the reality around him. He could only wonder if things would continue this way indefinitely, or if at some point matters would improve.

"Here." Kevin passed him his thermos flask.

The sensation of hot tea in his stomach didn't seem quite real either. Steven tried to work out what the difference was, what subtle thing no longer worked properly for him. He couldn't come to any definite conclusions.

"Maybe that'll wake you up," Kevin said. "You're seriously wasted, aren't you?" He sounded impressed.

"Yeah," Steven muttered, finding all expressions hard work.

When they packed up at five, he headed over to Helen's shop, needing to be able to talk about what had happened. He found her conversing with an earnest looking young couple, and pretended to be browsing the tarot packs until they departed.

"So what can I do for you?" she asked.

"I just thought I'd drop in."

"Hmm. You never just drop in. So what is it this time?"

"How do I seem to you?"

Helen spent a while scrutinising him before she attempted an answer. "You look tired, but then I don't think I've seen you without shadows under your eyes. You might be a bit paler than usual, a bit more distant. I don't know. What am I looking for?"

"I did some trance work with Cerridwen, and got eaten by a boar."

Helen chuckled at this.

"It's not funny," Steven protested. "I'm still there. I can't concentrate on anything properly."

"You do get yourself into some scrapes, don't you?" she said, not unkindly.

"I don't know how to get out of this one."

"It'll pass," she said, then chuckled to herself. "Yep, that's most likely your solution. Sooner or later this boar of yours will have to evacuate its bowels. If it's eaten you, it'll squeeze you out sooner or later, won't it? Shouldn't take more than a few days, I would think. Unless of course it's constipated." With this final remark, she collapsed into fits of laughter.

"You're taking the piss!" he protested.

Composing herself a little, Helen managed to reply. "Of course I am. What did you expect, walking in here and telling me you've been eaten by a boar? How am I supposed to resist?"

"Point." Steven managed to smile a little, and felt better for it.

"It's not healthy to take things too seriously. And, laughter is the best way of getting rid of unpleasant influences," Helen pointed out. "Lighten up."

"So my spiritual destiny is to be boar crap?"

"That's the one."

"And what's that supposed to mean, do you think?"

"I'd say it means you ought to get out more. Look, this isn't remotely my thing. But, if you want to go round attaching significance to your experiences, you might as well figure out what it means to you rather than getting some so-called expert to tell you."

"Ok."

"Now, are you going to buy something, or are you going to bugger off and let me close up for the night?"

"I'd better get home. Thanks Helen."

"That's all right. I needed a laugh."

"Cheers."

Walking home with the boar still digesting him, Steven looked at his surroundings with fresh eyes. The roads and cars seemed more unnatural than ever. Even the houses appeared in a new, uncomfortable light. All the little illuminated boxes in which people hid from each other and from themselves. The possibility of forest rose up all around him, the memory of trees still present in the soil. If everyone died tomorrow, it wouldn't be long before nature reclaimed this place, tearing down these fragile human constructions. Steven couldn't decide whether he liked this prospect or not.

Chapter Twenty-Six

Waking in the grey, pre-dawn light, Steven shook and sweated. He clung to the bed as it seemed to rock beneath him. The room spun and the walls writhed. Closing his eyes against these fevered imaginings he lay still, hoping it would pass. His head ached furiously, as though he had been caught in a giant vice. Fighting for breath, he threw off the covers, but it didn't help him much. The unpleasant sensation in his scalp spread downwards, so that his whole body felt squeezed and discomforted. Steven had the feeling of moving from darkness into light. His eyes throbbed and ached so he closed them, managing to mute the pain a little.

Awareness of the bedroom dwindled. Heat pressed around him, pushing him out, and then he fell, plummeting what seemed a great distance to the ground. The impact spread him, disintegrating what little form he'd emerged with. Light surrounded him, but he could not move. The pain had finally ceased, but even so he couldn't get to grips with his waking dream. Nearby, a creature grunted. It sniffed at him and he felt the brush of harsh bristles. Having no eyes with which to see, he couldn't really perceive it, but felt its presence clearly enough. Tusk and jaw, small eyes and powerful muscles. The boar had released him.

I'm boar crap, Steven thought, and laughter bubbled up inside him. Mad, untamed laughter that consumed everything in its path. He shuddered with it, weeping involuntary tears until his sides ached, and he remembered himself. Illogical though it seemed to him, he felt clean, as though passing through the boar had stripped something unwanted from his psyche. Through his mirth he travelled back to the room with its ravaged bed.

Outside his window, another day glimmered into life. He had work to do, and there were difficulties to face, but for the first time in as long as he could remember, his heart sat lightly within him.

"You seem more certain of yourself today," Cerridwen observed as Steven settled himself on her floor.

"I think our last session really helped me. It took me a few days to work things out," he said with a smile. "I'm not finished yet, but I feel like I'm on the right path now."

"Good. I'm glad to hear it. Tell me your intentions and we can begin."

"Take me into the heart of the forest if you can, please," Steven requested.

Cerridwen's floor felt entirely familiar now. He settled quickly, entirely focused on the task in hand. Although his previous visits to the woman had brought nothing but difficulty, he felt a buzz of anticipation as he waited for her to start. This time he didn't really expect solutions, but whatever they achieved, it might take him a little further along his own journey.

"Breathe deeply and let your body relax, releasing all tension as you become calm. Open your mind to the journey you need to make."

Her words carried him easily into the depths of his imagination. He still hadn't decided if he thought this was some internal place, a reality in its own right, or both. For a while he lay still, conscious of his breathing, and the swirl of colours behind his eyelids. Then the forest opened up around him, vibrant with soft light and humming with life. Seeing it brought a rush of joy to him. If his heart had a home, this could well be it. He knew these were the borderlands, the peripheries of the woodlands. How far they stretched, he had no idea, but the centre felt a long way off. Cerridwen had brought him further than before, but still a long way from the heart he sought. Why he couldn't travel there directly, Steven had no idea. He began to walk, wondering how to take himself further in to the forest's secrets. Going beyond this edge seemed hard. He had hoped Cerridwen could direct him to the centre, but no that hadn't worked he wasn't sure what to do.

Awareness of the boar came to him, like a scent carried on the breeze. This knowledge was not sensual in origin, but insinuated itself on a subtler level. The great boar snuffled and rooted amongst the old leaves, interested in him, but not approaching. He had the feeling it was waiting to see how he would respond, and after a moment's thought, Steven chose to greet it. After their last encounter, his feelings remained ambivalent, but much of is fear had gone.

"Hello," Steven said cautiously, wondering if it would hear him at this distance.

"Hello," the boar returned.

He hadn't entirely expected it to reply in such a human, verbal way, but finding it could speak eased his misgivings. This time the boar presented no obvious threat, but Steven didn't know if he could afford to trust that impression.

"Why are you here?" the boar enquired.

"I need to get to the centre of the forest," Steven said.

"I tried to take you there once before, but you resisted me," the boar pointed out.

"I was afraid of you."

"And are you still afraid of me now?"

"A little, yes."

"Good."

Steven wondered why his fear should be a good thing, but had not framed the question when his consciousness of the animal changed, becoming more immediate. Then the boar appeared alongside him, the sheer physicality of its presence capturing his attention.

"Can you show me the way?" Steven asked nervously. Now that the boar stood so close, he couldn't help but recall their last encounter in full detail. He felt decidedly unsafe. The large mouth and grinding teeth could rend him down again all too easily.

"I will carry you there, if that is what you truly want?"

"Yes, and thank you."

"Then sit upon my back."

When he tried to climb onto it, Steven realised the boar stood as tall as a large horse. Without a saddle or stirrups to help him, he struggled to raise himself up.

"You are too literal," the boar said. "Sit on my back."

Steven considered this for a while, before he understood the instruction. Then chose to be sitting astride the great beast and found that he had moved with all the speed and grace of thought. His legs struggled to wrap around the wild boar's girth, but he had found his seat, and the creature set off at a slow trot.

"Will is all in this place," the boar told him. "Know where you wish to be, and you will be there."

"So why can't I find the heart of the forest."

"Because you don't really understand where it is," the boar suggested. "Or perhaps your intentions are unclear for some other reason."

Around them, trees blurred past. Steven caught occasional glimpses of other creatures, but nothing showed much interest in them. Flashes of bright flowers, and glimpses of trickling water came amidst the trees. The trees they passed under increased in size, the earlier saplings replaced by gnarled trunks. Vast branches spread overhead, forming a high canopy. The heart of the forest must, he thought, be the oldest part. They might be moving through time as well as space, he supposed.

"Time has no meaning here," the boar said.

"Can you read my thoughts?"

"Sometimes."

"Oh."

The idea that his mind was not an entirely safe refuge perturbed Steven. For most of his life, his thoughts had been his fortress, the only place he could reliably hide from the rest of the world.

"I will not plunder your mind," the boar promised. "But thought is a power here, and if you think too intensely, I will feel it, that is all."

Reassured by this, Steven returned his attention to watching the scenery unfolding around him. There were vast pools only a short way from the track, edged by colossal, tangling root systems. The water looked clear, and inviting.

"What happens if we leave the track?" he asked.

"If you leave the track, you will get lost. You have come to find the centre of the forest. If your heart isn't in the journey, you will lose yourself. Perhaps only for a little while. Perhaps forever."

"And if I left the track with you?"

"That would be different, but it would still cost you the focus of your journey."

"I'm not sure I understand."

"Accept, for now. You will learn in time."

Ahead of them, the trees thinned, and Steven saw a clearing. Small flowers bloomed amongst the grasses, and light dappled between leaves from the canopy above. The boar stopped, and Steven slid easily from its back.

"This is the centre of the forest?"

"Yes."

"But there were standing stones, before."

"That was before, this is now."

"Why is it different?"

"Things change."

"You said time has no meaning here."

"That does not mean things remain the same."

Steven walked around slowly, bewildered. He had believed so strongly there would be answers here, but the quiet glade around him appeared ordinary enough. There were no obvious revelations to be had.

"I don't understand," he said.

"This is the centre of the forest, its heart," the boar said patiently. "Isn't that what you were looking for?"

"No," Steven said, realising his mistake. "I was looking for something else."

"Then that is why you haven't found what you wanted. Speak from your heart if you want truth."

"I'm sorry. I thought I knew what I was doing."

"Then you will know for next time."

"Next time?"

"You will come back, but on your own, and when you are ready. The woman calls to you, and she will rouse you, drawing you back to your body."

"But I haven't finished here!"

"That's why next time you will come to me unaided," the boar said.

Steven could feel his sense of the forest weakening. He tried to fight it, wanting to stay longer and ask more questions of the boar. There remained so many things he didn't have answers to yet. He still didn't understand why this creature had changed its attitude to him. Had it been trying to help all along? Cerridwen's voice played in his ears, the tone insistent, pulling him back. Although he tried to resist, all awareness of the forest disintegrated, returning him to himself and the hard floor beneath him.

"I have a feeling that went a little better," Cerridwen said as he opened his eyes.

"Yes. Thank you." He pushed his frustration to one side, accepting what she had done for him and that she had kept him safe.

"When do you want to come back?" she asked.

Thinking of the boar's advice, Steven shook his head. "I think I've done what I needed to do," he said. "Thank you again."

Cerridwen looked a little disappointed, but didn't argue.

"Perhaps our paths will cross again one day," she suggested.

"I expect so," he returned, smiling as best he could. He had the distinct feeling they wouldn't meet again in the immediate future, if not longer. Although he felt grateful to the woman for her assistance, there seemed no need to continue the connection and other possibilities called to him.

Chapter Twenty-Seven

A little after midnight, Steven set out from his flat with the intention of wandering the streets. He had spent a while planning this urban expedition, considering his route carefully, and the timing of his late-night foray. Initially, he had contemplated a physical attempt to see if he could lure the ominous man to him. The boar had counselled otherwise, coming to him as he waited for sleep, and teaching him new possibilities.

Now, his body lay peacefully on the bed, but his mind roamed out, into the near-empty streets and off towards the deserted town centre. The boar trotted along at his side, evidently as comfortable here as in the forest of his dreaming.

"And why not?" the boar asked. "This was forest once. I can feel the memory of trees. I can be here as easily as any other place."

"Nothing looks quite real," Steven said, gesturing towards the smudgy buildings and vague streets.

"You're only partly here," the boar said. "It's not exactly the same as your world. Think of it as another layer in the reality onion if you like."

"Could I be fully here, fully aware of it?"

"I can go anywhere because I am spirit. In some layers, I am more solid than others, it will be the same for you. But, to be wholly here, you would have to leave your body and it would die."

"I couldn't be here in the flesh?"

"I don't know, but I suspect not."

The boar's admission surprised Steven. He'd fallen into the habit of thinking of it as a wisdom source, able to answer his every question. That the boar had limits too gave him pause for thought as he reconsidered his ideas about this companion spirit.

"Call him," the boar suggested.

"How?"

"From the heart. Call with your need to understand, and to make peace with your troubled friend. Call with your anger and resentment, with your pain and fury."

Stood in what looked like an impressionist painting of Bromsgrove, Steven stopped to consider what he was doing. He had been over the plan more times than he could count, questioning the logic of it, and whether there might be a better way. Having failed to come up with anything else, he had stuck with this scheme. Still, he couldn't help but wonder if he would be better off avoiding this entity rather than trying to face it head on.

"Fear it and hide from it, and it will grow in power. Deal with it and it will not bother you again."

"Yes, but how? You still haven't told me how to do that."

"Because I have no more idea than you. To be free of this spirit, you must find your own way of dealing with it. Use your empathy and insight. Use your imagination. Trust to your instincts."

"And if it all goes horribly wrong?"

"I am here. I will not permit it to harm you."

"But it might be stronger than you."

The boar snorted in disgust.

"Sorry, no offence," Steven said hurriedly, "but you aren't the most powerful being that ever existed, are you?"

"True," the boar said. "But I am strong enough for this. You are stalling. Do not let your fear hold you back."

"Right," Steven said. "Call him to me."

He concentrated, forming an image in his thoughts of the gaunt figure in its long trench-coat, eyes blazing with a crazy light. He recalled his anger in their previous encounters, all the rage of violence, the fear and suspicion that had been building up over the summer. This creature, he reminded himself, may have driven Mindy to try and kill herself. Rage filled his vision, full of destructive potential, flowing through his awareness with its own dangerous poetry. He called to the ominous man, demanded his presence in this realm of spirit and imagination. There were questions to be answered, and a score to be settled. Until that moment, Steven hadn't fully appreciated how strong and volatile his emotions were regarding the unsettling figure who had haunted him of late.

"Good," the boar murmured.

Returning his attention to the street scene, Steven saw his nemesis had indeed appeared, standing a short distance from him. The figure looked more real than before, more substantial and detailed, while everything around it seemed hazy. For a while, the two of them stared at each other and the air crackled with the potential for violence.

"What do you want with me?" Steven demanded.

The dark man opened his arms wide, and rather than words, there came a rush of feelings and impressions, jumbled together. Flashes of Mindy's thoughts filled Steven's awareness. He had a keen sense of her isolation, her angst and emptiness. There had been a great wound in her, a void which no one else had been able to fill. There were drugs and painkillers, but nothing gave her much respite.

"Heroin," the ominous man whispered. "Only once, but once was enough for her to find me."

"What are you?"

"I am her."

"No you aren't," Steven said quickly, unable to see any connection with this sinister man and the girl he had been so besotted with.

"I am her dreams and her nightmares."

Steven shook his head.

"He speaks the truth," the boar commented. "As he understands it."

"I ask again. Tell me why you keep following me, and attacking me."

"It is my nature."

Steven fumed quietly, frustrated by all this wilful ambiguity. "What do you want?"

"You."

"So you aren't going to leave me alone, no matter what?"

"Correct."

"But what do you want me for?" Steven demanded.

"To be you."

Steven took a step backwards. "No way."

"It is the only way."

The ominous man took a step forwards as he spoke. Immediately, Steven reached out, touching the boar's hairy flank. With disorientating speed, the boar carried him back to his room, recognising his need to escape from the situation.

"I can't deal with that," Steven said.

"If you do not deal with it, no one else will," the boar pointed out.

"I can't make any sense of what he says. Is he really telling the truth?"

"Only so far as he understands anything. That is not a being of thought, but of feeling and not good at expressing itself," said the boar.

"Why does he hate me?" Steven asked.

"Does he hate you? Perhaps because you are everything he wants to be. Flesh and bone, and truly alive. It is a hungry spirit; it may try and feed on you."

"Is there nothing I can do?"

"There are all sorts of thing you can do, but you have to find the answer that will suit you."

"Can you help me?"

"Perhaps. But you should rest and think. Be sure of yourself before we proceed."

"He showed me something of Mindy. He is connected to her, isn't he?"

"Very much so."

"There was this painful emptiness in her. I had no idea. She felt so hollow, so lost. I recognised it, because I've spent so much of my own life feeling that way. It's only recently that things have changed for me."

"He is part of Mindy, she is part of him, but he is older than all of this," the boar said.

"I need some time to think about all of this," Steven replied. He didn't feel like he had all the pieces of the puzzle yet.

"There is time enough. I will watch over you. He will not approach unless I permit it."

Steven dreamed, fully aware that he walked in the realms of his unconscious. Streets twisted away from him in all directions, bending and distorting whenever he tried to focus on them properly. He was looking for something important, but could not remember what. It always seemed to be a little way ahead of him, beyond sight and reach. A frantic determination had hold of him, but recognising it as part of the dream, he resisted its impulses.

"Enough," he said aloud, and echoes of his voice rebounded from every nearby surface.

The manic urgency left him, making it possible to think a little more clearly.

"If you want me to find you, why don't you just come to me instead?" he asked.

For what felt like an age, nothing whatsoever happened. A person appeared at the far end of the street, made small by the distance. They walked towards him, moving cautiously and making slow progress. The street itself lengthened, the expanse of phantom tarmac between them increasingly hard to cover.

"I need you to find me," she called out. Steven knew that voice and his dreaming heart raced within him.

"I'm coming," he shouted back, and set off at a run, determined to traverse the impossibly expanding street.

Willing himself onwards, Steven made sufficient headway that he could see her clearly. The sight of her made him want to weep. Dark hair framed her angular face, and her lithe form looked its best in motion, displaying her poise and grace.

"Spirit of Arden," he breathed the title, but the sound of his voice carried as a wild shout of joy.

"You have to find me," she said.

"I have found you," he said.

"Not yet."

"Then tell me what to do."

"You have to find me inside yourself," she said.

"I don't think I understand," he replied.

"You will. These things take time."

Steven stopped running and focused his mind. "I will reach you." The distance between them contracted, until the forest spirit stood at arm's length. "I wish someone would give me a straight answer for a change. What is it with spirits? Why does everything have to be in riddles?"

"We don't mean to riddle, it's just how we see things."

"You touched Willow in some way, you show yourself to people through her," he said.

"I do," the spirit replied. "You see me as looking like her because you're used to that, but you also understand now that I'm not her and she is not me."

"Yes," Seven said. "I think I understand that."

She reached out, her fingers tracing along the edge of his jaw. Then she touched her lips to his and Steven felt himself falling. He'd never kissed like this before, with such intensity of feeling, such utter awareness of two forms meeting and melding in one expression. It seemed to go deeper than physical contact, her soul seemed to plunge into his, merging them.

"Understand yourself and you will be able to find me again," she said.

"Do you want me to find you?"

"Dear heart," she said, her smile full of mystery and promise. "Why else would I have said?"

"I'll find you," he promised.

The sappy, leaf litter taste of her mouth remained on his lips when he woke. Her kiss stayed with him, lingering in his flesh as though their mouths were still in contact.

Chapter Twenty-Eight

When the telephone rang, Steven thought for a moment that it might be Willow herself. He had experienced the same impulse every other time the phone rang in the weeks since the last time he'd seen her. Despite the absence of contact, he still hoped, clinging to the dwindling possibility that he hadn't lost her after all.

"Yes?" he said eagerly, gripping the receiver tightly to stop his hand from shaking.

"Mr Cooper?"

"Yes, that's me. How can I help?"

The formal tone and unfamiliar voice put him on guard. Steven took a deep breath and tried to concentrate on the actual call rather than thinking about the one he had longed for.

"This is Yvonne Redmond at Worcester hospital. Your mother came in to us a few hours ago, and as you are on her paperwork as next of kin, I've called to explain what's happening."

"Oh. Is she ok? What's happened?"

"She's had a heart attack. Currently her condition is stable enough. She's on a drip and conscious."

"Ok. Thank you for telling me." He felt numb and the whole conversation seemed to be happening in slow motion.

"Your mother is very frail, Mr Cooper. She has a weak heart and could very easily experience another failure."

"You're saying she might die?"

"I'm not really qualified to comment on her prognosis. Perhaps you should come in and speak to the consultant?"

"Of course."

The idea of seeing his mother again filled Steven with dread. There would be guilt and recriminations. On the other hand, he still felt he had a duty to do what he could for her, and he could hardly leave her in hospital and not show his face. He called work and left a message on the answering machine, then checked the train times. All of his recent experiences shrank to negligible proportions. His newly found confidence dwindled, leaving him the awkward son once more. She had a knack for making him feel like a child, and a fool. Even without any direct contact, it had already started – as though his experiences this summer were just games he had been playing while she represented the greater truth.

Briefly, Steven toyed with the idea of telling his mother about Mindy, and Willow, the moot and the boar. He could already hear her scathing responses in his mind.

"What is this drivel? I don't understand a word of it."

Part of him wanted to ignore the call, pretend it hadn't happened and get on with his life. Other feelings tugged at him, demanding that he do the right thing and pay a visit. She could die. He tried to imagine what life would be like with her gone. When she finally departed, all hope of every being accepted by her would vanish too. He would never win her approval, earn a kind word, a hint of praise or any other proof that she thought well of him. He sighed quietly and made his preparations for leaving.

The shrunken form in the bed looked smaller than he remembered his mother being. He still thought of her as the gaunt but imposing figure who had dominated his childhood even though he'd grown to be significantly taller than her. For a moment he stood in the doorway to the ward, looking at her and making the most of not having been spotted. Steven's emotions were in turmoil and he wanted to be calm before he made his approach. Familiar feelings of apprehensions stole through him, coupled with a profound melancholy. There had never been much joy in their relationship. He had always feared her, he realised. That hadn't gone away. Separation from her made it more obvious to him; that was all. Her words, her anger, her resentment – they all contributed to the fabric of his anxieties and evidently he hadn't broken free of it yet. Even without speaking or looking at him, she had the power to destabilise his sense of self.

There was nothing overtly intimidating about this husk of a person however. Steven approached the bed cautiously, wondering what to say. Had he forgotten how ravaged she looked, or had she deteriorated still further over the preceding months? Her skin looked like old, dry leaves, he realised, and what hair she had left clung to her scalp. With sunken cheeks and colourless lips, shadowed eyes and deep frown lines she looked more than twenty years beyond than her true age. There was something horrifying about her state. She breathed slowly, apparently asleep, but as Steven approached the bed her eyes flickered open and she stared at him.

"I wasn't expecting to see you," she said, her voice as dry and husky as her skin.

"I came as soon as I could."

"Hmm. Didn't think for a moment you'd want to be bothered with me. After you abandoned me."

Steven felt himself slumping under her merciless gaze. "I really couldn't look after you anymore. I did what I could."

"You had me carted off to a nut house so you could get at my money. That's all you ever wanted from me, isn't it? Did you sell the house? Did you?"

"Yes."

"I knew it," she said triumphantly. "Just like your father."

Steven had nothing to say to this. He'd heard that accusation enough times before. She used it whenever she didn't like his behaviour. Sometimes he had wondered if he and his father would get along – if his mother was to be believed, they had a great deal in common, but none of it good.

"You're looking even fatter," she said. "You've been eating too much."

"How are you feeling?" he asked.

"Took you long enough to ask, didn't it? Bloody awful, if you must know. They should have let me die. It's not like anyone wants me around. I'm just a burden, aren't I? Just a worthless nuisance. That's what you think, isn't it? That's why you never came to visit me in all those months."

"No. I was just tired of the way you talk to me." The words came out before he'd really considered them, and Steven felt shocked to realise he had spoken his mind.

"And what's that supposed to mean?" she returned acidly.

For a moment he hesitated, half afraid to continue, but exhilarated by the possibility of telling her the truth for once. She had never wanted to listen to him, never cared for his opinions. When his feelings did not suit her she had simply ridiculed them, or told him off, depending on her mood. Having had a taste of freedom and a little kindness in his life, Steven saw her treatment of him as never before. She had been needlessly cruel, and nothing obliged him to put up with it anymore.

"Do you listen to yourself at all? Have you any idea how you come over? All my life you've done nothing but criticise me and put me down. Why would I want more of that?"

"That's not true. I don't know how you could think such a thing," the whine had returned to her voice, tapping into all his natural capacity for guilt. For the first time in his life, Steven resisted her.

"Well, let's see, shall we? Let's just consider today. Since I got here, you've accused me of not caring about what happens to you, of abandoning you, putting you in a home solely so I could get at your money, and being fat. Not bad for a five-minute conversation."

"I don't know what's got into you Steven. You used to be such a nice little boy, but you've become so horrible lately. I don't know what's gone wrong."

"You see what you want to see," he said, trying to speak gently despite his anger. "Think what you like. It doesn't matter anymore. So I'm not the person you want me to be. Live with it." As he spoke these few words, a feeling of release passed through him. Maybe he didn't need her blessings after all.

For a while, they stared at each other. In the past, Steven would have backed down, long before this, and slipped away to some quiet place where he could hide. He had spent his life accepting her criticisms, taking them deep inside him to erode his self-esteem. Looking at her now, he could see his mother's bitterness in her face, and the pathetic mess of her life became apparent to him. He didn't have to let her take him apart too.

"I'm not well, Steven, not well at all. You shouldn't talk to me like that."

"You've hidden behind that one for a long time, haven't you?" he said, a hint of accusation escaping through his voice. "And why are you ill? Because you won't eat and you won't look after yourself."

"You don't understand."

"No, perhaps I don't. My father left you. It happens to a lot of women, and a lot of men. Relationships break up. Most of them get over it. You chose not to. If this is how you want to live, how you want to be, then there's nothing I can do about it."

"How can you say that to me?"

"Surprisingly easily it turns out. I should have said it years ago. All I've done with my life is help you stay like this. It's not done either of us any good."

Her mouth dropped open slightly in wordless disbelief.

"You never have a good word to say about my father, so why waste your whole life pining for him? Or do you think that by starving yourself to death you're going to punish him somehow, or punish me?"

"I'm not trying to punish anyone."

"No? You don't want me to feel guilty for putting you in a home and not coming to visit sooner? You don't want me to feel bad about that?"

She stared at him, silent and unrelenting. Steven knew he couldn't win, because he'd made small attempts before – although nothing on this scale. She ignored challenges and anything that didn't fit in with her take on the world – he could see it all too plainly now. Living with her, he had been too close to see what she was doing to them both.

"What exactly do you want me to do?" he asked.

She remained silent, no longer even looking at him.

"Is there anything I can do that would be right? Anything at all?"

Still she said nothing.

"Fair enough. I think we both know where we stand then, don't we?"

"Mr Cooper?"

Steven turned to see a rather striking woman who he guessed must have Asian ancestry.

"Yes?"

"I'm Doctor Adkins. Would you come with me please?"

Feeling distinctly uncomfortable, Steven followed the woman to a small office just off the ward.

"You are Mrs Cooper's son, yes?"

"Yes."

"Your mother has had a heart attack because her heart muscles are very weak. The consequence of her anorexia in all probability. I understand she's been in care for some months now."

"Yes. What's going to happen to her?"

"Difficult to say. A lot depends on what she chooses to do. I can't keep her in here on a drip forever, and that won't enable her to gain weight. None of her internal organs are functioning well and any one of them could fail at any time. But I would be wary about giving a life expectancy. A year, two years. Hard to say."

Steven took a deep breath, having considered every possible prediction during his journey, he was somewhat prepared for this news. Even so, it shook him.

"Thank you for explaining," he said.

"There's very little you can do for her," Dr Adkins said. "Mrs Cooper seems entirely aware of the harm she has done herself and shows no signs of wanting to change her behaviour."

"She's been like this for a very long time."

"That's not surprising."

"I don't really want to stay any longer, unless there's anything else you need me to know or do?"

"We will notify you if there are any sudden changes. Thank you for coming in, Mr Cooper. She had been demanding that we contact you, and refused to accept that we had."

"She's a difficult woman."

Dr Adkins nodded. "Most people are when they're ill."

Steven considered returning to his mother. She could after all die at any moment, with the latest round of ill feeling unresolved between them. He knew there was only one way of making peace – he would have to offer an abject apology and accept that she had been right all along. His mother would not bend or compromise, and would starve herself to death before she admitted her mistake. He pitied her then, and the tragic waste of her life.

As he stepped out into the hospital car park, Steven caught sight of a distant figure in a trench coat. He shivered, expecting another encounter, but the man just walked away. He wondered if he'd just seen some harmless goth kid, but his heart told him otherwise.

The possibility of guilt fluttered in his mind for some time afterwards. What could he have done though? His mother had an evident intention of starving herself to death. Sooner or later, a part of her abused body would cease to function and she would die. There could be no other outcome unless she put in some considerable effort to save herself. It occurred to him then that he had supposed himself partly to blame for this. *But why?* His child self could not have been responsible for her choices, and by the time he reached adulthood, she was too entrenched in her ways for any hope of rescue. The Doctor evidently didn't consider him culpable. Why should he blame himself for his mother's condition?

As he walked away from the hospital, Steven realised he was free to choose. If he wanted to, he need never see the woman again, and if he did return, it would not be as a contrite penitent, bending to her will. He accepted that her approval was unobtainable, that he would never be able to win the affection he craved. But there were other people in the world who thought well enough of him, who gave second chances, and offered hugs. A lifetime of longing for the love he could never have had carved a hole inside him, and he knew that might always be there. But he could chose to forgive and forget, to move on and try and do more than pin his entire existence around this one flawed relationship. At the very least, he didn't need to make his mother's mistake all over again.

Chapter Twenty-Nine

For a long time, Steven sat with the wooden boar in his hands, trying to think things through. During the last three days, the ominous man had drifted close along the edges of his life, constantly haunting him. The gap between them closed daily, but Steven had no idea where this might lead. There were no words, no direct encounters and no explanations. Every so often he would happen to glance round, and there the man would be, distant, watchful and quietly menacing. Things couldn't go on like this – he couldn't concentrate properly on anything. The need to find a solution pushed him deeper into himself, looking for answers and insights. He had none. Confess to anyone outside the pagan community that he was being harassed by a man invisible to others, and he could expect to be treated like he was delusional. The fear that he might be out of his mind came and went sporadically, making a hard situation worse.

"I can't fight you," he said aloud. Talking required him to assemble his thoughts into coherent forms, and he found it helped. "I can't destroy you, but I don't want to carry on like this, so what else is there?"

He glanced up at the Spirit of Arden painting on his wall, distracted by a moment of wonder and the feelings of hope she inspired in him. Those painted eyes seemed so full of compassion and wisdom. He would have given almost anything to hear her speak then.

"I haven't given up on you," he told the picture. "I just don't know what to do."

The flat felt even emptier than usual. Steven found the quiet oppressive, but it was late and he couldn't justify calling anyone. At least he had an autumn equinox ritual to look forward to on the following day, where there would be people to talk to. He considered going over to Helen's shop, but it was late already and she might well have gone home. Perhaps next week he would drop round to let her laugh at his paranoia, and that would alleviate this loneliness a little. He'd just tended to assume no one would want him around, he realised. That reason had kept him away from people for years. He expected rejection, but there were a few people now who appeared willing to put up with him. Everything he had assumed to be true of himself and his life looked suspect in light of his recent discoveries.

Steven lay back on the bed, closing his eyes and silencing the many competing voices in his thoughts. If he'd learned nothing else this year, that one meditation trick had proved invaluable. Gradually, his mind stilled. He considered calling for the boar to watch over him, but chose not to. It might be better to do this alone. A safety net could just get in the way.

There were layers to reality, as far as he could make out. The physical world around him was overlaid with a spirit realm, close to the tangible world, interlaced with it, but different in many subtle ways. Part of his own spirit could wander there, but his body could not. Concentrating hard, Steven envisaged himself leaving the bed, exiting the flat and walking down the echoing stairs. He imagined the familiar orange glow of street lamps and the noise of occasional traffic. Having no idea where to go, he pictured himself walking the route from the flat to Helen's shop. He couldn't recall much about most of the buildings clearly, but odd details came into sharper focus as he remembered them. Not long after setting out, he felt eyes upon him. Turning, he could see nothing, but remained certain the ominous man was close by.

For what seemed like hours, they hunted each other through the streets. Looming buildings stuck out at improbable angles against the night sky. There were no cars, but the hum of them, came and went intermittently, like listening to an un-tuned radio. A silhouette paused at the end of a road, watching and waiting. As soon as Steven headed towards it, it took off at a run. There were other things abroad in this place, he realised: Entities that skittered away from him or hid in the near darkness to watch. What they were, he didn't know, and he missed the boar's guidance and protection.

Steven had odd glimpses of his quarry, but for a long time he never drew close enough to get a proper look. Several times, he thought the dark man was watching him from a hidden vantage point. The niggling feeling of vulnerability ate into his nerves. They were playing some complex game, but Steven had the disadvantage of not knowing any of the rules. Eventually, he stopped trying, and just stood, waiting and wondering. Running and chasing hadn't done him much good so he supposed he had nothing to lose in trying a passive approach.

"Come and find me, if that's what you want. I'm not messing about anymore. Let's just get this over with."

Although he could see no visible changes, he felt the attentiveness of another presence, listening to his words and considering action.

"What do you want with me?" Steven asked. All the previous answers he'd had to this question didn't make much sense.

The ominous man appeared before him, taller than Steven remembered, and almost skeletal; the bones in his face showing all too clearly. The man's smile offered no hint of warmth.

"You have to let me in."

"In where?" Steven asked.

"Into your life, your heart, your soul. I will be in you, live in you."

"And if I refuse?"

"Then I will drive you mad. I will tear your mind apart, one small piece at a time."

"Why?"

"Because that is my desire and my intention. I will be your life and your death."

A chill crept through Steven's spirit form, making the solidity of his body seem all the more distant. Waves of hatred rolled over him, tasting of bitterness, malice and malevolence. The ominous man made him shudder inwardly, and long to be away from here, but he held firm, refusing to be frightened away so easily. The various alternative responses he could make flashed through his thoughts, none any more encouraging than its fellows. Ignore the entity threatening him, and things would be unlikely to improve. Fighting him hadn't worked. There might be occult means of protection, or that could exorcise the spirit, but Steven had no idea where to get that kind of help and no certainty it would work. Let this nightmare have its own way with him, and he suspected he would end up just like Mindy; driven from his wits and welcoming death with open arms. He imagined it would feed on him in some way, and then go on to its next victim.

Thinking of Mindy warmed him slightly. For all the suffering that had resulted from their connection, the innocent memories of sitting beside her cheered him. They had shared the midsummer sunrise, talked together, walked side by side. Those were companionable moments, full of optimism on his part at least. His thoughts turned to Helen, and from her, to Heathen John and their shared breakfast. Cheerful moments of working with Kevin occurred to him. Each good memory wrapped itself around him; a gauzy shield against the malice he faced. Finally, he thought of Willow, of the light in her eyes and the grace of her movements. He had been fully alive in her company, and the memory of it gave him fresh strength.

Steven imagined all those better moments from the recent past, feeling again the complex but positive emotions each had evoked. He stared at the ominous man, conscious of the ill will there, but no longer at the mercy of it. The seething mass of anger and cruel intent before him seemed brittle now: Hard perhaps, but fragile with it. It could be broken, shattered and scattered in countless fragments.

"You could do it," the ominous man hissed. "Why not? I tortured that girl until she bled for me. You could make it all stop. Have your revenge. Finish me. Explode me into a thousand little pieces."

And *each of those pieces nastier than the last* Steven realised with a jolt. If the uncanny man was egging him on to such an attempt, he had the suspicion the results would not be what he wanted. *Respond to it in kind, with anger and violence, and it grows stronger. But what does that leave?*

Steven took a step forward. His eyes locked with the flashing orbs in the uncanny man's face. They looked nothing like eyes when it came to the detail, and were just glowing points of unnatural light. The face before him held no beauty at all. Every line of it looked bleak and harsh, made for sneering and tormenting. None of the features seemed quite proportionate to the others, while the skin looked waxy and inhuman. Getting closer, he could see there were no real clothes beneath that impression of a trench coat – only shifting darkness.

The man laughed, the sound of it hollow and mocking. "Do I disgust you?"

Steven examined the thin, pale lips, the small, sunken eyes with their uncanny light and the sharp, ugly nose. He had never particularly believed that beauty equated to goodness, but had the feeling this thing wore its evil on the surface. A pleasant temperament might smooth those features with smiles and good humour, but everything about the face spoke of cruelty. Whatever lurked behind those eyes meant to cause harm.

Reaching out, Steven placed a hand on the ominous man's shoulder. It felt real enough to him, although he had half expected his fingers to pass right through. When he placed his second hand on the other shoulder, he saw a flicker of something across the ominous man's twisted features. *Uncertainty.* They were close now, chests a matter of inches apart. Steven became conscious of a smell rising up from the other man. The sickliness of a dead thing, mingled with bitter sweat, and other rank, putrid flavours.

It took all of the determination Steven could muster to see his hastily assembled plan through. Ignoring the vile smell, the dangerous eyes and the ever-present aura of malevolence, he leaned across those last few inches and pressed his lips against the deathly cold ones of his nemesis. The taste of earthy decay filled his mouth. The feeling of rising bile and disgust made him remember his body. Sickness would drive him back into that slumbering shell and there might never be another chance like this. He steeled himself, determined not to let repugnance overwhelm him.

The ominous man did not pull away, nor did he show any sign of resistance. Steven knew he must go further. His hands spread out over the man's narrow back, feeling a landscape of sharp bumps and protrusions beneath his fingers. He pulled the thing closer, pressing it against him, accepting the full extent of its horror. The being writhed, making the inhuman sharpness of its protruding bones obvious under his hands. Images of death and decay stormed his mind, of rotting corpses whose worm-laden tongues battered against his own, skeletal hands digging fingers into his skin. For a moment he thought he had given the spirit what it wanted, allowing it into him. It would take his body, and rend it apart from within.

The intimacy of contact made him all the more aware of the man's anger, as the rage reached out to touch him, filling his head with images of destruction. His grip held firm and it did not escape from him. Steven embraced his tormentor, clinging tightly to the hard, cold form, refusing to let go even though it repulsed him. For as long as he could remember, his greatest fantasy of all had been to embrace someone. He had never dared go beyond that, even in thought. To hold, and be held, locked close together in an overt gesture of love. Instead, he had this terrible parody of desire, clinging to the form of something he hated and which had sought his destruction.

"Good for nothing," the ominous man whispered. "You drove Mindy to nearly kill herself, not me. You made your mother hate you. Without you, she would have been happy."

The closer they came, the more readily this nightmare could feed upon his fears and regurgitate them to stimulate more. Steven felt as though every deep-seated anxiety and each moment of regret were rushing up to the surface of his awareness. A veritable sea of tiny mistakes threatened to drown him. Cold laughter echoed around him and his grip on the ominous man slackened slightly. He could not hold on, not in face of this – he lacked the strength, the courage, the worthiness.

"Why do you think your father left?" the ominous man asked. "You. Your fault. Little monster. Little shit. You ruined everything and he hated you for it."

In desperation, Steven tried to find some good thought to cling to. All the self-hatred locked away down the years had broken free.

"But you don't want to win. You don't want to destroy me, you want me to make it easy for you. You want to be broken and trampled on. You know you are worth nothing. I can teach you how to be nothing, and the world will be so much better a place when you are gone from it."

Clarity flashed through the fog of his despair. Steven thought of the lost forest, and the tranquillity he had known amongst those dreams of trees. Holding tight to his memories of this, he refused to succumb to the allure of self-loathing. The desire for destruction flowed through him and around him, but he did not lose control of himself even as its currents took him. He clung on again, more determined now than ever. The desire to ruin and destroy became all too clear in his mind. The ominous man's poison filled him and he could understand it, even though he did not let it overwhelm him this time. Hatred for all things generous and lovely entered his mind. Resentment of anything that did not suffer. Steven saw the creature in his arms for what it was – a being born of misery and isolation, hating all it was not. In that moment of insight, the last of his anger melted away, to be replaced by compassion. As that emotion swelled within him, the ominous man grew limp in his arms.

Steven parted his lips, feeling the flow of liquid darkness fill his mouth. The taste of it was worse than the smell had been. He longed to spit it out, forcing this rankness from his body. Still he stuck to his plan, determined to see it through. He kissed the dark man, giving utterly of himself, trying to put all the warmth, joy and love he could remember into that most intimate expression. With so little of his own to draw upon, it was hard to give, but he held nothing back. Bitterness flowed between his lips, along with age old decay and festering negativity. He took it all inside him, feeling the grim weight of it in his guts.

He would have kissed Mindy this way, given the chance. Memories of the love affair that had never been filled him with tenderness and compassion, which he lavished upon the strange creature in his arms. In dreams, he had shared embraces with the spirit of Arden, finding her playful and generous in her affections. He had learned from those unreal encounters, knowing how to convey passion and desire in the movement of his lips. The ominous man dissolved into him, melted by slow degrees and coming apart in face of this unconventional form of attack. Steven swallowed him down, taking drip after drip of that sinister essence. His mouth and throat burned with ingesting it, but he did not let up. Remembering the way the boar had consumed him not so long ago, he sought to replicate the trick, imprisoning this troubled being within him.

Naively, he had believed darkness to be familiar. Between the anguish Mindy had shown him and the miseries created by his mother, Steven thought he knew the midnight of the soul, that he had seen the worst. Those experiences seemed trivial compared to the thing he had ingested. The weight and breadth of torment within him went beyond anything he had experienced or imagined. Pain without end or reason. Hunger that could find no satisfaction. At the centre of it, emptiness, and that seemed the worst of all.

All outward signs of the ominous man had gone, but Steven could feel him all too keenly, down in the depths of his being, full of poison and resentment.

Chapter Thirty

By the light of a lone candle, a girl scratches runes into her pale skin. Drops of crimson blood trickle down her arms, one drips onto the bare floor beneath her. She watches it with curiosity, as though unaware that this is her own life force. With her full lips pursed, she works another mark into her skin, then catches up a few drops of blood on her fingertips and repeats the design on the exposed floorboards. Her concentration makes her look childish, but even so she can be little more than fourteen.

Her eyes are red, her cheeks puffy and blotched from crying. She does not weep now. The knife brings respite. She hurts, endlessly, but the physical pain makes the emotional distress easier to bear somehow. She cuts herself, and the blood pushes back the shadows. She knows they are there, beyond the circle of candlelight. They wait for her on the edges of sleep. They come to her in nightmares. Most nights, she wakes crying. No one hears her. She would not want their comfort anyway. She thinks she is too old for that now.

Moonlight streams in through opened curtains. She huddles against the wall, thin legs drawn up under her chin, knuckles white from gripping too hard as she hugs herself. Her eyes glisten and shine as she whispers to ward off her terror. These are not the prayers she learned at school, but other ones of her own making, like the blood symbols drawn around her bed. She is never entirely safe, but they help a little and she has to try or there will be no hope left. There are four hours until dawn. If she can stay awake that long, perhaps it will be all right. When she sleeps in daylight, the nightmares seldom come. Her parents do not like her sleeping late. They wake her. Chastise her for staying up all night. They assume she has been reading, sneaking downstairs to watch late night television, or listening to music. They do not ask why she fears to sleep and she takes this for disinterest. She is right. They would not believe the harrowing extremes of her emotional life even if she told them.

Staying awake is difficult. Being cold helps. Her body will not rest if she keeps it tense and chilly. The quilt seems so alluring, so warm and inviting. All she wants to do is lay her head down on the pillow and rest, but if she does, the nightmares will come again. They have given her no peace of late. Alcohol does not comfort her anymore and she fears the doctor too much to ask for help. She is sure they will think she is mad. There is no one who can help her. She thinks about the knife, but if she cuts herself too often someone might notice. This is not a cry for help. She doesn't want anyone to see.

A boy at school gives her a joint, and she sleeps easily afterwards. For a while, cannabis is her obsession. All of her money goes on procuring it. Each night she opens her bedroom window and draws the sweet smoke into her lungs. For a few glorious weeks it works and she imagines this must be what normal people feel like. Her thoughts become clearer. She feels less alone. Gradually, the bad dreams regain control, and it takes more and more weed to let her sleep. She takes money from her mother's purse, but this cannot last. She needs something stronger. Now she knows there might be a way of protecting herself, she has to keep trying. She wants to live, and this, to her, is self-medication.

They show her how to heat it up, how to use the needle. The familiar rush of pain as the metal enters her skin feels like an old friend. Then it is in her veins, painkiller for the soul, smoothing away all memory of suffering, letting her float and drift. She could stay here forever, if she had the money for another dose. This is the way she wants to die, high on heroine and oblivious to everything. She daydreams about taking an overdose, but never gets there. Once, and only once, but it is enough to open a door and let something come through.

He comes out of the haze of pain, blood and narcotics. "You want death?" he asks. His voice is a balm, a sweet caress.

"I want the pain to stop," she tells him.

"I can make it better," he promises in honeyed tones.

"What must I do?"

He tells her, late in the night when she can hardly think. He comes amidst the tripping, the wild highs and drunken melancholies.

She wonders how her parents haven't noticed, guesses they aren't looking. They see what they want to see, just like everyone else. Sometimes she thinks she has become invisible. He sees her, and when his barely audible voice comes out of the darkness, she feels relief. It is like the blessing of a good knife edge, giving her a different kind of suffering to offset the torments in her heart.

He guides her through strange rituals. She has always thought of herself as a witch and now his presence confirms that. Following his orders makes her feel powerful, as though she is the one in control, even though she knows she isn't. The magic burns in her veins, a whole new drug with which to blot everything out. She is bringing him through, making him real. He will save her.

He does not save her.

The old nightmares are nothing to this. At least she could wake from those. Now she hardly knows whether she is conscious or dreaming. He comes for her whenever she is alone, ice-cold hands on her body, vicious words on his lips. He tells her how much she likes it, wants it, needs it. There are days when she believes him, and that frightens her more than anything else.

When she fails several of her exams, her parents realise all is not well. They ask hard questions, which she answers partially. There are many things she cannot confess, but she says enough and they take immediate action. There are doctors and psychiatrists, help to get off the drugs. They will clean her up and make her normal again. There will be counselling, and she is going to be fine, they tell her. Why didn't she tell anyone when it happened? Why didn't she go to the police then, or the doctor or someone, anyone? All of this could have been avoided if only she had spoken up sooner, she is told. This does not comfort her. Mindy does not know how to explain that she knows how this goes and could not face the questions, the humiliations, disbelief, slut-shaming, and the odds of nothing being done to the young man who started all of this.

She knows that nothing will ever make her normal but there is no point telling them. They would not understand. She does not tell the psychiatrist about the unreal man who has become all too real. Instead, they focus on her self-harming and the trauma and she lets them think it is all her own work. She does not explain how the man who haunts her nights bit her and raked her skin. They probably wouldn't believe her anyway. She is not sure she wants them to know and believe. That might be worse. The solid, human lad who forced her is easier to talk about, but only slightly. Going into those memories is hellish and suddenly everyone wants her to repeat the details. Over and over, making her feel that she will never be free of it, never allowed to forget.

They do manage to clean her up, chemically speaking. Without the drugs, the phantom in her head does not appear so often. Still she does not feel safe. Without the drugs, there is nothing to insulate her from the rest of reality. There is so much horror out there, so much needless brutality. She is too sensitive to bear it. The news programs make her cry. She does not want to be here in this too-hard, too-cold world. There is only one way out, but she is too afraid to try it. Mostly she cannot sleep at night.

It is Halloween; night of cheap horror films, plastic tat and cheap candy. She walks among the tombstones, feeling safer with the dead than with the living. Death could be a friend, she thinks. There is a woman here too, moving amongst the oldest graves, touching the unreadable stones. They are so old that erosion and lichen have wiped away their words. Anyone could lie there, or no one at all. The woman strews flowers on the graves. They can't all be her relatives.

"What are you doing?" Mindy asks.

"Honouring the dead," the woman replies with a warm and friendly voice.

"Oh."

The woman walks over, her face looks kindly. "I assumed you were doing the same thing," she said.

"Sort of. Are you a witch?"

"Yes."

She has come home. She feels it at once. There is a place for her in the world after all. She is not alone and cannot recall the last time she felt this much happiness.

"What's your name?" the witch woman asks.

"Miranda." She says it without thinking and then wishes she hadn't, because it has never sat comfortably with her. She should have said something else, something cooler and more mysterious. If there is a name to fit her, she hasn't found it yet.

"I always feel closer to the ancestors tonight," says the woman.

"I thought Halloween was just an American thing. Trick or treating and all that crap."

"It's also Samhain, Celtic festival of the dead," the witch told her.

"Seriously? That's so cool."

"How old are you, Miranda?"

"Eighteen." The lie is automatic.

"If you want to learn more, you could come to the moot."

He is never far from her. She can see him in her peripheral vision, but if she turns and looks there is no sign of him. Even after all this time, she doesn't know what he is, but understands no one else knows he is there. Elspeth teaches her how to cast a protective circle, but this only holds true while she is awake. Sleep betrays her. Nothing keeps him at bay for long. There is no relief in the blades anymore. Pain draws him closer, makes him stronger. He twists her perceptions and there are days when she cannot be sure what really happens. No one else seems to see it. She can pass as normal, she has learned the trick over the last few years, but inside her head, nothing is ever good.

This is a new horror. She thought she knew all about fear, but he has gone further than before. She sees his face, pushing through the skin of another, leering at her with perverse delight. How he loves to see her distress. There is so much more he can do with a physical body. He has marked her before, but she knows it requires great effort for him to bruise or break her skin. Possessing the body of another, he could do anything to her. For now he just lets her see the threat. There is no one she can trust. If she lets anyone else get close to her, he can enter them, possess them and use them to hurt her.

Then Steven pulls away from her, his face confused. She has to get this man away from her, for both their sakes. Her demon will destroy them both, she knows this. He can poison anything good in her life. She must not let this happen again.

The allure of blades is so strong now. There are so many ways of doing it – slash the wrists or the throat, plunge the blade deep into the body cavity. She thinks about it endlessly, obsessing over the choices, wondering whether there is any point to living. An overdose. A noose, if only there was somewhere sturdy enough to hang one. Walk in front of a bus. Stop eating and drinking. Flood the room with gas and strike a match. Drink bleach. Her small kitchen offers so many ways of escaping, and the whispers in her head say 'do it' and promise that afterwards there will be more pain at all. She does not trust them. Why would they tell her the truth? They have never been friends to her. But even so, death sings her to sleep at night, and she cries on waking to find she must face another day. She does not want to live, but lacks the determination to end it. Her death would inconvenience others – her landlord, her parents. How can she justify that? Still the thoughts come – how easy it would be to find a river and drown in it, or drink so much water that it destroys her cells.

There are days when it takes all the courage she can find simply to get out of the flat and not harm herself. She thinks herself a coward for not having the guts to take her own life. Although she never speaks of it, she believes she has no right to live, that her existence is just a waste of resources. Suicide looks like the most environmentally friendly option; her way of contributing to not overpopulating the planet. It might be the only worthwhile things she ever does. She hopes it will bring oblivion, and absolute end to all awareness. The idea of an afterlife of any kind terrifies her. She does not want to exist, and wishes she had never been born in the first place.

There is only one way out. Most days she doesn't feel brave enough to do what is called for. For all of her self-hatred, life is a hard thing to let go of. It is all she has. What, beyond the grind of moving from one day to another, is there left to fight for? She can see her future stretching before her, full of fear. Even if her torturer vanished tomorrow, she would never stop waiting for his return. She would never feel safe, never be able to fully trust anyone, least of all herself. It does not seem like a life worth living. If she stays, then he may grow stronger, and more adept at taking over the bodies of others. What then? How many lives would he be able to blight? If she ends it now then perhaps she can take him with her, and do some small good.

The blood calls to him. He comes to watch, to gloat. The bath is warm, and it seems so easy finally to let go and forget.

"It gets worse than this," he tells her. "Life is so much better than what comes next."

"I don't care. It doesn't matter anymore."

"You won't be free of me, not even then."

"I don't believe you."

"Haven't you understood anything? I am you. I am all the monstrosity your nasty little mind could conceive of. You want to be punished. You want to suffer. That is why you made me."

"No," she breathes, but it is harder to shape the words now.

"Oh yes. Why can no one else see me? I'm you and I am yours and wherever you go, I go with you."

She cannot find the strength to answer. It doesn't matter. The creature is a thing of lies, and the greatest mistake she ever made was to trust it. She doubts it is telling her the truth now. Soon enough, all will be revealed. She hopes there is nothing on the other side of the darkness, that it all ends here. In the distance, she hears banging on her door and a familiar voice shouting her name.

"Mindy, if you're in there, just shout through the door so I know you're ok. Talk to me! Please Mindy just talk to me."

Chapter Thirty-One

The first thing Steven registered on waking was the awful smell. Initially he couldn't identify it but as he became aware of the stickiness, and the moisture surrounding him he had a nasty feeling about where the grim odours might be coming from. Sitting up, his worries were soon confirmed. All around him, the bed was covered in bodily excretions. Vomit. Urine. The dark brown stain of liquid shit. He could feel the unpleasant fullness of his undergarments. Never before in his adult life had he done anything like this. Once, as a child he had accidentally filled his pants thanks to a stomach bug. He could remember the list of things his mother had called him. "Filthy little runt" being by far the kindest.

With a light head and a painfully dry mouth to distract him, Steven couldn't think too clearly. He knew he had to sort the mess out, but where to start? He stripped off, depositing his ruined clothes in with the rest of the mess on his bed. Once he had showered, and his skin felt like his own again, he felt more able to deal with what had happened. Revolting though it smelled, he could cope. He'd cleaned up after his mother before now, so why should he own accident be any more of a problem? The whole mess of soiled fabric went neatly into one bin bag, while the mattress protector wiped down readily enough. Thankfully, he had kicked the duvet onto the floor and it seemed to have suffered no ill effects from his incontinence.

Only when he had the kettle boiling for a much needed coffee, did it occur to Steven he had no idea what time it was. There seemed to have been a power strike. None of his clocks were working and they all flashed different times at him. Flicking the television on, he skimmed through the channels looking for something to indicate the time. Only when he caught a news bulletin did he realise things were awry. According to the anchorman, it was Sunday the twenty third of September. He'd gone to bed on Friday the twenty first to try his spirit journeying and could scarcely believe he had slept that long. On the other hand, it went some way of explaining the disgusting mess in his bed. His stomach ached, and felt rather like it had done a few years ago when he had been struck down by food poisoning.

Then it crossed his mind that he had missed Diana's Autumn Equinox ritual. He hurried to the phone. She picked up after the first ring.

"Is that you Steven? I wondered where you'd got to."

"I've been ill. Touch of food poisoning I think. I was so out of it yesterday that I didn't even manage to call. I'm sorry. Did it go ok?"

"Good thanks. Are you better now?"

"On the mend thanks. I'll see you at the next moot, yes?"

"All being well, I'll be there."

Her voice, on the end of the phone, offered a much needed injection of normality and reason. The coffee helped too, grounding him and easing the ache in his skull. Piece by piece, his memories returned. Fragments of what seemed like strange dreams mingled with memories of his spirit walk. It took him a while to assemble those impressions in a coherent order.

Had he really glimpsed something of Mindy's life? Steven didn't really believe he could have imagined something so elaborate and horrible. Had those images come to him because he had eaten the man who haunted her? If so, did that mean the creature was what it claimed to be – a part of her? He had no idea what to believe, but there were things in his head now that frightened him, and a bad feeling in his stomach that seemed entirely consistent with having consumed something vile.

A cold wind sprang up, suggesting the first bites of autumn in the air. Steven walked out to Sandwell Park, feeling too confined in his flat, and in his head. The impressions gathered during his long journey were too intense to be written off as just dreams. It all seemed very real and being in a more normal environment did nothing to dispel that impression. Thinking back over everything, his insight during the spirit journey made sense. Mindy's continual wearing of long gloves might well have hidden evidence of self-harming. Her peculiar responses to him during their ill-fated encounter all fitted together with what he had seen. A lone voice in his thoughts still cried out that he was lying to himself, finding any excuse to not take responsibility for it all. Even in accepting his latest experience, there remained several things he didn't understand. Had she shaped that entity out of her inner demons, or had the anguish he'd glimpsed been the product of that entity abusing her psyche for years?

He had never really considered the implications of believing in malevolent spirits. His own dark days seemed modest enough compared to his visions of Mindy at her worst. *But what of other people? The ones who hear voices telling them to kill people, or harm themselves. What if the voices are real? What if my voices are real?* There had been enough times when he couldn't be sure if the ideas in his head were his own, or coming from elsewhere. What if there were beings full of malice and hunger, preying on the unwary? The idea made him shiver far more than the wind had. If he accepted the existence of the boar as an ally then why not believe there could also be dangerous things stalking oblivious humans?

There were children on the playground, laughing and chasing each other. He stopped for a while to watch them, drawn by the innocence of their laughter, their bright and lively noise. Steven didn't stay too long, conscious that as a single male, his interest might look threatening. Another dark thought to add to the many others swirling in his head.

A flash of movement drew his attention to a woman perhaps a hundred yards from him. She turned a cartwheel, then flipped from hands to feet in a smooth arc. Fascinated, he watched her gymnastics for a while, sunlight catching in her auburn hair. Steven set off in her direction, unable to think of a better plan, but intent on not looking like a threat. As he came closer, she stopped, brushing an unruly fringe out of her face and watching him. For a moment, she shone a brilliant smile in his direction. Assuming the bright welcome must be for someone else, Steven looked away, but when he glanced back, he could see no sign of her. He turned rapidly, viewing the park in all directions, but identifying no one who resembled the cartwheeling woman. It didn't entirely surprise him. There were many strange moments in life, he decided, if you paid enough attention to spot them and didn't try to convince yourself they hadn't happened.

There were small flowers growing in the grass where she had been and the nearby trees had countless tiny heads of toadstools pushing up amongst their roots. He had never seen so many together in one place before. High above him, the clouds shifted, and for a while the sun broke through, warming his skin and tinting the flower bedecked ground in front of the trees with gold. The beauty of it touched his soul and he felt blessed by the warmth and loveliness before him. There might be nightmarish things in the world, but there was goodness too. *Important not to lose sight of that.* However bad life might be, there would still be sunlight, flowers, the wonder of a tree with the first hints of autumn in its leaves. *It depends on what you choose to see.*

With his back against a tree trunk, Steven felt more secure than he had for a while. The distant sounds of children at play made it harder to think of troubled experiences. Closing his eyes, he thought only of the warm light permeating his eyelids, filling his awareness. It shone into him, illuminating every part of his being, down into the depths of his own fears and doubts. Sunlight filtered through even to the last recess where a tangled mass of serrated intentions still managed to retain its form. Partially broken and entirely consumed though it had been the ominous man had not gone. It merely rested inside him, biding its time and gathering what strength it could. He had not defeated it, just slowed it down for a while. He could see it now, and while it troubled him, he no longer felt afraid.

Steven coughed, his throat inexplicably tickly, as though he had swallowed a feather. When the first attempt at clearing his throat failed, he tried again, until a fit had hold of him. He leaned against the tree for support, hacking and gasping in turn. Then his guts began to retch and twist as well, until he doubled up and crumpled to his knees. The thing inside him rose and he could not stop it even if he wanted to.

It felt like a ball of barbed wire coming up from deep inside him. Its passing made his eyes water, and he couldn't work out if he should fight to keep it in, or let it go. Both options seemed equally unpleasant. Inch by slow inch, his body forced the thing out, rejecting it as an unwelcome visitor. He couldn't digest it. With a final, heaving cough it tore through his lips, tasting of metal and old death.

Steven saw a small, dark cloud hovering just above the grass. No bigger than his fist, it appeared shapeless, featureless, but he sensed its bile all too clearly. He made a grasp for it, but it slipped through his fingers like mist. It would not be destroyed so easily. Compared to what it had been, it didn't seem especially dangerous but even so it might latch on to someone else, to feed as it had done before. From past endeavours, he knew that any attempted violence would nourish it rather than destroy it, and restrained himself.

Steven tried to laugh. At first it sounded fake, but as he looked at the little ball of anger in front of him and saw how unimpressive it was, the laughter became genuine, rising up from his gut just as the remains of the ominous man had done. The much reduced spirit paled slightly, and moved away from him, surrendering to the wind. Steven watched as it rose like an abandoned balloon, lifting over the treetops and vanished into the grey of the sky.

He bought an ice-cream from a van and stood eating it. No one paid him any attention whatsoever. The sweet, melting flavours of vanilla and raspberry trickled into him, soothing the recent traumas his mouth and throat had suffered. It surprised him that the experience had been so acutely real. The spirit world did not appear to be so far removed from this as he'd been led to believe. Steven licked the last traces of ice-cream from his fingertips, savouring the sweetness and the pleasure of transgression. That was one old ghost he'd almost laid to rest. Why shouldn't he eat in public? Plenty of other people did and he didn't find them disgusting. Why shouldn't he eat whatever he liked, whenever he felt like it? There only laws against it were the weird ones cooked up in his mother's head. Those were her problems, and he didn't have to be governed by them. He could spit that out and let it float away on the breeze as well. Only when he'd got rid of it all would he be able to find out who he could be.

Maybe I need a new name. Something that doesn't belong to the past or represent who I have been. If I give up this name, and Steven Cooper, and everything that goes with it, I'll be able to work out who I am and what I want.

Where he would find a new name, he had no idea, but it felt like the beginning of a new quest, and he liked that. There were things he still needed to do for Mindy, and he would have to figure out how to go about it, but he no longer felt the weight of her suffering so keenly. It did not seem like his fault anymore, and he realised how much guilt he had been carrying over her attempted suicide. He was not to blame. Even if he had worked everything out at the time, the chances were he could not have done much for her. That seemed entirely clear now.

Chapter Thirty-Two

"You've done well," the boar said.

"Thank you."

"It would be beyond you to destroy such a being. As well not to waste your energies trying the impossible."

"I'd figured that, but I don't like the idea of it being out there."

"All things have their place. Where would we be without challenges? How would we grow?"

Steven said nothing to this. He didn't much like the answer, but could see the boar's point.

"And where are we going today?" the boar enquired.

"I don't know. Where do I need to go?"

"Hmm."

Steven climbed onto the boar's back, conscious of its wiry hairs beneath his hand. A part of him remained aware of his body, stretched out beneath the duvet. He wasn't as fully engaged with this journey as he had been in the previous one, but given what such intense journeying had done to his body, it seemed as well not to get so involved this time round.

"Correct," the boar said. "I won't let you go too far. You could have asked me to guard you."

"I think I needed to do that one myself."

"Your call."

The boar set off at a trot, travelling through what seemed like a series of dream sequences. The images around them blurred, bleeding into each other until only a smear of colours remained. As the boar slowed again, the colours coalesced into a fresh scene.

"Where are we?" Steven asked.

"You tell me."

Steven looked around him. It appeared to be early in the year, but the garden had high grass in it already. The place had an overgrown, uncared for feel to it. Nestling in the long grass, a small boy watched a beetle.

"That's me," Steven said with a start of recognition. He hadn't realised at first. The scrawny thing with a mop of windblown hair and grubby face didn't look much like his recollections.

"I'm thinner," he said. "How did that happen?"

The boy crawled back through the long grass to a makeshift den, fashioned from a large cardboard box and an old tablecloth. He slithered in, with enough room to sit alongside two well-loved bears. There was a tiny plastic tea pot with plates and cups improvised from the lids of old pots. The young Steven set about making a tea party, talking to his bears in careful whispers.

"Where are you, Steven?" a woman called from outside.

He shoved the tea things behind him. "In my house," he called.

A face appeared in the opening. "Are you playing another food game? You're obsessed with food. You'll end up fat like Granny Cooper."

The face went away again, leaving the boy with his head hanging.

"I don't remember Granny Cooper," he said to the boar. "She died when I was quite young."

"No memory is ever truly lost," the boar said. "Let's see if we can find her."

The warmth of arms around him and an amble bosom on which to lay his head. Wonderful aromas he hadn't known how to name then, but recognised now: Fresh bread, soap, lavender. A house full of warmth and food smells. Neither of his parents seemed happy there. His mother never wanted to go while his father spent the time on edge. The two women did not like each other. Steven could see that now. His grandmother, the full-figured earth goddess, giver of cake and sweet tea. His mother, bone thin and disgusted by the fat old woman who baked too much, ate too much and seemed unjustifiably happy.

In those strong, well-padded arms he had felt safe from the very first. She always had a smile for him, and a bit of something nice for him to eat.

"That boy's too thin, mark my words. You don't feed him properly."

"I don't want you giving him all that fatty stuff. And he's not to have salt. You put salt in everything."

"You need salt to live."

"Salt's bad for you. Don't you listen to the news? He's not to have any salt at all. Do you understand me?"

Then his grandmother would huff, puff and put the kettle on, preferring to be in the kitchen than around his mother. Steven would go to her as soon as he could, following her around and watching whatever she did. He was always hungry; a single fact that dominated all his childhood memories. Granny Cooper had cake and cheese, biscuits, and more. The older woman had no qualms about defying his mother, and the boy often went home with something good in his pocket. Food became a sin very early in his life. Then there came a time when Granny simply wasn't there anymore. Nothing was said, and he had already learned not to ask too many questions.

"What of your father?" the boar asked.

"I never really knew him. He's a shape in my memory, but nothing more. We weren't close. He worked away a lot, and worked late. I didn't see much of him, and when I did, I never knew what to say to him. I was quite young when he left. I felt like it was my fault."

"Why?"

"Everything else seemed to be my fault, it made sense. I didn't have any other explanations."

"Did he leave your mother instead?"

"Looking back it seems likely, but at the time that never crossed my mind."

"Did you never try and keep in touch or try to find him?"

"I didn't think there was any point. I didn't think he would want to hear from me."

"There is still time, if you want to try. He might have a different story for you. Another version of events. Perhaps you should hear that."

The scene shifted again and Steven saw himself in his mid-teens, pulling on a school jumper that he had long since grown out of. The arms were too short and it clung to his body ridiculously. His mother stood in the doorway behind him, her faced pinched and badly made-up.

"You've put on weight," she said. "I told you, you've been eating too much. You're getting fat. Who's going to want you looking like that? You look like a pig."

The boy Steven looked into the mirror, his expression sorrowful. His shoulders slumped a little lower.

"Does he look fat to you?" the boar asked.

Steven considered the figure before him, trying to look objectively rather than seeing what he had always seen in the mirror. The boy looked fairly normal – his skin wasn't good, it looked too pale and rather dry, but he wasn't overweight. He remembered the scene vaguely – there had been others like it and they had long since blurred together. Looking into the mirror at the time he had seen his unsightliness. Every spare ounce on him had seemed like a great sweating roll of pure lard. He had been ashamed of his body even then, convinced of its ugliness.

"But why is she saying these things if they aren't true? I believed her. I believed her for so many years," he said, his words emerging as a plaintive wail. "Did she hate me? I wondered sometimes if she did, if it was because my father left."

"She has her own way of seeing the world. That doesn't mean it is the only way of seeing things. You do not have to accept her version of you."

Steven looked at the boy again, and thought that even if he had been fat, that was no reason to be unkind. Bodies were just bodies, size didn't mean worth. Fat didn't mean unworthy or unlovable.

His boy self-vanished, as did the image of his mother. Steven looked around at the spartan childhood bedroom he had inhabited for so much of his life. It hadn't changed much down the years – same faded blue curtains, same grey carpet, the one lone bookcase, the wardrobe with woodworm in that somehow managed to stay upright. Looking round he felt a rush of gratitude that he had finally been able to escape. This room had been his prison.

"Face the mirror, Steven. Look with clear sight. Examine yourself as though you were appraising at a stranger."

Steven had never been keen on mirrors, disliking images of himself. However, at the boar's request he stood in front of this one and tried to look at himself properly. Usually he got in front of a mirror to shave every day or two, and at no other time did he raise his eyes to meet his reflection. His self-image, he realised, was of the unworthy boy he'd considered himself to be for most of his life.

Before him stood a lightly built man, with dark shadows around his eyes, and tousled, messy brown hair. He wore black, and stood uncomfortably as though trying to fold in on himself. Steven made a conscious effort to straighten up, and observed the improvement. Not handsome by any stretch of the imagination. Noticeable though. Striking even. The idea surprised him. Then he noticed his eyes. Steven hadn't looked at them properly in years, but now he realised just how rich a brown they were. He frowned slightly, not quite believing what he had seen.

"Is this how I really look?" he asked the boar.

"As real as anything ever is here," the boar responded. "More true in some ways, less true in others."

"That's not a very helpful answer."

"I know."

Steven raised his hand, covering the lower half of his face, and then looked at his eyes again. He shivered, excited and alarmed in equal measure by recognition.

Chapter Thirty-Three

"Spirits of the east, spirits of air and intellect, we call upon you to witness our ritual and guard us on this night." Elspeth's voice rang out clearly through the gloom, sending shivers down Steven's spine. There was real energy and possibility in the woodland tonight.

He didn't know quite where they were – the car ride had disorientated him, but there were trees, and he needed no more than that. In the centre of their circle, a small fire burned in a portable dish, hissing sporadically as droplets of water fell from the leaves above. Despite the cold and damp, they were in good spirits. Firelight and candles illuminated faces, creating strange shadows and distortions so that none of those people around the circle seemed quite themselves. Carol and Sean had agreed to lead the ritual, honouring Samhain and the season of the dead. Having missed the autumn equinox some weeks previously, Steven had never experienced a seasonal pagan ritual before. He found it compelling.

"Spirits of the south, spirits of fire and of summer gone, we call upon you to witness this ritual and guard us on this night," Heathen John called out with slightly less conviction. Steven knew this wasn't really his sort of thing, but he'd agreed to be involved anyway.

From a tree nearby, a lone night bird called out. Water drops slid down Steven's forehead. He mopped them away with a hand, brushing his hair back out of his face. It had grown considerably in the last month and had started getting in his eyes.

"Spirits of the west, spirits of water and emotion, we call upon you to witness our ritual and guard us on this night," Diana called. They'd picked this spot partly because it was so close to a cycle path they could get her chair in without too much trouble.

"Spirits of the north, spirits of earth and winter yet to come, we call upon you to witness our ritual and guard us on this night," Steven proclaimed. Carol had given him a script a week previously, and although she hadn't required him to say much, he'd still been nervous.

"We gather tonight to honour the dead. This is Halloween, All Souls' Night, and it is Samhain, Celtic festival of the departed." Carol paused, looking around the circle. "Let us speak of the dead. Let us name those we have loved and lost."

For a while they stood in silence, considering Carol's request. Diana was the first to respond. "I lost my great-aunt Christy this year. I think she wanted to go, in the end. I hope that she is in peace."

There were murmurs of agreement at this. Steven thought of his recent experiences. This night did not lend itself to silence. The surrounding trees were full of waiting energy, and he felt drawn to speak.

"I've been thinking about my ancestors a lot. The ones I didn't know, but whose stories and ideas have been passed down to me. Not all of those stories were good and I want to change them. Some of those stories are full of suffering, and I want to be the person that ends with." A respectful silence followed his words.

"I met Mindy for the first time at Samhain, years ago," Elspeth said. "She seemed like a lost soul then. I wanted to take her under my wing, but it never quite worked out and I don't know why. I could see her need, but I never knew how to respond to it. She's in my thought tonight and I'm aware of how close we came to losing her this year."

"I miss her. She's a nice kid, and I hope she finds the peace and healing she needs," Wiccan John said.

There was a long silence, filled with unvoiced emotions. Steven avoided making eye contact with anyone, his own heart too full for words. Carol took his hand, and they closed the circle spontaneously, reaching to each other in a gesture of unity. They had all suffered this summer.

Diana spoke up, "We can't change anything what went before. All we can do is choose how we respond to this. There's no point blaming her, or holding on to anger or beating ourselves up with questions about what we might have done differently. We have to look to the future and set our hearts on making the days ahead better than the days behind us have been."

The air tasted of damp leaves and autumnal decay. Breathing slowly and deeply, Steven let Diana's words wash over him. She was right, he had to let go. They all needed to.

"I honour all those who died in wars this year," Elspeth said, her voice muted but sincere.

"I honour those who died from sickness," Carol returned.

"I honour those who died because they stood up for what they believed in," Sean offered.

"I honour those who live with fear, who live too close to death," Steven said.

"I honour my ancestors, without whose blood and passion I wouldn't be here," Heathen John said, his voice gruff.

"I honour those who were never born. Children who died in the womb, and those who died in their cots." Diana said.

Steven looked up, meeting her eyes. "I honour those who face death with courage."

Round they went, offering thoughts and prayers, exploring all they knew of the pain and death in the world. Never before in his life had Steven been so conscious of the enormity of it all. There were so many people out there; so many lives cut short, so much brutality. He felt small and impotent, humbled by the scale of human suffering. There were tears, and their circle pulled in tighter, focusing around the fire dish. Beyond their ritual, the night pressed down, black and impenetrable. Steven could no longer make out the forms of the trees, but knew they were there. As Carol intoned a series of prayers, his mind wandered out towards the drowsy giants around him. With winter coming on, the trees were withdrawing into themselves, preparing for the cold days and sleep.

He wondered if he should have mentioned Willow None of the others knew her, but she had played such a huge role in his life of late and the loss of her still cut deeply. Marsden hadn't recovered from his stroke, and with the artist's mind gone, his only link to Willow had vanished. She could have been a dream. Only his picture of her suggested she had ever really existed at all.

"Willow," he mouthed, offering her name to the night so quietly that those around him did not hear.

Above him, the trees rustled slightly even though he could feel no wind. It seemed like a sign and he wanted to believe it had significance. Perhaps the Spirit of Arden was out there, beyond the circle of firelight. He could imagine her watching from the trees, amused but sympathetic.

"Steven?" Carol rested her hand on his shoulder and startled him out of his reverie. "North?"

He had lost track of the ritual, but remembered now that he had more to say. Trying to bring his attention back to their circle, he frantically sought for a recollection of the words Carol had asked him to learn.

"Spirits of the north," he began hesitantly, and it all came flowing back.

He lingered after the ritual, helping Heathen John to put out the fire and empty the dish. There wasn't far to walk and he couldn't hang about long with a lift waiting. Still he wanted a little time alone with the trees and his thoughts. With the fire out, most of the surrounding wood lay invisible to his eyes, but he could feel the plant spirits close by. Their presence reassured him. There had been no dramatic revelations or ghostly apparitions during the ritual, but even so he felt better for what they had done.

The forest held him. Its tranquillity felt like an embrace.

"I will find you again," he promised.

"Are you all right, Steven?" Elspeth shouted from some yards away.

"Be right with you."

Making his silent farewells, he hurried after the others.

"I'd almost hoped I might see something," he confessed to Heathen John later that evening.

He, John and Neil had gone back to John's house for hot drinks. It hadn't been an easy ritual and although he felt good about it Steven didn't feel inclined to be alone. As far as he knew, the other men were single and in much the same boat.

"Me too," Neil said.

"Well, if you follow the wheel of the year, it's supposed to be the time when the dead return," John said. "I'm not sure what I'd have done if anyone I knew had shown up."

"You don't follow the wheel of the year then?" Steven asked.

"Not really. I don't mind doing the eight festivals with you lot – its sociable, but it's not my calendar. I'd rather do something than nothing and I can honour my own festivals on my own."

"So how many festivals are there?" Steven asked.

"Loads. It's just modern Druidry and Wicca have settled on the big eight and they get all the publicity. There are all kinds of other festivals. It depends on what you're into."

"Oh." Steven realised he had a great deal still to learn.

"More mead?" John asked.

"Go on then."

Steven knew he'd end up asleep on John's sofa again. He had no desire to go home – the flat would be cold and empty. After the intensity of the ritual, he needed company and John seemed in no hurry to kick him out.

"You run one," Neil said.

"One what?" John asked.

"Ritual. Do a Heathen thing."

"Worth a thought," John replied.

Steven leaned back against the sofa and closed his eyes. The mead warmed his stomach, and eased away the sharpness of his feelings.

"Watch a film?" Neil suggested.

"Why not?" John replied.

Steven listened to their voices, and then to the soundtrack of the action film Neil had picked. There seemed to be lots of guns firing and people shouting, but none of it got through to impact on him in any way. He didn't care about the film. It was late, and he couldn't think anymore. The sofa felt good, and welcoming. He snuggled into it, wondering if he had ever been this safe and secure before.

Chapter Thirty-Four

After a while, the boar spoke. Steven had been drifting, not quite settled in his body, but not fully immersed in the forest either. The boar's measured response brought him back to the earthy scents of autumn leaves and a soft daylight that did not appear to owe its existence to any sun.

For a while, neither spoke. The boar moved closer to him and Steven became aware of its warmth. He felt sheltered by its company; protected as he had never been in ordinary life.

"You are hungry for that," the boar said. "For love and tolerance for care that comes without condition. You long to be loved for your own sake, but do not believe it possible."

Steven had no need to verbalise his agreement, the truth of it shimmered between them and required no acknowledgement.

"I went to a workshop once. The woman running it said how the universe is full of unconditional love. I can't believe her. It may be there for others, but not for me."

"If you find these things within yourself you might find it easier to see the same things outside of yourself," the boar suggested. "Love, forgiveness, tolerance, peace, understanding. It can begin inside you, not outside.

"I'm not sure how this works," he said regretfully.

"You are also a part of the universe. You can be the face the universe shows to others. You can choose what you want to put into the world and make real."

"That's a lot," Steven said.

Then they were travelling, space and time blurring into meaninglessness around them. As the scene resolved, he couldn't place it. There were tears wet on his cheeks, streaming forth like meltwater. His body shook, trembling violently beyond his control and the heart within him ached so desperately he thought it could burst from anguish. But these were not his memories. Beyond, a garden in early spring. A robin on the neatly mown lawn, washing on the line. Tears and more tears, fuelled by loss and hopelessness. Then, coming like glimpses of sun through heavy rainclouds, another feeling. Profound love. Earth shattering, life altering, soul stealing love. Desire and devotion beyond anything he had thought possible. A surfeit of emotion as likely to tear him apart as the grief that went with it. Then feelings of woeful inadequacy, self-loathing and an impulse towards self-destruction that he knew only too well.

"Where am I?" he asked the boar.

"Who are you?" the creature returned.

Peering through unfamiliar eyes, Steven looked out again at the pretty garden. The few trees in it looked familiar. In the distance, a small child cried piteously, setting off another round of desperate weeping.

Steven recognised the feelings of hopelessness, had lived with them too long himself. The sadness he understood, but those flickering moment of wildfire love shocked him. He touched on memories of a shared bed, her face against his shoulder, her arm around his waist. Peace and certainty. Each recollection of this powerful romance brought with it the most terrible, keening pain. She rocked with it, swayed under the force of barely articulated sounds as everything that had ever been good or beautiful withered and died within her.

In the end, only the self-hatred remained. Somewhere in the bitterness, he recognised her.

"Enough?" the boar asked.

"Enough," Steven acknowledged.

When he entered the ward, his old fear was there, strong as ever. Other emotions offset it. Although she must have known about the visit, his mother lay on the bed, her face turned away from him and towards the small window at the end of the bay. Without speaking, Steven sat in the chair beside her. Steadying himself with a few deep breaths, he reached out and covered her small, cold hand with his larger one. She started, and turned to look at him, her brow furrowed with confusion. For more years than he could number, the only physical contact between them came from practical necessity. They did not hug, there were no gestures of affection in that unhappy house.

"What is this?" she whispered.

"Me accepting you. As you are, not in spite of it. You aren't who I wished you to be, and whatever you wanted in a child, I know I wasn't it. There's not a lot of point blaming each other for that anymore."

She looked away from him again, her lips drawn in tight.

"I'm not asking for your forgiveness, and I'm not offering any either," he continued. "Acceptance I find I can do. It's a start."

She shook her head. "Why do you assume it was all about you? It was never about you."

Her words startled him. There was a sting in them, but at the same time he'd never considered that perspective before.

"I suppose I wasn't a very good mother," she said, staring fixedly at the middle distance. "I couldn't expect you to feel anything for me. Why would you? Why would anyone?"

He had no immediate answer, having never been able to deal with that issue for himself. They sat still, not looking at each other, not moving. His hand stayed upon hers.

"What else is there?" he asked after a while. "If there's no care, no understanding, no trust, we none of us have anything."

"You noticed."

"Perhaps I'm not so unlike you after all," Steven suggested.

"I hope not. I hope you're better than I am."

A lump formed in Steven's throat, and tears came unbidden. For the first time in his life, he felt a degree of empathy for his mother – a woman as lost and isolated as ever he had been. Perhaps she had not meant to hurt him so often, perhaps she knew no other way.

"You really loved my father, didn't you?"

She laughed bitterly. "It would have been kinder of him to kill me than leave me. But I had you, and a duty to you, and I tried to keep going. You were all I had left. I wouldn't have lived this long otherwise. When you lose the only thing that gives your life meaning... you go on, but you're just a shell. He took everything that was good about me, everything that was happy."

"I can't imagine what that must have been like," he said. "I've never loved anyone that much. But there was a girl back in the summer who touched my heart, and she very nearly killed herself. So I do know what it's like to be overwhelmed by despair, to want not to live, to see no point in it all."

"Not an insight I would wish on anyone."

"But there is hope, isn't there? Just the faintest hope that things might be better."

"Hope's a cruel thing, it keeps you going when you ought to give up," his mother replied.

"What else have we got? I'm not convinced I want to give up. This is not the sum and total of my life. There has to be something worth living for. More than duty, more than fear of death."

His mother laughed again, shaking her head slightly. "There was a time when I thought love made it all worthwhile, but when you give you soul to someone and they cast you aside... I wished I'd never been born. If I could have unmade myself, I would have done. After that, there was nothing but filling in the time."

"There are always other people to love, other people to care for," Steven said.

"But I didn't want anyone else. I only wanted him, and when he left..." she trailed off, her sentence decaying in a soft cry, like a small animal in pain. "Love like that, it's a once in a lifetime event."

"Then you were blessed, you had that for a while."

"Speaks the young man who has never been in love."

"That's why I think you were blessed. I've never had anything like that, probably never will."

"Love makes you stupid and vulnerable, and then it tears your heart to pieces," she said.

Steven smiled at this. "Perhaps it does. But maybe it's worth it even so. Can we be ok with each other?"

"Were we ever anything else?" she returned, and he realised that from her perspective, their relationship might have been very different to the one he remembered.

"Ok," he acknowledged. "Can I ask about my father?"

"What do you want to know?"

"You've never really talked about him, and I don't remember him – he's just a vague blur in my memories."

"What could I say? I don't think I ever really knew him. Was I in love with him, or the idea of him in my head? Why didn't he stay? What did I get wrong? I don't know the answers to any of that."

"He didn't love either of us enough to stay," Steven ventured.

"When his mother died, he came into a lot of money. I think that changed things. Money does that you know. It ruins people."

"I know."

"What's the point raking over the past now? It does no good, Steven. There's nothing there but pain. And if you want to find him… I lost contact with him years ago. I wrote to him at first. I hoped he'd come back, and then I hoped he would at least take an interest in you, but he didn't. But there you were, a little bit of good come out of it all."

"I don't think I can remember you saying anything good about me before."

"Didn't I?" she seemed puzzled and became distant for a while. "I thought you understood. I thought it was just one of those obvious things, that didn't need saying. I thought you knew that."

Steven shook his head, swallowing hard and trying to keep on top of his emotions. He had not known. In amongst the barbs and recriminations, there had been care. It had not been in a form he could understand, but it had existed. She had no idea how to express herself and he had not known how to look for it.

"Don't end up like me," she said. "I've made a mess of everything. I lost the love of my life. I lost my health, and now I'm dying."

"You could pull through this," he said. "All you have to do is start wanting to live again."

"You make it sound so easy."

"Isn't it?"

"No. It's easier just to give up. I'm tired Steven. I'm very tired and there's not much left to live for."

"What if I try to help you change that?" he asked.

She smiled, a touch amused perhaps, but also disbelieving.

"Give me a chance. Let me see what I can do," he offered.

"Will you come and see me again?"

"As often as I can."

She sighed heavily, the covers over her narrow chest rising and falling dramatically.

"Rest," he said. "I'll be back."

He lifted his hand from hers and stood, then leaned over her and planted a delicate kiss on her forehead. If he had ever kissed her before, he didn't remember it. This wasn't such a difficult thing to do, he realised. All those small gestures of affection made so much difference, and if you couldn't use words, touch could say a fair amount about your feelings.

As he walked from the hospital to the train station, Steven adjusted his posture, straightening up his neck and raising his head. He had nothing to hide, nothing to be ashamed of. He'd never expected the kind of exchange today had brought. There were wounds and old grievances that would not simply disappear overnight, but perhaps he could learn to live with them.

Chapter Thirty-Five

For a long time, Steven gazed at his own reflection. He experimented, brushing his dishevelled hair into different shapes around his face. From time to time, he placed a hand over his nose, isolating his eyes and forehead. The impression remained compelling. He had seen enough Marsden paintings to know that sometimes he depicted the Spirit of Arden with brown eyes, sometimes with an improbably bright green hue instead. In those images, the shape remained the same, the intent and the deep soulfulness. His eyes were not identical to hers; they lacked the wisdom he saw in her gaze. But all the same, the similarity could not be denied. With his hair growing out, dark brown locks framed his face. Considering his light build and fairly delicate bones, the effect gave him a peculiar feeling of familiarity.

Does it mean anything? And if so, what do I do with it?

He ran a finger over his slightly stubbly cheek, trying to relate what he saw in the mirror to his ill-formed sense of self. Steven seldom spent much time looking at his own face, and had only a vague notion of how he appeared to others. Glancing at his watch, he realised time was getting on. He had booked that Friday afternoon off work especially, planning on seeing the midwinter sunset. It seemed strange that midsummer was only six months behind him. That wondrous night seemed a world away.

Neil and Heathen John were already on the platform when he bought his ticket. He hurried out, joining them as the train to Barnt Green pulled in.

"Lousy weather," Neil said.

"I don't think this is going to be a good one somehow," John agreed. "But, who wants to be a fair-weather Pagan?"

Neil chuckled at this. "It's real," he said. "Really really real."

The woods on the flanks of the Lickeys were cold and quiet, with dense mist swirling between the trees. They could see the path well enough, but all sense of the wider woodland disappeared. Dry leaves from the previous autumn crunched underfoot. There were rustling sounds in the undergrowth, and Steven caught sight of grey squirrels, blackbirds, and other small birds that he couldn't identify. Occasional bursts of song came from the nearby trees, but otherwise the woods were quiet, disturbed only by a few horn blasts from passing trains.

"You know, there's a myth about a bloke called Harry Canab, I think that's his name. The Devil's Huntsman. He supposedly hunts around here. Keeps his hounds over at Halesowen," John said as they walked.

"Explains a lot," Neil muttered.

"There's a lot of myths about these hills, with giants, and other things," John continued. "And of course the beacon must be ancient."

They didn't talk much as they walked, pausing occasionally to point out toadstools, birds and the like to each other. Steven preferred the quiet. These two were good companions to walk with, he decided. With more eyes watching, he saw more than he did on his own. The other men knew something about trees and birds, and shared their insight with him, their knowledge enriching his experience.

By the time they reached the road at the top of the hill, the mist had started freezing. Tiny ice crystals clung to every tree, painting them brilliant white and emphasising the delicacy of each narrow twig. Steven looked around him at this frozen beauty, shivering but alert to every detail.

Along the lane to the beacon, every tree stood ice-decked, like a vision from a fairy-tale. They walked in single file, silent in their individual contemplations. Turning a bend in the road, Steven saw there were a few cars parked on an expanse of exposed, sandy soil opposite.

"This is it," Heathen John said. "We turn our backs towards Birmingham, and our faces towards the setting sun."

"Where exactly is it setting, do you think?" Steven enquired, gazing into the mist. He could see no trace at all of the sun.

"Over there somewhere," John replied, with a vague hand gesture.

"Setting in a couple of minutes," Neil added, looking at his watch.

Steven faced the direction of the setting sun, as the shortest day faded into the longest night. He shifted his weight from one leg to the other, trying to stop his feet from going numb. He'd hoped for a dramatic wintery sunset. There was nothing to see. The sky remained uniform grey, and he couldn't tell if it had grown darker by some small measure. For a while, he considered it to be a bit of an anti-climax. But the walk had been good, and even if he couldn't see it, the sun was setting, and the wheel of the year turned past this dark point and towards the light.

"Makes you glad to be a Pagan," John said, grinning. "Who would want to be tucked up in a warm, dull church on a day like this?"

Neil nodded, and Steven couldn't suppress a smile. *Who indeed?* The cold and the long walk had a beautiful reality to them, and the loss of comfort seemed a price entirely worth paying to have experienced this afternoon.

"See you in the New Year," John said as they parted at the station.

"Have a good one," Neil put in.

"You too," Steven said.

He stood for a while, watching as the two other men wandered off in their separate directions. He had a few days off work for the festivities, but had no idea how he would spend them. Christmas had always been such an uncomfortable time of year. Back before his mother stopped cooking entirely, she'd usually try to do something but more years than not it ended in disaster. He associated the day with tears, frustration and recrimination. Given her food anxieties, he supposed the emphasis of feasting must have been a real nightmare for her. They didn't have much wider family to turn to, nor did she have any friends. It tended to be the loneliest time of the year, and this one showed no signs of being better. With no public transport running on the day, he could not visit his mother and he had nowhere else to go.

"It's not my festival," he said to himself. "It's just a few days off work."

He woke early on Christmas morning, with the orange glow of streetlights permeating the curtains as the sun hadn't risen yet. Pausing at the window a while, he greeted the day, marvelling at how quiet the world beyond the glass appeared. He made a point of eating a decent breakfast, then packed a bag with everything he might need for the day.

The streets were almost entirely empty when Steven set off. He imagined that behind every window, happy families did whatever it was normal people got up to during this festival. Of all the days of the year, he hated this one the most. The adverts full of perfect families. The endless demand to buy and spend, purchasing happiness in the form of that one ideal gift that would inspire love. All the hope and expectation, the half-formed notions of how it should be that bred bitter disappointment. *Not this year* he promised.

After a while the flow of traffic began. Steven supposed there were some people whose jobs demanded it, and others who journeyed towards family members, loved ones. As soon as he could, he left the road, striking out along the first footpath he could find, travelling in random directions and following his feet. In the hedgerows, small birds fluttered and called. Grey skies threatened rain, and a chill wind kept his face cold. Steven stopped in the middle of a field and looked around him. Countryside prevailed in all directions, although he couldn't see a great distance. Muddy grass beneath him and open sky above. Cows lowing sporadically nearby. It occurred to him that out here, Christmas did not exist. With no one to sell it, put twinkling lights on it or make a fuss over it, Christmas had no reality at all. The thought cheered him. Today was just another day, no more or less meaningful than any other cycle of light and dark. He did not have to buy into the compulsions that held everyone else in thrall.

The solid certainty of earth beneath his feet inspired him. This was real, as were the sporadic bird songs, the cutting cold of the wind and the wild crashing noises behind him. He froze, straining his ears as he tried to make more sense of the sound. An angry snort suggested the presence of a sizeable creature. For a few seconds he envisaged a farm animal, escaped, injured, in need. He turned at once, compassion outweighing lack of knowledge and skill. Steven hadn't the faintest idea what he might be able to do, but he hurried in the directions of the crashing noises.

Along the side of the hedge ran a deep ditch, with water lining its muddy bottom. Steven could see a gaping tear in the hedge, as though something massive had recently forced its way through it. The field curved with the contours of the land, and he followed it round until a large, dark shape became apparent. At first he had no idea what it was. The animal snorted, scrabbling for a purchase on the muddy bank of the ditch. With a snort and a momentous heave, it broke free of mud and ditch, and cleared the top, scattering filthy water as it crashed down. Steven halted, unsure of the best course of action. He tended to imagine farm animals as docile, harmless things. This creature looked huge, its dark coat wiry, shoulders broad. He had the distinct feeling this was no tame beast to be shooed off with a loud word.

When it turned towards him, Steven had a decent look at the head shape, the nose, the small eyes. At first the dark skin had thrown him – his mental image of a pig included pinkness as the most significant feature.

Nor had he appreciated just how large a pig could be. Its gaze met his, fearless, challenging. *Not a pig,* he realised. *A boar.*

"The Boar, even," suggested the boar.

Steven took a step back. He had heard the voice clearly. "What is this?" Steven asked, perturbed.

"You can walk in the other worlds. Why should I not walk in this one?"

Steven gaped, silent and stunned.

"Everything is as real as everything else," the boar said in conversational tone. "Here is as real as there."

"But..." Steven began, stopping when he realised he had no idea what to say.

"Shall we walk?" the boar suggested, manifestly amused by his unsettled state.

Having nothing better to suggest, Steven walked alongside the boar. For a long time, he said nothing. He wondered what would happen if they met some lone dog walker. Would anyone else be able to see his strange companion?

"Where am I?" Steven asked.

"Here," said the boar.

"But where is here?"

The boar looked around, sniffing the air. "It looks like a field to me," he said. "An old field, that has been field for a long time and has lost all memory of every being a wild place."

"Why are you here?" Steven asked.

"Why are any of us here? That's one of the greatest questions. What does it all mean? What is it for? I suspect there isn't any meaning."

"I meant more why are you in this place right now?"

The boar glanced at him, its expression toothy. Steven had the uncomfortable impression it had smiled at him.

"We have unfinished business, do we not?"

"Do we?"

"Your search for the Spirit of Arden, or had you forgotten?"

The name sent a jolt through Steven. It rang with notes of inevitability, with fate.

"Here?" he asked, thoroughly confused.

"Why not here? Why not anywhere? Once you understand what you search for, you can find it anywhere you choose to look."

"Right," Steven replied, less than entirely convinced.

"Do you understand what you need to do?" the boar enquired.

"I don't know." He looked at the boar for a while. It occurred to Steven that however peculiar he might find his own ideas, he had nothing to lose in confessing them. Given his current companion was a creature of dubious reality, the situation could hardly be any more mad. He took the plunge.

"Willow explained to me how she had chosen to embody the Spirit of Arden. How she tries to bring the lost forest into the world. I dreamed about her, but it wasn't her."

"Real and not real, I would imagine," the boar said. "Why shouldn't you both have been touched by the same dream, reaching towards the same truth? Life can be very plural sometimes. A tangled wilderness of possibilities, not an open field."

"Every depiction of Arden I've seen, based on her, has been so feminine. So I've been looking for her outside of myself. Someone to follow. But that's not it, is it?" He still didn't quite dare put it into words.

"I see just the place for you," the boar said, trotting off across the field towards a metal water trough.

Steven followed unhurriedly, realising that on the uneven ground, any attempt at speed could land him on his backside.

He leaned over the edge of the trough, looking at the greenish water inside it. A striking creature peered back at him, not exactly pretty, but captivating. Long hair framed an angular face, generous lips folded into a warm smile. Steven gazed into the water and nodded, watching as she nodded with him. When he brushed the water with his fingertips, the image collapsed. Looking round with a question at his lips, Steven realised the boar had left him.

"What are you?" he whispered to his re-forming reflection. "What am I?"

"All that you have lost," his feminine counterpart whispered. "A spirit is not a sturdy thing. Anguish, torment and madness can tear a spirit apart, can break off fragile pieces."

"And you are that? The parts of me I have lost?"

"Oh no. I am the spirit, and you are my lost dreams, my wounded hopes." She laughed then. "We both are. We are fragments of the same whole, but even together, we would not be complete. But it would be a start."

"How?"

"Let me in. Surrender to me. Give up your old life, your old sense of self. Let me be your breath and your truth."

Steven let go and slid. Cold water shocked his senses, drenching him, surrounding him. In the near darkness, hands reached for his, holding him, guiding him downwards. He felt no fear, and wondered at this as he sank.

The impression lasted for seconds, and then he was back in some anonymous field, and it was Christmas day. Steven breathed in, feeling the presence of his own lost self. Places within him that he had only ever known as gaps and wounds seemed full and alive now. He had found something, reclaimed something. All he had to do was make it real.

Chapter Thirty-Six

While Steven knew what he wanted to do, he had no idea how to go about it. Did he need a ritual of some kind? Who did he know who could help him? He went to Helen's shop and went through every title on the shelf but couldn't find anything that connected with what he wanted to do.

"Stuck?" she asked, but only once he's given up.

"Yes," he admitted. "I've read a bit about drawing down the moon in rituals, but it all seems to be about using the right text. So what would you do if you wanted to do something like that only different?"

"You want to draw down a deity?" she asked.

Steven thought about this. "Actually, that's not it either. It's not for ritual, it's more about bringing something into the world."

"Aspecting," Helen said.

"That's a new word," Steven admitted.

"I don't have anything that really deals with it. I have seen quite a few conversations online but nothing I could usefully point you at. But I can tell you the gist," she said.

"That would be really helpful," Steven said.

"First up it doesn't have to be massive drama, you don't have to let someone possess you. At the most basic level it's like acting on their behalf in the world. Embodying what they represent. Speaking on their behalf could do that. I reckon anyone could do that. Nothing woo-woo called for, just think about a deity you like and undertake to do what they're interested in."

"That makes a lot of sense," Steven said. "I reckon I could do that on my own."

"Of course if it works, they might start showing up," Helen said.

Steven nodded. He had no idea what to do with that possibility, but supposed he could deal with it is it happened.

January brought a protest march to Birmingham. While the cause was social rather than environmental, it seemed like a good place to start. In a crowd of people, it wouldn't really matter what odd things he did so long as he didn't bother anyone else. As he thought about the march, Steven had a growing sense of what he wanted to do, along with a feeling of confidence in his ability to do it.

On the way to the train, he picked a length of ivy and twisted it into a headband. Now that his hair had grown out a little, he felt more in tune with the Spirit of Arden. He had dressed in earthy colours, but didn't want to stand out too much. From New Street Station he headed up into the streets, and found a place to pause.

Closing his eyes, Steven focused on the ground beneath him. Somewhere beneath him lay soil. Somewhere in the soil layers was a physical memory of the time when there had been a forest here. He breathed deeply, letting the idea of the forest fill him. He thought about the way he'd seen Willow embody the Spirit of Arden, and he asked to be allowed to do the same.

She came as a buzz of energy, a tingling on the edge of his awareness. He felt connected to the ground as though he had roots reaching down into the earth beneath him. Steven opened his eyes and saw the street anew. The present seemed like a thin layer of reality stretched over the vast breadth and depth of the past. All he had to do was walk, breathe and bring that forest consciousness with him.

Steven spent the entire day walking the streets with countless protestors. He thought about the deep peace of ancient woodland, and the natural balance of forest ecosystems. Whether his presence, and his attempt at aspecting the forest made a difference, he could not say. No one around his spontaneously sprouted leaves or turned into deer. The city tarmac did not erupt into verdant growth, although he pictured it doing so.

No one paid him much attention, but that seemed fine. Steven did not feel the need for affirmation from anyone else. What mattered was that he knew he could do this. He could feel the forest inside him and the Spirit of Arden with him. He could be a means by which the forest came back into the world.

All the things that both the spirit herself, and Willow had said to him now made a lot more sense. He'd been looking for wonder outside of himself, when what he needed to do was figure out how to manifest it inside himself. He needed to become wonder, and magic, not to chase after it in other people. They'd been trying to steer him this way all along, and so had the boar. He just hadn't understood that such things might even be possible.

Walking through the city he felt wild and alive, with the forest inside him and around him. He could be in the present, carrying the past. Given time, he might be able to do a lot more with this way of being. As yet Steven had no idea what he should be doing with any of this, although tree planting seemed like a good idea. He wanted to go to the places where the trees were young and help them remember that there had once been an ancient forest here. He wanted to open people's eyes to the possibility of magic and to enchant others as he himself had been enchanted.

Turning a corner he caught a fleeting glimpse of an older woman who was also an owl, walking alongside someone who radiated wildness and mystery. Steven knew that he was not alone, that forest-touched people were around him and that he would find his people. He had not been given some special mission, he was just one of the many hearing the call of the land and the lost forest. That gladdened his heart. He had no desire to be alone in this, and the idea that there wasn't anything remarkable about him felt comforting. Connecting to the forest wasn't some rare gift, it was something anyone might do given the chance.

Looking around at the crowds on the street, Steven saw in each one of them the potential to be touched by the forest. These were people who already cared enough about something to be out and making a noise. If enough people cared about the forest, there might be some way to bring it back. A forest of people with dreams of trees. A forest of intentions. And if enough people planted trees, there could yet be something like a forest, scattered across the place that had once been Arden.

This he could give his life to.

Ahead, he saw Willow, moving towards him. Then, in a moment of uncanniness, Steven realised he had encountered a reflection of the crowd in an angled window. He wasn't walking towards Willow, but towards himself. Long-haired and with a crown of ivy, he saw his own magic properly for the first time, and joy filled him. With it came an overwhelming sense of love for the strangers around him, and the ground beneath his feet. Everything could change and he felt ready to step up and make better things happen.

Fin

Some notes from the author

I started writing this at some point after 2004 when I was living in Redditch. This was the novel that got away. I wrote it nearly to the end and then found I just couldn't finish it. The project haunted me thereafter.

In the autumn of 2023, I had a conversation with Jessica Law about the book that got away and she suggested I try to finish it. Somehow I still had a version stashed on a hard drive in a very out of date file format, and was able to coax the project back to life.

That I was able to fix the problems in the first draft and finding an ending has a lot to do with Mark Hayes, and his novels Cider Lane and Passing Place. Both have relevant themes and made me think about how I need to handle this kind of content. Reading those books also gave me the confidence to venture into the difficult places. I cried a lot over Mark's stories and it was a helpful, healing process.

All of the places in this book are real apart from Helen's shop. Some of the events are real, or owe a lot to things that happened. The characters are all fictional, but they owe a lot to real people. For every character, I drew on personal experience and stories people shared with me. I've tried to reflect something of the diverse and lively Midlands Pagan culture I encountered while entirely missing out the witch-wars that raged at the time.

During the timeframe this is based on, I was involved with Hedd Wyn's Grove in Birmingham, Circle of the Greenwood in Redditch, various moots, and then a ritual group called Bards of the Lost Forest. I look back with great affection to the many wonderful experiences I had with those communities.

I first ran into the concept of aspecting through Jane Meredith's work. Not having that concept initially was one of the things that made the first draft impossible to finish.

This story has been a collaboration between the person I was in my late twenties, and the person I am now. We got along pretty well while we were working on this. I've been through a lot since I began this story, I know more than I did when I started. I'm glad to have got the whole thing to a point where I could say 'the end' and it feels like closure on a lot of different levels.

Printed in Great Britain
by Amazon